# The Obituary Writer

ALSO BY ANN HOOD

*The Red Thread*

*Comfort*

*The Knitting Circle*

*An Ornithologist's Guide to Life*

*Somewhere Off the Coast of Maine*

# The
# Obituary Writer

## ANN HOOD

W. W. NORTON & COMPANY

NEW YORK • LONDON

For information about permission to reproduce selections from this book,
write to Permissions, W. W. Norton & Company, Inc.,
500 Fifth Avenue, New York, NY 10110

For information about special discounts for bulk purchases,
please contact W. W. Norton Special Sales
at specialsales@wwnorton.com or 800-233-4830

Manufacturing by Courier Westford
Book design by Brooke Koven
Production manager: Julia Druskin

Library of Congress Cataloging-in-Publication Data

Hood, Ann, 1956–
The obituary writer / Ann Hood. — First edition.
pages cm
ISBN 978-0-393-08142-8 (hardcover)
1. Housewives—Fiction. 2. Women journalists—Fiction.
3. Loss (Psychology)—Fiction. 4. Regret—Fiction. 5. United States—
Social life and customs—Fiction. 6. Psychological fiction. I. Title.
PS3558.O537O25 2013
813'.54—dc23
2012040074

W. W. Norton & Company, Inc.
500 Fifth Avenue, New York, N.Y. 10110
www.wwnorton.com

W. W. Norton & Company Ltd.
Castle House, 75/76 Wells Street, London W1T 3QT

1 2 3 4 5 6 7 8 9 0

*This is dedicated to the ones I love*

# The Obituary Writer

# ONE

*First of all, the ones in sorrow should be urged if possible to sit in a sunny room and where there is an open fire. If they feel unequal to going to the table, a very little food should be taken to them on a tray. A cup of tea or coffee or bouillon, a little thin toast, a poached egg, milk if they like it hot, or milk toast.*

—FROM *Etiquette*, BY EMILY POST, 1922

# 1

## The Missing Boy

### CLAIRE, 1960

If Claire had to look back and decide why she had the affair in the first place, she would point to the missing boy. This was in mid-June, during those first humid days when the air in Virginia hangs thick. School was coming to an end, and from her kitchen window Claire could see the bus stop at the corner and the neighborhood children, sweaty in skirts and blouses, khaki trousers and damp cotton shirts, pile out of it like a lazy litter of puppies. Their school bags dragged along the sidewalk; their catcher's mitts drooped. Jump ropes trailed behind a small group of girls, as if even they were too hot.

Watching this scene, Claire smiled. Her hands in the yellow rubber gloves dipped into the soapy dishwater as if on automatic. Wash. Rinse. Set in the drainer to dry. Repeat. The kitchen smelled of the chocolate cake cooling on the sill in front of her. And faintly of her cigarette smoke, and the onions she'd fried and added to the meatloaf. Upstairs, Kathy napped, clutching her favorite stuffed animal, Mimi, a worn and frayed rabbit.

A stream of sweat trickled down Claire's armpits. Was it too hot to eat outside? she wondered absently, still watching the children. It was hard for her to imagine that in a few years Kathy would be among them, clamoring onto the bus at eight-fifteen every morning, her braids neat, her socks perfectly rolled down, and then, like these kids, appearing again at three-thirty, sweaty and tired and hot.

That June was when Peter had said he was ready for another child, and Claire had stopped inserting her diaphragm before they made love. She wanted more children. The families around them in Honeysuckle Hills all had at least two, more likely three or four. Like divorce, only children were rare and raised eyebrows. Everyone suspected that the mother in a family with an only child had female trouble of some kind.

After all, it was 1960. The country had put war behind it. New houses were springing up around the city, in Arlington and Alexandria, clustered together in neighborhoods like Honeysuckle Hills, neighborhoods with bucolic names like Quail Ridge and Turtledove Estates. They had wide curving streets, manicured lawns, patios with special matching furniture. Men wore suits and fedoras and overcoats to work in D.C.; the women vacuumed the wall-to-wall carpeting that covered the floors. They polished furniture tops with lemon Pledge and baked casseroles with Campbell's soup and canned vegetables. They went to the hairdresser every week and got their hair sprayed and flipped.

On long summer evenings, the families sat outside watching their children bike up and down the streets, or balance on scooters or roller skates. The girls chanted songs as the sound of their jump ropes slapping the pavement filled the air, beside the whir of lawn mowers and the distant noise of someone's radio. On Saturday afternoons, adolescents gathered, clutching bath towels and shaking their still soft bodies trying to learn the Twist. They walked on a mat with plastic footprints, doing a clumsy cha-cha.

Even now, Claire could hear Brenda Lee crooning "I'm Sorry" from someone's transistor radio. The dishes done, the children from the school bus dispersed, Claire removed the rubber gloves and touched the top of the cake to see if it was cooled enough to frost. Not quite. Soon enough, Kathy would wake from her nap, a little cranky, and insist on sitting on Claire's lap, keeping Claire immobile and unable to get anything done. She glanced at the clock. If she was lucky, twenty minutes stretched before her with nothing to do. She thought briefly of the basket of laundry waiting to be folded, the summer linens that needed to be aired before she put them on the beds.

But instead of doing any of these things, Claire poured herself a tall glass of ice tea, adding ice cubes and saccharin and a sprig of mint she kept in a glass by the window. She grabbed the new issue of *Time* with its stark cover of an illustration of a woman and the headline: THE SUBURBAN WIFE. A yellow banner across the corner reported that one third of the nation lived in the suburbs. Settling onto the chaise lounge in the backyard, Claire glanced at the lead story.

*"The wreath that rings every U.S. metropolis is a green garland of place names and people collectively called Suburbia. It weaves through the hills beyond the cities, marches across flatlands that once were farms and pastures, dips into gullies and woodlands . . ."*

Really, she thought as she flipped the pages of the magazine, who needed to read a description of her own life? Her own happy life, she added as she took in bits of information. The Negro songstress Eartha Kitt got married. So had Mussolini's daughter. Judy Holliday and Jimmy Stewart both had new movies opening. President Eisenhower was off to Japan—he always seemed to be off somewhere, Claire thought—and the Prince of Cambodia needed to lose twenty-two pounds.

She closed the magazine and set it on the grass beside her

chair. The smell of roses was heavy, almost hypnotic. Claire heard bees. Across the Parkers' yard next door, she could see a gaggle of boys walking down the street, the tops of their summer buzzed haircuts shining in the late afternoon sun. She recognized them all, and took comfort in the familiarity of her surroundings. A white car passed the boys, then disappeared around the corner. Closer now, the kids' voices grew louder, their excited tone one that only children can have. They were talking, from what Claire could glean, about going to the moon.

That white car appeared again, slower this time. Probably someone lost in the maze of streets that made up Honeysuckle Hills. People used to the grids of city streets, the logic of numbers and letters, got confused when they had to navigate Mulberry, Maple, and Marigold Streets.

Kathy's sharp wake-up cries cut through the air, halting Claire's private time. Forgetting the tea and the magazine, Claire made her way back inside, up the stairs to Kathy's room.

"Bad Mommy," Kathy pouted.

Claire patted her daughter's bottom to be sure she hadn't wet the bed. Dry. A small victory.

"Come here, Kitty Kat," Claire murmured, lifting the rigid girl. Kathy always woke up on the wrong side of the bed.


After a snack of graham crackers and milk and playing paper dolls, Kathy finally grew less crabby.

Claire let her help set the table, to carry the napkins and the silverware out to the patio. She taught her how to fold the napkins into triangles, and to place the forks on the left, the spoons and knives on the right.

"Four letters in left. Four letters in fork," Claire explained.

"Five letters in right. Five letters in knife and spoon. That's how you remember."

Kathy nodded, even though she hadn't yet learned to recite her ABC's and still watched *Romper Room* and *Captain Kangaroo* every morning as Claire cleaned the house. Kathy liked to sing along with Miss Bonnie: *Bend and stretch, reach for the stars. Here comes Jupiter, there goes Mars.* Still, Claire didn't think it hurt to spell words and explain complicated things to her now. Maybe it would help her understand eventually.

"Now it's time to make Daddy's martini," Claire said.

Kathy padded back inside right behind her, climbing her little stool so that she could reach the counter. Claire carefully measured the gin and then the vermouth, letting Kathy pour the jiggers into the shaker.

"Shake, not stir," Kathy said proudly.

Claire laughed. Her daughter might not know her ABC's, but she knew the secret to a good martini.

"That's right, Kat," Claire said.

By the time the martini was chilled and the cheese was sprayed onto Ritz crackers and the potatoes mashed and the canned green beans warmed, Peter's car pulled into the garage. Everything right on schedule.

Looking back on that evening, Claire tried to find the beginnings of a rupture, the way they say the San Andreas fault is already cracked and over time shifts more and more until the earth finally cracks open. But she could never find even a hairline fracture. She remembers feeling satisfaction over the dull predictability of her days. If she did not feel a thrill at the sound of Peter's key in the front door each evening, she did feel a confidence, a *rightness*, to the way the hours presented themselves.

Peter walked in, handsome, a bit slumped from his day having the admiral rant at him and everyone around him. They both took pride in the fact that Peter was the only civilian who worked for Admiral Rickover at the Pentagon, an honor that made up for the admiral's erratic behavior and famous temper. Peter kissed Claire and Kathy absently on their cheeks, loosened his tie, and took his place on the turquoise couch he hated, waiting for Claire to appear with that martini, now perfectly chilled. She always wet the glass and placed it in the freezer so that it was frosty and cold too. For herself, she poured a glass of Dubonnet, adding ice and a twist of lemon. On a warm night like tonight, Kathy got Kool-Aid, poured from a fat round pitcher with a face grinning from it.

"I thought we'd eat outside," Claire said after settling onto the pink chair across from him.

"Mmm," Peter said, already distracted by something in the newspaper he'd opened on the coffee table.

"Eisenhower's off to Japan," Claire said, because a woman always needed to keep up with current events.

Peter gave her a half-nod.

"Doesn't it seem that he's always off somewhere?" Claire said. "I read somewhere that he's traveled almost one hundred thousand miles in his presidency." Of course she knew exactly where she'd read it. Just a couple of hours ago in the new *Time* magazine.

"Well," Peter said. "He is the president."

Claire handed Peter a cracker, admiring the squiggle of cheese on top. Ever since she had first bought cheese in a spray can, she'd gotten better at making even lines or perfect bull's-eyes. One afternoon, her neighbor Dot had all the neighborhood women over for Grasshoppers and a lesson in how to use the damn spray can of cheese. That had done it, even though the Grasshoppers made her half drunk and Peter came home to find her asleep on the sofa, no dinner made and a tray full of dozens of crackers and cheese.

She watched as he popped the whole thing in his mouth without even looking at it.

"Did you know, darling," Claire said, "that one third of the nation is living in the suburbs now?"

At this, he looked up at her, impressed or surprised, she wasn't sure which.

"Is that so?" he said.

Claire nodded.

In the weeks to come, she would hear him repeat this statistic like he knew something about it. Like he had discovered the fact himself. By that time, she had already begun to dislike him, so this boasting made her hate him even more.


It was after dinner that Joe Daniels appeared in their yard, looking worried and hot.

Claire and Peter were still sitting at the patio table, sipping B & B. Claire had already put Kathy to bed, and the evening was winding down in that gentle way June evenings do. Peter's stockinged foot ran lightly up Claire's bare calf, a sign that he would want to make love tonight, despite the heat. She thought fleetingly of the fans still up in the attic. The heat had come on suddenly and she'd been unprepared. She wondered if she might convince Peter to get them down. Or at least to put one in their bedroom. The thought of him sweaty on top of her was not appealing.

His foot moved up and down, up and down. His cigarette was almost finished. If she could move this along, they might be done by ten, in time for *Hawaiian Eye*. With that in mind,

Claire inched her chair closer to her husband's and put her hand on his thigh.

"Hello!" Joe Daniels called into the yard.

Claire jerked her hand back and got quickly to her feet, her face hot as if they'd been caught actually doing something.

Peter got to his feet, one hand already extended to shake Joe's. But Joe didn't seem to notice. Instead of looking at either of them, his eyes swept the backyard.

"Joe," Claire said. "Would you like to join us for a B & B?"

"No, no," he said. "I'm looking for my boy. For Dougie," he added.

Claire detected panic rising in his voice.

"He didn't come home for dinner," Joe said, "and Gladys is practically hysterical. She's called just about everybody and no one's seen him."

"I saw him," Claire said. "This afternoon."

She pointed to the chair where she'd sat and read the *Time* magazine, which still lay in the grass where she'd left it. Claire made a mental note to bring it inside or it would get soggy and Peter would complain that she was careless.

"He was with a bunch of boys talking about space, about going to the moon," Claire told Joe.

For a moment, Joe looked relieved. But then his face grew worried again.

"When was that?" he asked.

"Around four," Claire said.

"Are you sure?"

"It was right before Kathy woke up from her nap," Claire said. "I came out for a breather." She pointed to the magazine and the abandoned glass of ice tea.

"All right," Joe Daniels said, nodding. "All right. But then, where could he be now?"

Claire had no answer for that.

"You know how boys are," Peter said. He touched the other man's arm. "He's probably catching frogs or fireflies or some such."

Joe nodded again. "It's just so late, that's all. Almost nine-thirty."

"Is it that late already?" Claire said, thinking not about Dougie Daniels but about how she would certainly miss *Hawaiian Eye* tonight.

"And it's a school night," Joe said.

"I hate to bring this up," Peter said quietly, "but have you called the police?"

Joe gulped air as if he were a drowning man.

"I guess that's the next step," he said.

"I'm sure Dougie is fine," Claire said brightly. "Boys will be boys."

"It's just so late," Joe said again.

The whole time that Peter and Claire made sweaty love later that night, the teenage girl next door played the same song over and over. It started with a train whistle, then a vaguely familiar voice sang about giving ninety-nine kisses and ninety-nine hugs. As soon as the song ended, the girl played it again. She must have just gotten the 45, Claire thought, not liking the song or her husband's sweat dripping on her. Finally, his thrusts quickened and she heard that welcome long low grunt.

"That was nice," she whispered in his ear once his breathing had evened.

Peter kissed her, right on the lips the way she liked, the way she wished he kissed her more often. But usually she only got these kisses afterwards. She kissed him back anyway. Why was it that as soon as he finished, she began to feel stirrings? Even now, too hot and too sweaty, she held him tight, her mouth opening, something in her tingling.

"Whoa," he chuckled. "I just finished."

"I know," Claire said. "I just . . ."

She just what?

"I just love you," she said, though that wasn't what she meant at all.

He rolled off her and lit a cigarette.

"Want one?" he asked.

"All right," Claire said.

Peter handed her that one, and lit another for himself. She always liked when he did that.

The 45 started up again.

"I can't tell if Peggy's just fallen in or out of love," Claire said. "She's playing that record so much, it must be something."

She inhaled and closed her eyes. An image from that afternoon floated across her mind.

"Peter," she said. "When I saw the boys this afternoon—"

"Boys?"

"Dougie Daniels and the others. There was a white car driving around the neighborhood. A car I didn't recognize."

"Are you sure?"

"I thought he was lost."

"So you saw the driver?" Peter asked her. He was sitting up now, and pulling the phone onto his lap.

"I don't know," Claire said, straining to remember.

"You said you thought *he* was lost," Peter said as he dialed the Danielses' number.

All of the neighborhood's phone numbers and emergency numbers were right there on the phone, neatly typed and alphabetical.

"I just meant the driver came by a couple of times, real slow."

"Joe," Peter said into the receiver. "Sorry to call so late but Claire just remembered that when she saw Dougie this afternoon she also saw a white car   "

Peter glanced at Claire.

"A Valiant maybe?" she said, shrugging. "Or a Fury?"

"Really?" Peter said into the phone. "Well, I'll be damned. Call us if we can be of any help."

"The boys reported it too," he said after he hung up. "They all noticed that car. D.C. plates apparently."

He kissed the top of her head and turned off the light.

"Did someone take Dougie?" Claire said into the darkness.

"I'm afraid that might be what happened," Peter said. "Joe said the cops were leaning in that direction."

"Someone kidnapped Dougie?" she said. Her heart beat too fast. She could hear it.

"Don't think about it," Peter said sleepily.

But that was when it all began.


That Saturday night was the dinner party at Trudy's when she first met Miles Sullivan. By then, her world had already started to shift. Peter looked different to Claire. Rather than comforting her, the similarity of her days made her edgy. She kept thinking back to that afternoon, to the tops of the boys' heads, their new summer buzz cuts, the white car circling them. Circling the neighborhood.

The heat grew worse. The air felt like pea soup. And still the police could not find Dougie Daniels. The boys had given a description of the driver to the police. A short olive-skinned man with close-cropped curly hair and a plaid short-sleeved shirt. He had slowed down, they reported, and looked right at them, taking in the sight of each of them before driving past.

Claire sent a pan of lasagna to the Danielses' house. The next week she sent an angel food cake. No one knew what else to do, and the food piled up on the Danielses' kitchen table and refrigerator shelves and in their freezer. At night when Peter reached for her, despite the now-installed window fan, Claire squeezed her eyes shut and tried not to think about how much she wanted it to be over. When he kissed her afterwards, she did not hold him tight and kiss him back.

Two weeks after Dougie disappeared, Trudy had a cookout and Claire drank too much sangria. She felt sloppy and silly, and when Roberta's husband accidentally brushed against her as he walked past her in the hall, it seemed as if he had electrocuted her. She studied him drunkenly. Claire had never found him attractive before. She had never considered his looks at all. But suddenly he seemed not only attractive, but desirable. Such a different type than her tall, angular husband. Ted was beefy and ruddy-faced, with unnervingly light blue eyes. She smiled at him.

"We are all so drunk," he said.

Back at home, in bed, the room spinning slightly, Peter reached for her.

"Kiss me right on the mouth," she whispered, and when he did as she asked a need in Claire seemed to make itself known. Dougie Daniels had been kidnapped and possibly even murdered. Nothing in the world made sense anymore, and Claire felt like an idiot for having lived so safely, for having believed that this was what she wanted: this man, this house, this life.

That night, when he finally moved on top of her, Claire's hips met his thrusts. Her fingernails dug into his back. Something was happening to her. Something, finally, unexpected. It wasn't Peter who let out that predictable groan, but Claire. More a yelp really, as waves seemed to grab hold of her and not let go.

In the morning, hungover, Claire felt embarrassed about what had happened. She could not meet her husband's eyes. Instead, she scrambled his eggs, made his toast, squeezed oranges for juice, all the time wondering what in the world was she going to do next.

Of course all the mothers of Honeysuckle Hills watched their children more closely after Dougie Daniels went missing. They stood on street corners and front steps, making sure their own sons and daughters arrived wherever they were going and then back home, safely. They made casseroles and cakes for the Danielses, but they didn't linger when they delivered them. To see Gladys Daniels, her hair unwashed, her eyes wild with grief, made them nervous, the way they had been before Dr. Salk calmed them down with the polio vaccine. If Dougie Daniels, an ordinary boy, a B student and average second baseman in Little League, could be kidnapped, then anyone could.

"It's not contagious," Claire said one afternoon to Roberta and Trudy. "We should go and sit with her."

They were standing vigil as their own kids ran under the sprinkler in Roberta's backyard. It had been a month since Dougie disappeared, and there was no sign of him being found.

"She just kind of scares me," Roberta said, her eyes never leaving her Sandy and Ricky, not once.

"I think she could wash her hair," Trudy said primly. "They said she didn't even bother to wash it when the newspeople went over there."

"I think we should sit with her," Claire said again. "I'm going to make calls for Kennedy tomorrow night, but I could go in the morning."

"And bring our kids?" Roberta said. "That would just make her sad, to see our kids safe and sound while Dougie is . . . gone."

Dougie Daniels was an only child. Gladys had had a hyster-
ectomy at a very young age. Or so the women thought.

"What would we possibly say to her?" Trudy asked.

"I made her a Jell-O salad," Roberta said. "With canned
pears and walnuts."

"That's always nice on a hot day like today," Trudy added.

And that was the end of that.

The next night, Claire walked into an empty law office and
sat beside Miles Sullivan, the man who would change everything. When Dougie Daniels' body was found in the C & O
Canal over Labor Day weekend, she wished she had gone that
morning to visit with Gladys. But wasn't it too late now? Wasn't
a dead child—a murdered child—even harder to talk about than
one who had simply vanished? If kidnapping seemed possibly
contagious, no one wanted to think about this even worse thing.

Claire sent flowers and a fruit basket. She signed up for the
neighborhood meal rotation, leaving a casserole on the Danielses' front steps every Thursday. The curtains were never
opened, the blinds always drawn. It was as if all life had been
removed from the house. One afternoon, when she dropped off
a pan of chicken divan, she saw a catcher's mitt and a bat on the
front lawn. The sight of them made goosebumps climb up her
arms. Had they been there all this time? Claire hesitated at the
door. But then she laid the casserole, wrapped in a blue-and-
white-checked dish towel, on the stairs and hurried off, avoiding
the sight of Dougie's Little League gear as she walked back to
her car.

By October, when the leaves on the trees in Honeysuckle
Hills had turned scarlet and gold, the Danielses had moved
away. At first, no one bought their house—Who would? Roberta
had wondered aloud, and all the women had nodded, understanding that a house where a murdered child had lived was of

course undesirable—but two weeks before Christmas a new family moved in. The wife was pregnant with twins and on bedrest, but the husband was friendly. He could be spotted shoveling snow, or hanging Christmas decorations. He always waved when someone went past.

If Dougie Daniels had not gone missing, kidnapped practically right in front of Claire's eyes, she thought it was possible that she would still be moving through her life as she had been, in a pleasant, mind-numbing routine. But Dougie did get kidnapped. And after that afternoon, nothing felt the same to Claire. Nothing felt right anymore. Until Miles had looked at her in that way. Then something shifted. Not into place, but rather completely off-center. Claire had recognized it, and jumped in.

# 2

# The Obituary Writer

## VIVIEN, 1919

The obituary writer, Vivien Lowe, usually did not know her clients. They came from Silverado and Calistoga; from Point Reyes Station and Sacramento; from San Francisco and Oakland. She had even had clients come from as far away as Ashland, Oregon, and, once, Los Angeles. They read about her gift for bringing the dead to life, and they came to her clutching their tearstained handkerchiefs, their crumpled notes, their photographs of their deceased loved ones.

They were all very much like Mrs. Marjorie Benton, who sat across from her now on the small deep purple velvet loveseat. It was a rainy March afternoon in the town of Napa, California, in 1919. Outside the window, the leaves on the oak trees were wet and green. The office looked like a sitting room, with its Victorian furniture salvaged from the old apartment in San Francisco, the loveseat and chairs and ornate, beaded lamps. The obituary writer lived above her office, in one large room that looked down on Napa's main street. On the rare occasions when she parted the draperies that hung on the windows upstairs, she could watch small-town life unfold before her. The farmers with their wagons of fruit; the vintners with their hands stained purple from Mission grapes; women clutching children's hands. But she preferred to keep the draperies closed. Downstairs, however, in her office, she let the light in; she believed sunlight had healing properties.

Mrs. Benton was crying softly. Her cup of tea, which sat on the small table between them, had grown cold.

Even though they did not know it, Vivien knew that grieving people needed food and something to quench their thirst. She believed in the powers of clear broth and toast, of sustenance. So she always put out a small plate of cheese and crackers, or cookies, or fruit. She always offered her clients a drink. Cool water, hot tea, even a glass of wine from her friend Lotte's family vineyard up Highway 29. Mrs. Benton had asked for tea when Vivien offered her a drink. Long ago, in another lifetime, she had learned about tea from David's law partner, Duncan, who had spent his childhood in India. Duncan liked to pontificate about everything from tea to séances to the mating habits of tigers. *I only trust about ten percent of what he says*, David used to say. *But he is entertaining.*

Vivien kept many varieties of tea on hand. Mrs. Benton had chosen Earl Grey. It sat now, amber in its china cup, forgotten.

"My Frank," Mrs. Benton was saying, "graduated from the University of California at Berkeley in 1899."

Vivien did some fast math. Frank Benton was only a man in his early forties. Not much older than Vivien herself; she was thirty-seven. Mr. Benton had died after having a tooth pulled.

"His degree was in mathematics," Mrs. Benton added. She frowned. "Aren't you going to write any of this down, Miss Lowe?"

Vivien shook her head. "That isn't how I work," she explained.

She didn't tell Mrs. Benton that these facts—degrees and numbers and jobs and affiliations—were not what made a life. Everyone who came here to her small office in Napa answered her request of: "Tell me about your loved one" with facts. Vivien let them tell her about places of birth and accomplishments, number of grandchildren and siblings. Then, when they were finished, she would say again, "Tell me about your loved one." That was when the person began to come to life.

"We were married on June 17, aught four," Mrs. Benton continued. "Lost everything in aught six."

Vivien felt that lump in her throat, the one that seemed to appear at the mere suggestion of the earthquake. *Lost everything,* Mrs. Benton said matter-of-factly, and Vivien nodded, willing herself to be calm. It had been thirteen years and she was getting better at holding her own grief at bay.

"That scared the bejesus out of us," Mrs. Benton said, "so we moved up to Monticello."

Vivien waited. With a sigh, Mrs. Benton went on. "Three children. Owen, fourteen. Maxwell, twelve. June, ten." She frowned again.

She was a plump woman with saggy skin that made Vivien think of elephants. Of course, Vivien had never actually seen an elephant, except in books and magazines at the library, which was where she spent her free time. There and at Lotte's place. And here, of course. Alone.

Even in her grief Mrs. Benton had applied red lipstick and too much face powder. Out of habit, no doubt. Grieving people operated by rote. They went through the motions of living, pulling their hair from their faces or pinning on a brooch without thinking.

"Are you going to write *that* down?" Mrs. Benton said.

"No, no, I have it. Owen. Maxwell. June," Vivien said.

"I don't know," Mrs. Benton said, shaking her head and sending her folds of skin into a tremble. "I came because of what you did when Elliott Mann died. Do you remember that obituary you wrote? Why, people went up to his wife for weeks afterwards saying that after reading it, they felt they knew him better than when he was alive. Why, no one at all knew that he had rescued those boys from drowning way back."

She waited for Vivien to say something. When she didn't, Mrs. Benton said, "You put in that poem by Emily Dickinson. Remember?"

"Of course," Vivien lied. In truth, after she wrote an obituary, she pushed that person's name, that life, out of her mind. It was too much of a burden to keep so many deaths so close.

"I liked that poem," Mrs. Benton said. "Maybe you'll use it for my Frank?"

"Perhaps," Vivien said.

The women sat across from each other in silence. Vivien was very aware of the grandfather clock's loud ticking. She wondered if Mrs. Benton heard it too.

Finally Vivien said, "Tell me about Frank."

Mrs. Benton's overly powdered face seemed to fall in on itself. "When I think of him, it's always with his birds, you know?"

"Birds?"

Mrs. Benton nodded, no longer trying to control her tears. "He raised songbirds. What will become of them all now? Cages and cages of songbirds. He could exactly imitate each of their songs. Couldn't carry the tune of a regular song, mind you. But the man could chirp."

*Yonder stands a lonely tree, There I live and mourn for thee,* Vivien thought. Would Mrs. Benton be satisfied with Blake instead of Dickinson?

"I used to accuse him of loving those birds more than he

loved me. I didn't really think that. If you had seen him, Miss Lowe, when I was sick with consumption a few years back. How tenderly he cared for me. How gently he brushed my hair and laid cool cloths on my forehead. He was a gentle man, my Frank. And to think something as simple as a tooth . . ." She shook her head, unbelieving.

Vivien thought again of "The Birds," when the voice of the woman asks: *Dost thou truly long for me? And am I thus sweet to thee?* Yes, Blake was exactly right for Frank Benton's obituary.

"It had to come out, didn't it?" Mrs. Benton asked suddenly, her eyes wild. "It was infected. You know the pain an infected tooth can cause. I told him to go and have Doc Trevor take it out. I told him that. But it had to come out, didn't it?"

"Of course, darling," Vivien said, reaching for Marjorie Benton's doughy white hands. "Of course."

Grief made people guilty. Guilty for being five minutes late, for taking the wrong streetcar, for ignoring a cough or sleeping too soundly. Guilt and grief went hand in hand. Vivien knew that. The morning of April 18, 1906, threatened to creep into her mind. She saw it there at the edges of her thoughts, her younger self in their bed with the bedclothes  they had bought in Italy crumpled around her. The room was still dark, and Caruso's voice still rang in her ears.

David bent to kiss her goodbye. "Last night," he said. "It was musical."

She smiled, even in her drowsiness. This was a game they played. "It was delicious," she said, remembering the lamb chops, the potatoes dauphinoise, the baby peas.

"Intoxicating," he whispered.

"That was mine!" she said, swatting his arm.

"Sexy," he whispered.

"Go," she laughed.

"Not until you say one."

Vivien sighed. "Too short," she said finally. "Last night was too short."

"Yes," he agreed. "Damn Duncan for insisting we meet so early. It's not even light yet."

"Ah! So you're leaving me to meet someone else," Vivien teased. She ran her fingers up his arm, enjoying the goosebumps that rose beneath them. David and his partner in the law firm were opposites: Duncan flamboyant, loud, flashy. He drove a Rolls-Royce Silver Ghost all around town, and wore a white suit. He had grown up in India, and threw huge parties where he served curry so hot he provided linen handkerchiefs to all the guests so they could wipe the sweat from their faces.

"Everything's an emergency with Duncan," David said. He caught her fingers in his hand, and raised them to his mouth, kissing each one.

"You will put out yet another fire Duncan started," Vivien said.

"I hope so. It's difficult to deal with Duncan on three hours' sleep," he added, laughing.

"You will," she said, stifling a yawn. "You are heroic. You can do anything." She was teasing him, but Vivien did believe it. She had watched him in court, the way he argued cases, the way he saved men's lives.

"We'll find out soon enough," he said, kissing her again.

Vivien listened to his footsteps move away from her. She imagined him downstairs eating bread and jam, drinking a cup of espresso he had made from the temperamental machine he used. Finally, the door opened on its hinges that needed oiling, and closed shut.

She snuggled deeper under the blankets, and closed her eyes, knowing that in a few hours Fu Jing would arrive noisily, banging doors and shaking dishes. Fu Jing would appear in the doorway with her breakfast tray, muttering in Chinese about Vivien's laziness. And about her immorality. Vivien wondered which of the angry Chinese words Fu Jing muttered meant mistress or whore? Which meant homewrecker, kept woman? She didn't care. If she did, she wouldn't be here in this lavish apartment that her lover paid for while his wife woke alone across town in their house in Pacific Heights.

Vivien closed her eyes and drifted off to sleep. Less than an hour later, she woke not to Fu Jing rattling about and cursing, but to the entire house shaking and rolling as if it were riding waves across the ocean. Vivien sat up with great difficulty, and clutched the sides of the bed. The clock, the one that chimed so beautifully on the hour, the half, and the quarter, with whimsical paintings across its face of all the astrological signs, said 5:12. Outside, people had begun to shout and things had begun to fall—streetlamps and stairways and windows. The noises grew louder and more frantic. The light grew brighter outside her window. But all Vivien could do was sit holding on to her bed, as if it were a life raft keeping her safe.

The clock chimed and Mrs. Benton shifted in her chair. Vivien pushed away the memories. And that small illogical part of her rose, the part that believed, ridiculously, that perhaps David was still alive somewhere. Perhaps he had hit his head during the earthquake. Hadn't entire walls and columns and roofs fallen that day? Wasn't it possible that he had hit his head and had amnesia? She had spent hours in the library researching that condition. The word came from the Greek, *amnestia*. Not remembered. She knew it was, in simple terms, the loss of memory, and that it came from a head injury or psychological trauma. She knew too, that it was possible that David suffered one or both of those that terrible day of the earthquake.

It sounded foolish, Vivien realized that. But she clipped arti cles from newspapers and journals about amnesia, about people who suffered from it, and people who had recovered. She clipped these articles and pasted them in a large leather book and kept it by her bed. There was hope in those stories. One of them dis-cussed a different kind of amnesia, one in which a person has the inability to imagine the future. Funny, Vivien had thought when she read that, how she and David were perhaps both suffering from amnesia. His, the more common type, and hers this other one. The inability to imagine the future.

Mrs. Benton sighed. She glanced toward the window and touched her own powdered cheek as if to prove that she was still alive.

"People always say how nice his feet are," she said softly. "Isn't that the craziest thing? A man's feet? Once we were on Stimson Beach and a man came up to us and asked Frank if he could take a photograph of his feet. The man said he was a photographer and that he was certain that Frank could be a foot model for catalogues. Do you know that I think for a minute Frank considered it?" She blinked and then narrowed her eyes at Vivien. "Listen to me go on about nonsense," Marjorie said. "But they were beautiful, my Frank's feet."

It was dusk. The sky was turning violet and the lamps on the street were lit.

"I think I have enough," Vivien told her.

Already a person was taking shape. Mrs. Benton had arrived an hour and a half ago, her hair and coat wet with rain, and she had brought with her a dead man, a blank thing without breath or life. But she had left behind a living man who could perfectly imitate a bird's unique song.

"Thank you," Mrs. Benton said, surprising Vivien by pulling her into a suffocating hug.

Mrs. Benton smelled sour. Vivien guessed that since her husband had had that tooth pulled two days ago, and come home looking ill and feeling, as Mrs. Benton said, "not quite right," and gone to bed where he had died by suppertime, Marjorie Benton had not washed. She had cried and screamed and pulled her frightened children close to her. She had applied powder and lipstick without thinking because that was what a woman did when she went into town.

Now, she held Vivien close, pressed to her, for a long while. Vivien felt the sobs rising in Mrs. Benton's chest, felt her shuddering. Finally, Vivien was released. She stepped back and took a deep breath, letting the soothing smell of lavender fill her. She kept dried lavender in small dishes placed all around the office. Lavender was known to calm and comfort. The people who came to her needed that. Vivien needed it too.

She walked her client to the door. For a moment she was afraid Mrs. Benton would hug her again, but instead the woman just pressed Vivien's hands in her own soft ones before hurrying out.

Vivien stood in her small office, listening to the clock tick and breathing in the scent of lavender. She stood for some time, trying not to think about those three fatherless children in Monticello, or Mrs. Benton's sour smell, or her own long-missing love. But as always, this last was impossible.


Vivien Lowe met David Gardner on an afternoon in May on Market Street in San Francisco. She was wearing an oversized, ridiculous blue hat that she had owned for exactly ten minutes. It was spring and she was twenty-two years old. She saw that hat in an expensive milliner's shop and without thinking about it at all, she bought it. The hat made her feel foolish and sophisticated. She pretended she was a Frenchwoman, a Parisian, instead of an English teacher at the Field School, a private school for girls on Nob Hill. Lotte would laugh at the hat, Vivien knew that. She would laugh and then beg to borrow it. Lotte had been her best friend since they themselves were students at the very school where Vivien now taught. Both of them had been orphaned young, and this sad history had made them instant friends.

Catching her reflection in the window of the Emporium, Vivien smiled. Perhaps she would go inside and take the elevator to the fourth-floor tearoom and have a sandwich, pretending to be French. She would order her sandwich in a French accent, and pretend not to understand when the waitress in her pink and white uniform asked if she would like lemon or cream in her tea. Vivien giggled at the thought.

"I've never seen a woman who enjoyed herself quite so much as you do, mademoiselle," a man said.

Vivien saw his reflection in the glass too. He was tall and broad-shouldered with golden hair. He was smirking.

*"Je ne comprends pas,"* Vivien said. She had always received A's in French.

The man replied in such rapid French that Vivien turned away from their reflection to see him better.

He laughed at the look on her face.

"That is quite a magnificent hat," he said.

Embarrassed, Vivien turned and continued down Market Street, wondering how he had known her fantasy of being a fancy Frenchwoman. She wondered what Lotte would say about this, if Vivien mentioned it. In three weeks, Lotte was getting married and it was hard to get her attention and keep it for any length of time these days.

Footsteps rushed up beside her. "Pardon me," the man—that rude man—said. "I couldn't resist teasing you."

Vivien wished she had not bought the hat. Or that she could take it off now. Maybe she would just give it to Lotte, although her friend certainly wouldn't be needing it up in that one-horse town she was moving to. In Napa, people grew fruit and made wine and had babies. The thought of losing her friend made Vivien's eyes tear. They had been together forever, since they were six and wore the gray jumpers that all Field girls wore in the lower school. Now Lotte was moving a world away.

The man, whom Vivien had stopped noticing, touched her elbow. "I've upset you," he said.

She shook her head. "I forgot you were here," she said honestly, missing Lotte already.

They stopped walking. Vivien saw her streetcar approaching but did not move to catch it.

"What then?" he asked her.

She did not know how to articulate her loss. It seemed too large for words to capture it.

Without warning, the sky grew dark and large fat drops of rain began to fall hard and fast. The man took her elbow again and guided her into a small restaurant at the corner. Already, Vivien's skirt was wet. The hat drooped.

A waiter rushed over to them and offered a table for two by the window. He pulled Vivien's chair out for her, then slid it back to the table, handing her a large, heavy menu. It was, she noticed, all in French. The stranger was sitting too, ignoring his menu and staring at Vivien instead. Outside, rain lashed the window, which rattled from the wind.

"A storm," Vivien said.

"Quite," the man said.

"Forgive me," she said. "I'm not in the habit of picking up

strange men on the street and allowing them to take me into dim French restaurants."

The man grinned at her. He was older than she, with fine lines at the corners of his green eyes.

"And I," he said, "have never fallen immediately in love with a hat. Until now."

The waiter hovered nearby.

Vivien knew that some people believed that in the moments before death, a person's life flashed through their mind. Although she did not believe she was dying as she sat in that French restaurant on that May afternoon during a rainstorm, her life did pass before her. The vague shadowy images of her parents; her Aunt Irene and the house on Fremont Street; all of those years at the Field School for Girls with their Latin and French and Literature; holding Lotte's hand; the small room in the boardinghouse across the bay in Oakland where Vivien lived while she studied at Mills College; her first beau, Langston Moore, who kissed her with such passion her teeth ached afterwards; the classroom at the Field School that was hers now with its neat rows of desks and the girls in their gray skirts and white blouses and the smell of chalk dust and books being opened; her first glimpse of the blue hat in the window of the milliner's shop.

The man, this stranger sitting across from her, was speaking to the waiter. Ordering supper, she realized.

Vivien stood abruptly, banging her knee against the table and spilling some water onto the starched white tablecloth.

"I can't eat supper with you," she said. "I have to be at Lotte's bridal shower at the Fenn Club." She was going to be late, she realized, and without even telling the man her name, Vivien rushed outside into the rain. Her streetcar was there, ready to close its doors. She shouted to the conductor, and lifting her skirt, ran across the street, hopping onto the streetcar, wet and out of breath. From the window, she saw the man standing in the doorway of the restaurant, still holding one of the white linen napkins, like a soldier offering surrender to his enemy. For the first time since he'd spoken to her in front of the Emporium, she saw the thick gold band on his left ring finger.

"It's infatuation, that's all," Lotte told Vivien.

It had been three days since Vivien had met the man on Market Street, and she had not had a good night's sleep or been able to keep him out of her mind. Even as she sat with Lotte recording the wedding gifts for her, murmuring over the heavy silver and delicate crystal lined up on the dining room table, all she could think about was that man.

Sometimes she blurted, "The audacity of him! Assuming I'd want to eat dinner with him."

To which Lotte, tracing the bluebells on her china, replied, "And him a married man too."

Or Vivien would say dreamily, "He is handsome, though."

"And married."

Vivien sighed. She hadn't told Lotte that part of what kept her up at night was imagining his wife, hoping she was ill or insane or something that would allow him to pursue Vivien. But then she would worry over how he would ever find her again. She was just a nameless stranger in a blue hat.

"Love is something else," Lotte was saying now.

Vivien, bored with her job of carefully writing down each item and the name and address of who had sent it, was contemplating how she might find him. If she went to Market Street and stood in front of the Emporium every afternoon, would he pass by again?

"It's a more practical feeling, Vivvie," Lotte said as she

unwrapped yet another china plate. She admired it as if she had not already received six others. "Love is reliable. Infatuation is temporary."

Vivien realized she'd been holding a sterling silver fish knife for far too long, and lost track of who had sent it.

"Have you recorded that yet?" Lotte asked her.

The thank-you notes, engraved with dark brown letters on thick cream paper, waited on the sideboard to be written.

"Yes," Vivien lied, and laid it on the table. "It doesn't matter," she continued. "I'll never see him again."

"Which is a good thing," Lotte said. "Since he's—"

"I know."

"You'll see at the wedding. Robert has some very handsome friends. And a cousin who's a dentist in Boise."

"Idaho? No thank you, Lotte. You might be willing to move to the country, but I prefer to stay right here, thank you."

"Boise is a city, Viv."

Vivien made a sound in her throat which she hoped Lotte took as agreement.

Lotte walked dreamily around the table, her fingers fluttering over her wedding presents as if she were already placing them in her new home.

"If I went back to the very spot where I first saw him," Vivien said, pretending to admire a sterling silver ice bucket, "do you think he might pass by?"

"One of Robert's friends also owns a vineyard. We could be neighbors," Lotte said, her eyes shining. "Our children could be best friends too. And we could grow old together."

Vivien smiled. "That sounds nice," she admitted.

It did sound nice. More than nice, Vivien thought. It sounded right. She and Lotte had been like family to each other ever since both of their parents had died during the influenza epidemic. By coincidence, they each had a spinster aunt who took them in. By coincidence, those aunts lived next door to each other in Pacific Heights. Although both of those women were loving and kind to the girls, Vivien and Lotte found comfort with each other. At night, Lotte always turned her nightlight on and off three times. And Vivien responded by doing the same. It was their way of saying *Good night. I'm here.*

Now of course Lotte was leaving San Francisco. Leaving Vivien. Lotte was starting a family of her own, with Robert and her china and silver. What was Vivien supposed to do by herself?

"What's this friend's name?" Vivien asked Lotte, a panic rising in her chest. "I'll pay special attention to him."

Perhaps that was what she should do. Fall in love with the vintner, move to Napa, manage a vineyard and have babies and keep Lotte close.

Lotte brightened. "Thomas," she said.

"That's a good strong name," Vivien said, carefully unwrapping white tissue paper and lifting a crystal goblet from its nest there. "I always liked the name Thomas."

"There," Lotte said, her voice heavy with relief. "You'll forget all about this other man. You'll see."

But it wasn't infatuation. That's what Vivien understood almost immediately when she saw David again. That very afternoon, as she and Lotte opened the wedding gifts, the doorbell rang and a letter was delivered for the woman in the blue hat, in care of Lotte.

*"I had just two clues. Your friend's name was Lotte and her bridal shower was at the Fenn Club. I trust this will find you and we can have our dinner together, though by now it has probably grown cold. Tonight? At eight-thirty? Yours, David Gardner, Esq."*

"You can't go," Lotte told her.

But of course, Vivien did.

.    .    .

*Ah, David,* Vivien thought, that too-familiar ache of sadness filling her.

Mechanically, Vivien collected the teacup and saucer, the small plate of cookies, from the table. She would wash them in the kitchen, then climb the stairs to her bedroom and take a long warm bath. She would enjoy a glass of Lotte's wine, and climb into bed to read until she grew drowsy and could finally sleep. Her nights were often exactly like this one. But rather than causing boredom or loneliness, this solitary routine brought her comfort.

Vivien rinsed first the teacup, watching as the Earl Grey disappeared down the drain, then its saucer, both of them rimmed with a silver stripe. Her wedding china, she and David called it, even though there had never been a proper wedding. Exactly half of it had survived the earthquake. The irony of this was not lost on Vivien, herself a surviving half. Vivien took a cookie, a lacy Florentine, and nibbled it as she rinsed the plate. She realized she had not had any supper and considered making herself a little something. There were good fresh eggs in the icebox, and mushrooms, the dirt still clinging to them, waiting on the counter. Vivien imagined cracking two eggs in the cobalt blue bowl, and stirring them with some salt and pepper. She imagined wiping the mushrooms clean, slicing them, then sautéing them in butter.

In her mind, she could see the result, a golden omelet, earthy with mushrooms and a snip of the chives she grew on her windowsill. But instead, Vivien turned off the light in the kitchen and went upstairs. A book lay open on the night table. Without undressing, she picked it up and settled onto the bed. She could almost hear Lotte reprimanding her. *Eat! Take a walk!*

*Let the Italian man who adores you buy you dinner in town.* She could hear Lotte telling her, *You are wasting your life on a dream, Vivvie.*

Vivien placed her finger on the page, and closed the book. If David had died, she thought for the millionth time, she would have felt it. She would have felt his life leaving. By now, he would have come to her somehow—in a dream, as a ghost, *somehow.* She shook her head, as if she were actually arguing with Lotte. He had to be out there. He had to. If not, then Lotte would be right. She had wasted so many years on the dream of him, on this sliver of hope.

These kinds of thoughts could keep her up all night, Vivien knew. She opened the book again, and forced herself to focus on the words there.

*"I used to wish I could have this flattering dream about Antonia,"* she read, *"but I never did . . ."*

And soon, Vivien was back in Willa Cather's world, safely removed from her own.

# TWO

Persons under the shock of genuine affliction are not only upset mentally but are all unbalanced physically. No matter how calm and controlled they seemingly may be, no one can under such circumstances be normal. Their disturbed circulation makes them cold, their distress makes them unstrung, sleepless. Persons they normally like, they often turn from.

—FROM *Etiquette*, BY EMILY POST, 1922

# 3

## Super Constellation

### CLAIRE, 1961

They called her mother-in-law Birdy. Everyone did. Even Peter called her Birdy instead of Mom or Mother. Claire never liked it. To her, birds were small, delicate things with hearts beating fast in their chests and lovely feathers and songs. This Birdy was tall and big-boned. No bright plumage. No catchy songs. *Think pelicans*, Peter teased. *Think flamingos*. Still, the nickname always caught in her throat. *It's what my father always called her*, Peter had explained. *But she's so un-bird-like*, Claire insisted.

Claire glanced out the window at the snow falling steadily. In her hand she held the invitation, a formal one on heavy paper with green embossed leaves climbing up one side and the words:

*Come Celebrate Birdy's 80th Birthday*
*January 19, 1961*
*8 p.m.*
THE HOPE CLUB  PROVIDENCE

The truth was, she didn't want to go her mother-in-law's—to *Birdy's*—birthday party. What she wanted was to stay right here and go to her neighbor Dot's inauguration brunch tomorrow morning. The entire neighborhood would be there, and they would watch John F. Kennedy take the oath of office. All of the women were guessing what color Jackie would wear, and the winner got a daiquiri party. Pink, Claire had guessed, and she felt certain she would win. She could picture Jackie in pink. That dark hair against pale pink, against the winter sky. Now she wasn't even sure if she'd get to watch the inauguration at all. Would Birdy want to sit around and wait to hear what Kennedy had to say? Or what Jackie wore? Claire had considered using her condition to stay home, and let Peter go off to Rhode Island alone. But she owed him. She knew that.

Still, with him out of the house, Claire thought she might be able to breathe, to think straight. Because the truth was she had not really thought straight since Dougie Daniels went missing. The baby inside her rolled lazily, and Claire put her hand on her stomach as if to say good morning. Outside the window, the snow was accumulating fast. This storm was supposed to move all the way to New England, and they would be right in it. They should have left last night, Claire thought. They should stay home.

At the corner, their big green Chevy station wagon turned, inching along the slippery road. Peter, always prepared, an Eagle Scout still at thirty-two, had gone to fill the gas tank and check the oil and tires.

"Romper!" Kathy was saying. "Romper! Romper!"

"You're right, Kitty Kat," Claire said, lifting her daughter from the high chair. "It is time for *Romper Room*."

She carried Kathy, clutching her stuffed rabbit Mimi, into

the den and turned on *Romper Room*. Miss Bonnie was already
looking through her Magic Mirror.

"And I see Debbie, and I see Wendy," Miss Bonnie said.

"See Kathy!" Kathy shouted at the television. "See Mimi!"

Claire went back into the kitchen and stood at the window
again, staring out at the snow, her husband's headlights moving
straight for her. She didn't love him. Every time she had that
thought, she felt like she was strangling. Literally, she gasped for
breath. She didn't love her husband and she was pregnant with
a baby that she didn't think was his. Just six months ago, she
would never have believed that she would be a woman standing
by a window in a situation like this. But here she was.

"Reach for stars!" Kathy sang from the living room.

Claire leaned forward, barely able to lean across the expanse
of her belly and press her head against the cold pane of the
window.

She heard the car stopping, its engine dying. She heard the
car door open and then shut, her husband stomping across the
snow.

Gulping for air, she tried to shut out her thoughts. A woman
in 1961, who did not love her husband, had nowhere to go. A
woman who'd had an affair and been caught, had no choice but
to hope her husband forgave her and would let her stay. So then
why did Claire want neither of these things to happen, not for-
giveness, not to stay? What was wrong with her?

The kitchen door opened.

Miss Bonnie sang, "There goes Jupiter, here comes Mars
. . ."

"Claire?" Peter said.

She swallowed as much air as she could take in.

Her husband was walking across the gold-speckled linoleum

floor toward her. She could see his wingtips covered in rubber galoshes.

"Honey?" he was saying. "Are you okay?"

She lifted her head and gave him a weak smile. "Just dizzy," she said, her hands floating above her belly as evidence.

"Come sit," he said.

He put his hands on her shoulders and guided her to the chair at the head of the table, the one called the captain's chair. Their eyes met briefly. Claire was the first to look away.

"Water?" he asked, already moving to the sink.

But Claire shook her head.

Peter stood in the middle of their kitchen, looking lost.

"Do you think it's safe?" she asked him. "To drive all that way in this?"

His jaw tightened. "Jesus, Claire. It's her eightieth birthday. We can't miss that."

Claire waited, hoping he would say the next thing on his own. *You stay, Claire.*

But instead he said, "The car's in tip-top shape. You packed?"

She nodded. The kitchen table was strewn with the remains of a roll of wrapping paper, dark red and white, and threads of silver ribbon. Claire picked up Birdy's present, a collection of poems by Robert Frost. Birdy loved poetry. And Frost was reading a poem tomorrow at the inauguration.

"I'll get Kathy," she said, heaving herself to her feet.

At night, Claire put herself to sleep by doing the math to determine just how pregnant she was. At five months with Kathy, she'd only gained ten pounds; this time she'd gained more than double that. Did that mean she was more than five months pregnant? In which case this baby was indeed Peter's. But no matter how she calculated, she always got the same answer. This baby was not her husband's.

"Claire?" Peter was calling from down the hall. "Just the one suitcase?"

She stared down at the pretty wrapping paper, the mess of ribbon and scraps and tape.

"You fit everything in just the one?" he was saying.

"Yes," Claire said, deciding to leave the mess until they got back.

Her lover's name was Miles Sullivan, and he was not her type. Or what Claire had always thought was her type, which was tall and well-muscled with a face that seemed to be carved from marble. No, Miles—though tall, taller even than Peter—had the start of a paunch, his stomach pressing against his belt, and a fleshy ruddy face with almost a cartoonish nose. In his way, he was handsome, she supposed. Black Irish, he had described himself, which meant a head of thick dark hair that he wore slightly too shaggy and round bright blue eyes. His smile dazzled, but it was not those blue eyes or his imposing size or even that smile that attracted her to him from the start. It was the way he listened to her. He cocked his head, and turned his eyes on her as if she had something important to say. That very first night at Dot's dinner party, Claire had noticed this and wondered if Peter had ever listened to her in quite this way. He had not, she decided. Not once.

Of course, there was desire too. A desire like Claire had never felt before. And she was embarrassed that somehow this desire was wrapped up in Dougie Daniels' disappearance. Yet once that happened, something stirred in Claire for the first time. She remembered a night in Rome when she was an air hostess and she and her roommate Rose had met two men at a trattoria, gotten drunk with them, and then taken them back to the hotel.

That night, Claire had done things she'd never before imagined doing with a man. It was the wine and the summer Roman air and all the Sambuca and the riding on the Vespa with the wind in her hair. But she'd never seen that man again. And she'd never spoken of that night, not even with Rose.

Now this thing, this *stirring*, could not be satisfied. Embarrassed after what happened with Peter, she'd tried to feed it in other ways: tennis and hot baths and even some of the diet pills Roberta's doctor gave her (those only led her to do things like vacuum or polish the silver, and lose five pounds too many). At first, talking to Miles seemed to work. His head cocked like that, his questions, probing, asking what she thought and felt, what she wanted. But soon, her desire grew into something more, as if she wished he could actually climb inside her and fill her, fill this unnameable need she had. To both of their surprise, she had been the one to lean in for the first kiss, the one to unbuckle his belt and reach her hand inside. *I'm suffocating,* she had told him that first time. With him, she could breathe. She could say whatever was on her mind, wonder aloud about why a soufflé had failed to rise or what she would bring to a desert island or anything, really, that popped into her head. No matter what it was, Miles listened.

That was why she invited him into her home, a stupid idea. But with Peter at work in the city, and the neighborhood settled into its routines, she imagined a whole day with Miles. She'd made a pitcher of perfect Manhattans, carefully measuring the sweet and dry vermouths, dropping six neon-red cherries into the amber liquid. She put on a lace bra and matching panties in a color called champagne, bought at Hecht's just for this day.

"A tryst," Miles had said when he arrived, his hand slipping into her silk blouse to discover the lace waiting there.

It was a gray September morning, the kind of day that

reminds you that summer is over and fall is on its way. Claire had dropped Kathy at the sitter's, spurting lies about errands and appointments that would keep her out all day.

"Manhattans in the morning?" he'd said as he watched her place ice cubes into the heavy glasses, then pour the drinks.

"Why not?" Claire had said.

"Why not indeed," he said, raising his glass to hers and clinking. "Obviously," he said, "to us."

They had talked that day too. About the election—that was all anybody could talk about. About Claire's fascination with Jackie. About his fascination with Marilyn Monroe. But then the talking stopped. They were half drunk, having sloppy sex first on the sofa Peter hated and then on the twin bed in Kathy's room, the one she'd never slept in yet, which they were planning on moving her from the crib onto by Thanksgiving. Miles had ripped her new lace bra. She had banged her knee on his chin, then laughed at the fact that her knee was even near his chin.

Outside, she heard voices, someone getting into or out of a car.

She felt reckless and alive. She clawed at Miles. He was saying something to her, his breath boozy and sweet, all bourbon and cherries. The air around them seemed electrified. That stirring in her, that thing, was an abyss, a chasm, something that needed to be filled. She told him that she needed to run away. *Do women ever do that? Run away from their perfect lives?* Miles had looked at her hard. *No*, he told her, *they run away from their imperfect lives.*

He kissed her, and she opened her mouth to him, tangled her fingers in all that dark hair.

Then Claire opened her eyes.

In the doorway stood Peter, his tie in a perfect Windsor knot, a pulse beating in his temple.

"Get out," he said calmly, and at first she thought he was speaking to her.

But then she realized that he was talking to Miles, who was struggling to his feet, dragging the white sheet patterned with daisies along with him.

"Get out of my house," Peter said.

Claire had the comforter around her now, covering herself with it, the daisies everywhere.

Miles gathered his clothes. When he walked past Peter, Peter seemed not to notice. He could only look at Claire, as if he were trying to find his wife somewhere in that bed.

"Get dressed," he said finally.

"I . . . need some privacy," she said. "I need a minute."

Peter didn't leave. He watched her clumsily pull her blue silk blouse on over her torn bra, watched her try to button the buttons.

"Are you drunk?" he asked her, his voice for the first time since he'd walked in revealing emotion.

Claire nodded. What was the point in denying any of it?

"Peter," she said, "I'm so unhappy."

"Unhappy?" he said, almost in wonder.

"I don't know what I want or what I feel. I thought I wanted this. Us. But now I'm not so sure." Her only lie that. She couldn't hurt him more than she already had.

Peter shook his head.

"I can't look at you," he said, and he turned and walked out.


To Claire it seemed they would be trapped in the overheated car forever.

Peter had barely spoken since they started driving north. His hands in the brown leather driving gloves Claire had bought him for Christmas clutched the steering wheel hard, and his nose was red from the cold.

Outside, the snow fell furiously. Claire sat uncomfortable and frightened beside him. The station wagon, that massive green thing that she hated to drive, even on sunny days or for short errands, fishtailed and slid on the slick road.

"She's so excited about this party," Peter said. He let out a low whistle. "Eighty years young," he said.

Claire chewed on her bottom lip, the waxy taste of her lipstick almost pleasant. They hadn't eaten anything since they left five hours earlier. She didn't dare ask Peter to stop, even though she would love a grilled cheese sandwich and a cup of coffee. Every so many miles, she saw the orange roof of a Howard Johnson's through the snow on the side of the road. But she didn't bother to mention it.

Peter was hunched over the steering wheel now. "Goddamn it! I can't see anything."

Claire took a tissue from her purse, and wiped away the condensation on the windshield.

"Don't do that," Peter said. "It's leaving smears."

He had always been this way: demanding, a perfectionist, someone who wanted things done his way. Until last summer, Claire had accommodated him. She hadn't liked it, the way he could be so critical of others, including her. Especially her. She hadn't liked that when she tried to tell him what she thought or felt, he might walk out of the room, saying, "Keep going. I can hear you." And Claire would be alone in an empty room, feeling foolish. Still, he loved her. She knew that. He loved her the best way he could. But Claire wasn't sure that was enough anymore.

She shook her head, as if to shake these thoughts away. For weeks now she'd been doing nothing but worrying about what to do about her marriage. Women did not leave. Unless there had been adultery or abuse, and even then, they usually stayed. She remembered the story of a woman who had lived a few streets away, long before Claire and Peter moved into the neighborhood. She'd left her husband and the judge had not let her take her children. *She abandoned them,* Dot had explained, her face set in disgust. If she left Peter, would a judge let Claire keep her children? Or should she stay and possibly never feel happy again?

Claire swallowed hard, then offered, "There's a Howard Johnson's up ahead. Maybe you could use a cup of coffee."

"Maybe," he said, softening.

He liked when she took care of him; Claire knew this. But it was getting harder for her to take care of him when she didn't really like him very much anymore. She had to keep reminding herself that it was her job to care for him. That was what wives did.

"It might be a long night. We might as well have a little something in our stomachs." He added gently, "You, of course, already have a little something in yours."

Claire laughed politely. This baby did not feel at all little. It jammed up against her ribs and pressed on her bladder. It made her short of breath and short on patience. When Peter made love to her now, she kept her nightgown on. She didn't feel very pretty these days.

Relieved, Claire felt the car slow even more and make a slippery turn into the Howard Johnson's.

"Maybe I can call Birdy and be sure the party is still on," Peter said, opening his door and stepping into the night.

The snow seemed to gobble him up. *If only,* Claire thought. She imagined that when she too stepped out of the car, Peter would really have vanished. She would go inside and wait out the storm, sipping coffee and dreaming of her new life, free of her husband. Stop it, she told herself. You are married to this man, for better or worse. When she had spoken those words four years ago, she had meant them, hadn't she?

Peter's voice cut through the storm. "What are you waiting for?" he called.

Claire sighed and got out of the car. She opened the back door, and awkwardly lifted their sleeping daughter into her arms.

"Come on, baby," Claire murmured to Kathy.

Kathy wrapped her arms around Claire's neck and hung on her like a koala bear. The parking lot hadn't been plowed yet, and Claire had to pick her way slowly across it, trying not to fall. Peter stood in the harsh light by the front door, smoking and waiting for them. Claire could feel his impatience in the air.

"Of all days for the world to come to an end," she heard him saying.

Kathy's breath, sour from the potato chips she'd eaten in the car, warmed Claire's cheek.

Finally, they reached the entrance. Claire panted from the walk and the weight.

Peter dropped his cigarette and crushed it with his boot.

Claire grabbed at his arm.

"What?" he said. His eyes were bloodshot from the hard drive.

"I'm sorry," she said. "If I could take it back, I would."

Their eyes met briefly before he walked over to the hostess, stomping snow from his overshoes as he did.

Claire watched him. She was sorry. Sorry about the blizzard. Sorry that she'd fallen for another man and had an affair with him. Sorry Peter had caught them together, Claire and this man. She let herself remember him for a moment. How they thought so alike he sometimes could finish her sentences. The way he kissed her with such ardor. His ability to laugh and be—oh, the word that Claire thought of was carefree. He could be carefree while Peter always seemed so serious, so burdened.

Standing in this restaurant, her husband's angry eyes on her, the storm raging outside, Claire even let herself miss Miles.

Peter was in the orange vinyl booth now, opening the large menu.

Claire walked clumsily toward him.

"I always like the fried clams here," he said, without looking up.

"They are good," Claire said, even though all during this pregnancy fried foods made her sick. Also certain fruits— melon, pears, grapes. And tomatoes. Or were tomatoes fruit too? She wasn't certain.

She glanced around for a high chair for Kathy. The restaurant was oddly bright and very crowded. Travelers had decided to pull over, out of the storm, like they had, and there was a buzz in the room, a sense of being in something together. The name Kennedy swirled above the noise, adding to the excitement of the blizzard.

"Are you going to sit?" Peter said, as if he had just noticed her.

Kathy, asleep against her shoulder, mumbled.

"I was looking for a high chair," Claire said.

*He's the man we need,* she heard. *Things will be different now.*

"Oh, for God's sake," Peter said. "Does anybody work here?" He waved at a waitress who carried a large tray overflowing with plastic baskets of food.

Claire's cheeks grew hot. He was always short, even rude, with people in service jobs: waitresses, the washing machine salesman at Sears, Roebuck, bellboys and meter readers. It embarrassed her, the way he snapped his fingers and ordered them about. Even on their first date, a romantic steak dinner at Frankie & Johnnie's on West 45th Street in Manhattan, he'd acted like that. Claire had two brandy Alexanders and French wine and crème de menthe afterwards. She'd blamed the drinks for the flush that crept up her chest and neck when he complained about the temperature of their soup, that his steak was overdone. When he'd snapped his fingers at the busboy, she'd looked down and sipped her cocktail.

The waitress delivered the food to a large rowdy group of men and boys, all wearing red shirts with logos, a team of some kind. When she was done, she came over to their table. Her uniform was splattered with ketchup and brown gravy and she looked exhausted.

"Two fried clam dinners," Peter said, snapping his menu shut. He didn't even glance at the waitress.

"Oh, just one," Claire said.

He frowned, confused. "You just told me you wanted the fried clams. You said you loved them."

In her wet boots, Claire could feel her feet swelling. She looked at the waitress, a tired woman with rings of smeared mascara beneath her eyes and a drooping ponytail.

"Just a grilled corn muffin for me," Claire said. "And a hot dog for Kathy."

The waitress wrote the order on her pad.

"I'm sorry," Claire said. "And a high chair?"

"Right," the waitress said. She lumbered off in her white nurse's shoes.

"Why do you do that?" Peter said.

"Do what?" Claire lowered herself to the very edge of the booth, the only place her belly and the sleeping child could fit.

"Apologize," Peter said, leveling his gaze directly at her in a way that made her look away. "For everything."

"I don't," she said.

"You did it just now. Apologized for asking her to get a high chair when that's part of her job."

In the booth behind her, two men argued about how Kennedy's Catholicism would affect the country. *The pope's our new boss,* one man said. *You'll see.*

"Claire?" Peter said.

"It's just politeness," Claire said. "That's all."

"Well, it's annoying."

Claire nodded. Since Peter had walked into that room that day, the traits of hers that annoyed him had multiplied. She touched her hair too often. She wasn't a good listener or a careful shopper. She could not parallel-park. Claire did not argue with him when he attacked her this way. It was her guilt that kept her silent. She knew that. Her guilt and her foolish idea of how to be a wife. Of course, she reminded herself, if she truly believed that foolish idea, she would not have slept with another man.

The waitress arrived with the high chair, banging into tables as she did. The high chair was covered in vinyl with a cowboy pattern. Claire stood to put Kathy into the seat. The waitress helped her to hold the child while she buckled the strap and slid the tray in place. Gently, Claire lowered her daughter's head onto the tray, smoothing her tangled brown hair.

"Where's our coffee?" Peter said.

"You didn't order coffee," the waitress said, flipping the pages of her pad until she found their order. "Two fried clams, then one fried clam, a grilled corn muffin, and a hot dog."

"And coffee," Peter said.

The waitress didn't answer him. As she walked away, she squeezed Claire's shoulder.

*We'll all have to become Catholics,* the man behind her said. *You know that, don't you?*

Claire leaned across the table. "Can you hear this?" she whispered, motioning with her head.

Peter nodded. "Foolish, isn't it?" he said.

"Yes," she said.

"What do you know about it?"

"Well," Claire said, "for one thing, I know we won't all have to become Catholics."

Peter laughed. "Some people worry about what's next. If we have a Catholic president, then who knows? We might even have a Jewish one someday."

"Or Negro," Claire said.

Peter grinned. "There will be no stopping anyone."

With the tension diffused momentarily, Claire relaxed a bit. How ironic, she thought, that Miles had been the man to talk these ideas out with her. And now this was what her husband found interesting. Four years earlier, on Election Day, Peter had told her as he left for work, "Remember to vote for Stevenson," as if she wouldn't know who to vote for. But they were newlyweds then, and she'd found it charming, how he liked to think for her.

"I thought when you worked on the campaign it was just out of boredom," Peter was saying, watching her face.

"I told you I believed in John F. Kennedy. I told you it was a passion."

"Yes," Peter said. "You did."

The waitress arrived with their food, announcing each item as she placed it on the table. Fried clams. Grilled corn muffin. Hot dog. Claire saw that she wore a wedding ring, a thin gold band with a small diamond ring above it.

The greasy smell of the clams made Claire queasy. She took a quick bite of her muffin, hoping it would settle her stomach.

"We never got our coffee," Peter said. He had already begun

to eat his clams, dipping them in the tartar sauce and splashing ketchup on the French fries.

The waitress sighed.

"Busy day, huh?" Claire said to her.

"I'm working a double," the waitress said. "Some of the girls couldn't get in 'cause of the snow."

Claire wondered how late the woman would have to be here working. By the matter-of-fact way she had helped get Kathy in the high chair, Claire thought she must also have a child. Or children. And a husband at home while she served cranky people food all day. And then drove home through this blizzard.

"Sorry," Claire said as the waitress went for the coffee.

"You just did it again," Peter said. "Why should you be sorry because she can't get the order right?"

Suddenly, all Claire wanted to do was sleep. She wanted to be in her own bed back in Alexandria with its layers of warm blankets and the familiar pattern of violets on the wallpaper, the curtains drawn against the snow.

"I don't know, Peter," Claire said wearily. "I just am."

He looked confused. "You're sorry because she's not good at her job?"

"I'm sorry she's working in this storm instead of being home with her husband."

The waitress returned. "Two coffees," she said, placing the cups on the table.

"Thank you," Claire said. Steam rose from them, and the bitter smell comforted her. She wrapped her hands around the cup to warm them.

Peter added milk to his coffee, then to Claire's. A small gesture of kindness that she appreciated since he was so rarely kind to her anymore. She smiled to let him know that and, for an instant, his face softened.

"Peter," Claire said. "Look."

The waitress was standing across the aisle from them, taking orders from new customers who had just come in, noisily shaking snow from their coats and stomping their boots. At this angle, Claire saw clearly that the waitress was pregnant. As far along as Claire, maybe more.

Peter followed her gaze. "Jesus," he said.

"Poor thing. Working two shifts."

"People do what they have to," he said.

"Still."

"It's not right," he said.

Claire reached across the table and took his hand, oddly grateful for her own easy life. Instinctively, he recoiled at her touch. She almost apologized, but stopped herself.


The afternoon that Peter discovered them, after Miles left, after she'd dressed and gone into the living room where her husband sat on the turquoise Danish sofa they had argued over buying, she sat across from him in the square pink chair. He had thought that modern furniture wasn't comfortable or inviting enough, and sitting there that afternoon, Claire understood what he meant. It was all angles and wood, this Danish contemporary.

Peter had demanded details. Not when or where they had met, but what they had done. "How many times?" Peter asked her. "Did he come inside of you?"

Out of spite or fear or something else, Claire told him. "I have lost track of how many times," she said. "And he does come inside me. Yes."

Peter jumped off the sofa, his eyes wild. As he loomed in front of her, she thought for a moment he might hit her. But he just stood with that scary look on his face, a look that told her he was capable of anything.

The clock, the one she thought looked like a sunburst and he thought looked like a spider, ticked into the silence.

"I have to pick up Kathy at the sitter's," Claire said finally.

She stood. He didn't move. She put on her white car coat, not because the weather had turned cool but for protection. From the pocket, she took a tube of lipstick, Rio Red, and smeared it across her lips. She took the car keys from the little ring where they hung.

When she reached the door, Peter said, "If you see him again I'll kill you."

Claire turned to her husband. "No you won't. You're not a murderer," she said.

Her heart was beating so fast she thought she might be having a heart attack. She didn't wait for him to answer, she just walked out.

Despite everything, she did not end the affair right away. Instead, she waited until after the election. Perhaps it was part of her recklessness then, but she kept meeting Miles. Every Monday night she went to campaign headquarters in the law office and sat beside him, calling people to urge them to vote for JFK. They sat at big desks, and drank cold bottles of Coca-Cola, the fat White Pages open in front of them. At nine o'clock, they left along with everyone else, and went to their separate cars, and drove around the block, meeting back in the parking lot where she got into his car and they drove off together. They had one hour to say all the things they wanted to say to each other, to touch each other, to wonder how they could be together. Usually, they parked in an empty bank parking lot down the street. Claire believed that they were in love, and they had just that one hour on Monday nights and Wednesday afternoons together.

On election night, in the Hilton Hotel ballroom, under a ceiling of balloons and streamers, she had kissed him for the last time.

"We won," he'd said into her mouth. His hand was on the small of her back, and she stood slightly on tiptoe to reach his lips.

By then, she had learned she was pregnant.

"We won," she said back to him, letting him press his body against hers. She said it, even though she knew it wasn't so.

While Peter went to call Birdy, Claire tried to feed Kathy the hot dog. She had woken up, fussy and disoriented. In their rush to leave, Claire had forgotten to take Mimi, Kathy's stuffed bunny, and now Kathy was in a panic, demanding it. "I need her!" she wailed. "Go get her! Get Mimi!"

"Mimi's at home asleep," Claire said.

"I need her!"

The waitress walked by, carrying a tray of empty glasses.

"Excuse me," Claire said, stopping her. "Could you fill this bottle with warm milk please?"

Kathy's cries pierced the restaurant.

"Tough having to take her out in a storm like this," the waitress said, taking the bottle.

Claire busied herself with getting Kathy out of the high chair. All of her movements were so clumsy now it was hard to imagine she had ever been graceful. Her face and hands were puffy, her breasts achy and large. She felt like she inhabited the wrong body.

Finally she wrangled Kathy out of the high chair. The child had made her body go rigid, and Claire held her awkwardly on her lap.

Peter appeared beside them. "Well," he said, "the party's on. *You only turn eighty once,* she said."

He frowned down at Claire. "Can't you quiet her?"

"The waitress is getting some milk," she said. She didn't mention that she'd forgotten Mimi.

"What a mess," Peter said.

Kathy's screams were giving Claire a headache. The baby inside her rolled. The bright noisy restaurant was almost too much. Tears fell down her cheeks. Everything was a mess. She was a mess.

"Claire," Peter said. "Come on. Stop that." She could hear in his voice that he still loved her, despite himself. Despite everything.

He tugged on her arm, pulling her up and out of the seat. Claire felt everyone's eyes on her, a pregnant woman with a screaming child and an angry husband. She cried harder, awkwardly holding her stiff wailing daughter as Peter urged her forward. At the door, the waitress ran up to them, holding out the bottle of milk.

"You'll need this," she said, looking at Claire with pity.

Outside, the snow covered everything. It seeped into the tops of Claire's boots. She pulled Kathy's hood up.

"Wait here," Peter said. "I'll bring the car around."

Claire watched as his charcoal gray coat disappeared in the snow. Again, she found herself imagining him really disappearing, and never coming back. She imagined calling her old roommate Rose and asking her to come and pick her up. Rose would take her and Kathy back to her house and help her figure out what to do next. Claire squinted at the line of cars inching along beyond the parking lot. Rose had married a pilot and moved to New London, Connecticut. She wondered if that was nearby.

But then Peter drove up, the station wagon skidding to a halt.

He leaned across the front seat and opened the door for her. When the interior light came on, Claire paused to study his face illuminated like that. He was handsome, her husband. Even with his dark hair wet with snow and the beginning of stubble along his sharp jaw. Even with his face set hard and his eyes cold.

"Hurry up," he said. "All we need is for Kathy to get sick on top of everything else."

Claire sighed, and handed Kathy to him. She had fallen asleep again. Her cheeks were red from the cold and she had snot hardening between her nose and mouth. Peter placed her on the backseat, tucking her little powder blue blanket around her.

He didn't shift into first gear. Instead, he stared out the windshield, already covered again with snow.

The car grew dark as the snow accumulated on the windows.

"Claire," he said, his breath a puff in the cold air.

She waited.

"This baby," he said, but nothing more.

Claire reached for his hand. The leather of his glove was cold beneath her woolen ones. She was glad he didn't pull away.

Peter turned to look at her. She thought he might be crying.

"Peter," she said softly, her heart breaking for him, for the mess she'd made of everything. "Don't even think it," she told him.

He looked away. "I need to clean off the windshield," he said, and got out of the car.

They had met on a flight from New York to Paris. Claire had been a TWA air hostess for exactly five years. You flew until you found a husband, that's how it went. By the time they had stopped to refuel in Gander, Claire already thought Peter would make a very good husband. He had gone to Columbia University, and graduate school at MIT, and now he was off to work at the Pentagon for Hyman Rickover, the man known as the Father of the Nuclear Navy. Peter had an air of importance about him; all of the other girls noticed too. But he only noticed Claire. In Shannon, as they waited to refuel again, he asked her if she'd have dinner with him that night in Paris. They ate in the Eiffel Tower, and had their first kiss at the top. Such a storybook beginning could only lead to happily ever after, Claire had thought.

She had loved her light blue uniform with the silver wing pinned to her chest and the way her hat fit just so above her blond French twist. She loved mixing cocktails for the passengers and the way the men eyed her when she walked down the aisle past them. She and Rose shared a one-bedroom apartment in Manhattan on East 65th Street. They placed an Oriental screen in the middle of the bedroom, with their beds on either side of it. Before they fell asleep, they shared stories about their layovers: the places they'd seen—the Acropolis and the Pyramids and the Eiffel Tower—and the men who had taken them to dinner or for a tour of the city. *He's the one*, she told Rose when she got back from that trip. They would move to a big house outside Washington, D.C., and have babies and always remember that dinner in Paris, that dramatic first kiss.

She was lucky, that's what Claire thought. She was a pretty girl from a small town in Indiana, and she had the whole world right at her fingertips. Then Peter walked onto that Super Constellation, and everything changed.

# 4

## The Key to the Majestic

### VIVIEN, 1919

E very Friday morning Vivien went to the library. Today she would return the Cather novel, and Booth Tarkington's *The Magnificent Ambersons*. The library was small, just three rooms and a sagging front porch. On cold days like today, a fire roared in the hearth in the largest room, and Kay Pendleton, the librarian, had a pot of strong coffee warming. Vivien poured herself some in a chipped cup decorated with pink roses and sat in her usual place at the long oak table in the Reference Room. Kay collected castoffs, like the mismatched coffee cups she kept here and the out-of-print books she bought at estate sales and the like. The books lined a shelf with a handwritten sign hung from it: *Kay's Personal Oddities and Curiosities.*

Kay Pendleton herself was something of an oddity and a curiosity. She appeared to be a woman who could plow a field and birth a dozen babies easily. But as far as Vivien knew, Kay was a spinster like her. Her fine blond hair was always falling in soft tendrils from the bun she wore, and her pale blue eyes behind her wire-rimmed glasses showed a hint of mischief. Kay wore low-cut blouses that showed off her ample cleavage and the sprinkling of freckles that dotted her chest. Sometimes, Kay Pendleton wore men's trousers that on her looked feminine and chic. But more often, like today, she wore skirts that hugged her hips seductively. Vivien had seen men have to avert their eyes when they checked out their books, or risk blushing or ogling. How she had landed here in Napa, unmarried and working in a library, remained a mystery to Vivien.

As she did every Friday, Vivien opened her leather-bound scrapbook and read the first page, a habit now since she could recite it by heart.

*The causes of amnesia have traditionally been divided into the "organic" or the "functional." Organic causes include damage to the brain, through physical injury, neurological disease or the use of certain (generally sedative) drugs. Functional causes are psychological factors, such as mental disorder, post-traumatic stress or, in psychoanalytic terms, defense mechanisms.*

Her fingers touched the words, as if she were reading Braille. Physical injury. Post-traumatic stress. David, she knew, could have suffered either. Vivien thought of that April morning, how she had run into the street, Fu Jing screaming at her in Chinese. After that first shock, Vivien had climbed out of her bed and crawled under it. She couldn't remember what a person should do in an earthquake, even though she had read it somewhere.

When she heard the heavy front door slam, she had been certain it was David coming home to rescue her. Vivien had slid from beneath the bed and run downstairs, calling his name. She could still smell sex on her, and taste him on her lips. Barefoot, her ice blue silk nightgown tangled around her, she'd found not David, but her maid Fu Jing, wild-eyed and covered in dust, speaking in rapid-fire Chinese. *What has happened?* Vivien said, taking hold of the woman's shoulders and shaking her roughly.

*Zai nan,* Fu Jing had said. She said it over and over. *Zai nan.*
Later, Vivien would learn that *zai nan* meant catastrophe.

A hand on her arm startled her and Vivien let out a little yelp.
"I'm sorry," Kay Pendleton said. "I didn't mean to frighten
you."

Vivien, eye to eye with Kay's breasts rising above her lemon
yellow silk blouse, got to her feet. "No, no," she sputtered. "I
apologize for overreacting."

Kay was holding out a newspaper. *The Denver Post.* "I thought
something in here might be of interest to you," she said. She was
a person who looked you right in the eye when she spoke, another
unnerving trait of hers.

"Oh?" Vivien said.

"Page nine," Kay said. She placed the newspaper on the table
and sashayed back to her desk in the other room.

Without sitting again, Vivien opened the paper, flipping the
pages impatiently until she got to page nine. Her Friday morning
routines were a comfort to her, and she didn't like them interrupted. She glanced at an article on mountain lions, and another
on a disease affecting cattle in Colorado and New Mexico. From
where she stood, she could clearly see Kay adding books to her
shelf of oddities and curiosities, her body a curvy figure eight,
her bun lopsided. Vivien sighed. Sick cattle? She shook her head,
trying to think of a polite comment to give Kay when she asked
what she'd thought of the article. But then a smaller headline
caught her eye. *Man Found Wandering Down Colfax Avenue;
Claims He Has No Memory of His Past.*

Sinking into her chair again, Vivien lifted the paper closer
to her face, as if it would bring the man himself closer to her.
Phrases leaped out. *No identification . . . Utterly confused . . .
Otherwise healthy . . .* And then: *Doctors confirm that the man is
suffering from amnesia.*

Vivien glanced over at Kay, who had paused to watch her.

"How did you know this was my particular interest?" Vivien asked her.

"I see what's in that book," Kay said. "I don't ask questions."

Vivian nodded and returned her attention to the newspaper article. The man was estimated to be fifty to sixty years old, in good health except for his lack of memory, and had in his pocket a key to a room at the Hotel Majestic on Sutter Street in San Francisco. The Hotel Majestic, the article continued, opened in 1902, and was one of the few hotels to survive the devastating earthquake of 1906. Vivien's heart beat faster. She and David had spent a weekend at the Hotel Majestic. Not just any weekend, but their first weekend together. Despite Lotte's warnings, Vivien had met him for dinner that night. He was older than she'd remembered, ten years older than her.

They'd finished dinner before she'd blurted, "What about this wife of yours?"

"We're unhappy," he'd said matter-of-factly. He sipped his cognac, then stared into the glass. "But she won't give me a divorce."

"So you seduce young women to stay happy?" Vivien asked.

He'd smiled up at her. "Have I seduced you?"

She blushed.

"It is my intention," he admitted, which made her blush deepen.

"I don't go out with married men," Vivien said. It was what Lotte had told her to say.

"But you're out with me now."

He was teasing her, she saw that. But it angered her enough to bring her to her feet and pull on the jacket she'd draped over the back of her chair. How she wished that she'd kept it on instead of revealing her collarbone and flesh below it to him. Had she intended to reveal so much of herself so readily?

David stood too. He reached over and very carefully buttoned her jacket for her.

"There," he said. "Now I'll call a taxi to take you home."

For three miserable weeks, she heard nothing from him. In that time, Lotte got married, and Vivien dutifully danced with the dentist from Boise and even let the neighboring vintner kiss her outside as the band played the last dance of the evening. He kissed her too roughly, and groped at her, and invited her to come to Napa soon. She'd agreed, anything to keep David out of her thoughts. Then Lotte and Robert left for their honeymoon in Yosemite, and for the first time in her life, Vivien was alone. She had other friends, of course. But there was only one Lotte, who had been by her side from the start.

When finally David's calling card arrived in her mailbox, Vivien almost cried with relief. The way he'd buttoned her jacket that night, so tenderly, had made her feel safe. With Lotte ensconced at Robert's family's vineyard in Napa, Vivien needed to build a new life for herself, to create a new family.

*I will find a way. Trust me,* he'd written.

*Don't trust him,* Lotte had warned her.

That very night she had hurried to meet him at Coppa's, and she had decided that, yes, she would trust him.

She could imagine what Lotte would say, that this was a coincidence. The fact that Vivien and David spent their first night together—a night that turned into an entire weekend—at the Hotel Majestic, and that this amnesiac who happened to be the age David would be had he survived had a key to a room there, all of it Lotte would write off to coincidence.

But how could Vivien dismiss it so easily? She went to the atlas that lay open on a table behind her, and flipped first to the United States, and then to the western United States. There was Colorado, a big square state roughly a thousand miles, Vivien guessed, from where she stood. She allowed herself to believe for a moment that the only thing between her and David was one thousand miles. That she could be on a train this very afternoon, heading eastward. That she might walk into the hospital where he was held for observation and that his memory would return when he saw her. Thinking these things made her breathless, and Vivien gulped air, trying to breathe normally again.

She had barely known him when she'd agreed to go with him to the Hotel Majestic that spring night. They had gone to Coppa's in North Beach for dinner and Vivien had recognized the writer Jack London there, sitting at a big table in the middle of the restaurant.

David was telling her about the case he was preparing for trial, and Vivien had put her hand on his—the first time they had touched, really—and whispered, "I can't hear a word you're saying. All I can do is stare at Jack London."

David took her hand in his, closing his fingers over it, and followed her gaze to the crowded table. "Which one is Jack London?" he asked her. "So I know which one to beat up."

"He's the handsomest one at that table," Vivien said.

"I'm going to have to break that perfect nose of his," David said, leaning into her. His mouth on her ear made her shiver, and Vivien leaned her head back, allowing his lips to graze first her ear, then her neck. "Would you find me too forward if I invited you to come with me to the Hotel Majestic for the night?" he whispered.

She did not look at Jack London again as she placed her stole around her shoulders and left hurriedly with David.

Lotte would tell her to be sensible. She would tell her that rather than get on a train and travel a thousand miles, she should contact the hospital in Denver. Vivien's breathing slowed. Yes.

That would be the sensible thing to do. More than anyone, she could tell them about the thin white scar beneath his chin. She could even tell them how he got that scar as a young boy, trying to jump a fence. She could describe the constellation of freckles on his back, and the distance one would have to travel to reach his thighs from his toes.

The sharp smell of earth and spice brought her out of her reverie. That Italian man, the one who knew Lotte and her husband, who always asked her to dinner, stood in front of her, a worried look on his face.

"Miss Lowe," he said in his halting English, "you need to sit? You need some water?"

"No," Vivien said. "I'm fine."

He peered at her. "Your face," he said, "it's very . . ." She watched him struggle for the word. "White," he said finally, defeated.

"You mean pale," she said.

"Pale," he repeated, giving the simple word too many syllables.

"Well," Vivien said. "Nice to see you again."

"Sebastian," he said.

She had started to walk away from him, but she turned. "What?"

"I am Sebastian," he said. *Se-bah-sti-ahn.* He held a black hat in his hand, and worried the brim as he spoke.

Vivien nodded. "Yes. Of course. Sebastian."

The light was changing, morning becoming noontime, and here she did not even have her books yet. She left the Reference Room and went into the smaller room where Kay sat at the circulation desk, immersed in a book.

"Is the new Zane Grey in?" Vivien asked her.

"I put it aside for you," Kay said. She retrieved it from the Reserved shelf behind the desk.

"How's that one?" Vivien said, motioning to *The Four Horsemen of the Apocalypse* opened in front of Kay.

Kay hesitated. "I have no idea," she admitted, blushing.

Vivien laughed. "I knew you were listening."

"Guilty," Kay said. She lowered his voice. "Poor guy. He comes in here every Friday morning, just hoping to have a few words with you."

"You sound like my friend Lotte. Just have coffee with him, she says. What could it hurt?"

The two women watched as Sebastian studied a copy of *National Geographic*, frowning over it.

"I think he's handsome," Kay whispered.

He was short and well-built, with dark wavy hair and a voluminous mustache. No matter what time of day Vivien saw him, he appeared to need a shave, his cheeks always covered in five o'clock shadow. His eyes were large and deep brown, and gave him an air of sadness somehow.

"I suppose," Vivien said. "I . . ." She considered explaining to Kay Pendleton how she was in love with a ghost, but stopped herself. Vivien knew too well how easy it was to open your heart to strangers.

Kay waited, but Vivien just shook her head.

"I'm not interested," she said finally.

Kay held up her book. "You can have this one if you'd like."

Relieved for the change of subject, Vivien agreed.

Kay stamped the books in red and handed them to Vivien. "I would remind you when they're due," she said, "but I know you'll have them back next week."

Vivien tucked them into her bag, beside her scrapbook. "I wonder," she began.

"You want that newspaper?" Kay said.

"I know the rule is not to let them leave the library—"

Kay leveled her gaze at her. "I've never followed a rule in my life," she said. "And I suspect you've broken a few yourself."

Vivien looked away from her.

"Go on," Kay said. "Take it."

"Thank you," Vivien said.

She went back to the Reference Room and carefully folded *The Denver Post*, sliding it too into her bag. When she looked up, Sebastian was watching her. He *was* handsome, in a way, Vivien thought.

Sebastian smiled at her, and she noticed that his front teeth were slightly crooked, which made him even more attractive.

"Vivien," he said, "tonight I will see you perhaps?"

"Oh, I don't think so," she said as she hurried past him.

"*Ciao*," he said.

She murmured a goodbye.

Outside, Vivian paused on the sidewalk. The rain yesterday seemed to have washed everything clean—the sky was a bluer blue than it had been, the morning glories climbing the fence a more vivid pink. The air itself smelled of spring and new beginnings. Vivien breathed in a deep lungful. It was almost April. In just a few weeks it would be thirteen years since she had last seen David.

She remembered how only a few nights before the earthquake they had gone to Coppa's for dinner and David noticed that someone had written on the wall: *Something terrible is going to happen.* Vivien had feared it was prophetic, but David had laughed. "Probably your friend Jack London," he'd said. "Afraid that I'm going to marry you sometime very soon." He'd asked his wife for a divorce, and even though Vivien was afraid to hope she would grant him one, David had been full of optimism

Vivien closed her eyes against the memory and thought instead of that man in Denver. The room they had stayed in at the Hotel Majestic was number 208. She imagined that key held in David's pocket all these years, waiting for her to find it.

"This is crazy," Lotte said. "You know that, don't you?"

"But that key," Vivien said for what seemed like the hundredth time. "To the Majestic."

Lotte sighed and went back to attending the large pot of beans on the stove.

*What if it was Robert?* Vivien wanted to say. *Wouldn't you try anything to find him?* But maybe Lotte wouldn't try anything. Her friend had always been practical, the one to worry over consequences and risks. As children, she'd kept Vivien out of danger many times. Lotte had warned Vivien not to get involved with David in the first place. *He's married, Viv,* she'd said, horrified and concerned. *You just don't do that.*

Lotte lifted the long wooden spoon to her mouth and tasted, frowning. She took a hefty pinch of salt from the canister and tossed it in, stirring. Lotte's life had a rhythm, a predictability that Vivien sometimes envied. The tending to Robert and their three children, feeding her family and all of the workers at the vineyard. In September, when it came time to harvest the grapes, Lotte was out there with all the men, from first light until it grew too dark to work. Her once-smooth ivory complexion had grown ruddy from years in the sun, and lined enough to make her look her age, or more. Although her long legs were muscled and her arms strong from the physical labor of having babies and working the vineyard and doing the laundry and cooking for so many people, Lotte had gone thick around the middle.

"You probably won't hear till Monday at the earliest," Lotte said, hoisting a ceramic platter of chicken. The chicken had been sitting in oil and lemon and garlic all day, and pressed flat under heavy bricks.

"I know," Vivien said. She'd gone straight from the library to the Western Union office: MIGHT HAVE INFO ON AMNESIAC IN YOUR HOSPITAL. STOP. IS HOTEL KEY FOR ROOM 208? STOP.

Lotte paused on her way to the large outdoor grill where she would cook the chicken. "I just don't want you to get hurt again," she said softly.

"Grief is a strange thing," Vivien said. "There isn't an again. Not really. It's always there, always present. Again implies it can end and then start up anew. But it never goes away in the first place."

"Once a teacher always a teacher," Lotte said, laughing softly.

Vivien watched her friend's broad back as she walked outside. Were all old friends this way, somehow stuck in time? To Lotte, Vivien was still a teacher acting foolish over an older married man, instead of an obituary writer, a woman who had lived alone for over a dozen years. A widow, Vivien thought, though Lotte wouldn't grant her that status.

"Vivvie!" Lotte's daughter Pamela screamed. "I didn't know you were coming today!"

"Well, here I am," Vivien said, scooping the child into her arms. At six, Pamela had the same brown curls as her mother, and the same vivid blue eyes. Looking into her face, Vivien could see the child Lotte all over again, as if thirty years hadn't passed and they were still sitting side by side at the Field School.

"I'm mad mad mad at Bo and Johnny," Pamela said, her whole face seeming to frown. "They won't let me ride the ponies with them. They say I'm too little but I'm not. I'm big, right, Vivvie?"

"Quite big, darling," Vivien said. "And getting bigger every minute." She hugged Pamela good and hard before setting her back down. Poets and mothers spoke of the lovely smell of children, but to Vivien they smelled acrid, like vinegar. And in Pamela's case, earthy too, like the soil here in Napa.

Pamela dragged a small wooden chair with a straw seat over to the stove so that she could inspect the beans. "Do you wish I were a boy, Vivvie?" she asked, tasting one.

"Not at all," Vivien said truthfully. Lotte's boys were not at all like the boys she'd grown up with in San Francisco. They thought nothing of shooting and skinning deer or rabbits. There was always dirt under their fingernails and in the creases of their palms. She couldn't remember seeing them dressed in anything but blue jeans and flannel shirts. No, Bo and Johnny were mysterious creatures to Vivien, and even to Lotte. When Pamela had been born, Lotte was the happiest Vivien had ever seen her. *At last*, Lotte had told her, *I won't be alone.*

"Well, sometimes I wish I were a boy," Pamela was saying. She stirred the beans, just like her mother had, with confidence and assurance. "Like in *Treasure Island*, right, Vivvie?"

"You want to be an adventurer," Vivien said. Whenever she visited here, she read to Pamela at night. Robert Louis Stevenson was their latest favorite.

"Yes!" Pamela said. "I want to fight pirates and crocodiles and sail around the Cape of Good Hope!"

Vivien laughed. "Girls can do that too," she said. "See? You don't have to be a boy at all. Just older than six."

"That's a relief," she said. Pamela jumped off the chair and scurried toward the large open doors that led outside to where Lotte stood cooking.

. . .

The fullness of Lotte's life always struck Vivien. While hers was solitary and isolated, Lotte's was populated with noise and work and people. Like tonight. At the long picnic tables behind the house, neighbors from other wineries sat talking and sharing their own wines, nibbling cheese made from one of their goats. Mexican and Italian workers from Lotte's vineyard sat beside them, speaking in Spanish and Italian and broken English so that the air seemed to buzz with syllables. Children ran past, holding empty jars as they searched for fireflies. Someone had brought a large wooden bowl of rocket and small red tomatoes from her garden. The salad was dressed with olive oil from one of the vineyards, and a splash of a vinegar Lotte made from pouring leftover wine into an earthenware jug she kept by the kitchen door.

Vivien stood beneath the string of white lights Robert had hung from the patio roof, weary from the abundance, the fresh food and wine, the life that seemed almost palpable here. A hand on her shoulder forced her to look up, into the face of the Italian man from the library.

"Mrs. Lowe," he said, smiling beneath his mustache.

She didn't correct him. "Sebastian, right?" she said.

"If you must pronounce it like that, it's okay," he said. "I just like the word, how should I say this? In your mouth. It sounds like the song of a canary."

His hand felt heavy on her shoulder, like a burden. Would it be impolite to move it away? Vivien wondered.

"We will get food," he was saying, "and then sit together?"

Vivien shook her head. "I'm sorry, no. I'm sitting with Lotte." Even as she said this she caught sight of Lotte already at a table, surrounded by her neighbors, the ones who made the goat cheese and the other ones who pressed the olive oil.

"Do you know the story of Saint Sebastian?" Sebastian asked her.

"I'm afraid I don't know very much about saints."

He raised his bushy eyebrows. "No? A pity."

"I wasn't raised Catholic," Vivien explained.

"Saint Sebastian," he said. "He is patron saint of athletes because of his . . . endurance. So you see? I wait."

Vivien blushed. "You are certainly a romantic," she said.

Flustered, Vivien walked away from him and squeezed herself on the picnic bench beside Lotte.

Lotte's eyes followed Sebastian as he made his way to the table where most of the workers sat talking noisily.

"He's sweet on you," she said.

"Please," Vivien groaned. She took some chicken from the platter and some of the salad. "Don't encourage him, Lotte."

"Thirteen years," Lotte said. "It's too long to wait." Her voice sounded tired of this conversation.

Luckily, Pamela came running up to them, holding out her jar. In the darkening night, the fireflies inside glowed bright.

"I caught five!" Pamela said. "More than Bo!"

Lotte kissed the top of her daughter's head. "My girl," she said softly.

Unexpectedly, tears sprang to Vivien's eyes. For the first time, she realized what made her so weary here. The noise, the companionship, the children. She envied her friend. The idea made her whole body heavy, as if stones weighed her down. In their youth, it had been her, Vivien, who had attracted suitors and other friends. She'd always had invitations, to parties and dances and shows. She used to have to practically drag Lotte along. And now, what did Vivien have? The stories of dead people. A foolish belief that her lover was waiting for her to find him. While Lotte had . . . Vivien dared to look up. Pamela had climbed onto Lotte's lap and the two of them were laughing over something Vivien was not privy to. Someone had put on a record, and Caruso's scratchy voice rose above the laughter and conversations. While Lotte, Vivien thought, had everything.

# THREE

*No one should ever be forced upon those in grief, and all over-emotional people, no matter how near or dear, should be barred absolutely.*

—FROM *Etiquette*, BY EMILY POST, 1922

# 5

## *Just Like Jackie*

### CLAIRE, 1961

Peter's voice startled her awake. "Home at last," he said.
For a moment, Claire thought he might have turned
around and they were back at their own home. She
squinted out the window, but the snow hid everything.

"We'll just have time to change and get to the party," Peter
was saying.

"Okay," Claire said.

She opened her purse and took out her compact and lipstick.
She powdered her cheeks, and rubbed at the dark circles under
her eyes. Then she carefully put on fresh lipstick.

"Why are you bothering with that now?" Peter said.

Claire snapped the compact shut. Because it's what is expected
of me, she thought. Because even though I am unhappy and I
don't know if I love you anymore and I'm pregnant, I still need
to do the things I have always done.

But she said none of it. She just pulled a comb through her
hair as he parked in front of his mother's house.

"You're not going to meet anyone here," he said, motioning

toward the green triple-decker. "No one cares if your hair is done or if you have lipstick on."

"I care," Claire said.

She stepped out of the car, slipping as she did. A small yelp escaped before she caught herself. By the time Peter arrived at her side, she was steady again.

"Careful," he said, his hand firm on her arm.

Was he being kind? Or simply safe? Every word he said, Claire found herself weighing, trying to determine what emotion lay behind it. Would he forgive her? Or would he punish her forever?

It was dark and snowy and cold. This street of working-class triple-deckers, which appeared sad even on bright sunny days, looked gloomy and deserted. The house seemed to sag, its porches heavy with snow and ice, the faded green duller than she remembered. The houses in most of this neighborhood held generations of families. Grandparents on the first floor, their kids and grandchildren in the second- and third-floor apartments. But Peter's mother lived alone on the top two floors and rented out the bottom floor to the neighbor's youngest child and her family. Peter had gone away to college and never moved back. He'd tried to convince his mother to move to the smaller first-floor apartment, or to sell the house altogether. But she refused. *This is my home,* she always reminded him.

The front door opened and the Galluccis peered out. Connie Gallucci had had three babies right in a row, and she'd never lost all the baby weight. But she still dressed sexy, even now. She already had her party dress on, a garish too-tight green one, low-cut and revealing her ample cleavage. Connie's hair was still in giant curlers. No, Vivien saw as she got closer. She'd rolled her hair in empty Campbell's soup cans, like Vivien had seen in some fashion magazine at the hairdresser's recently. Her husband Jimmy had gained weight, and his stomach pressed against his white sleeveless T-shirt, hanging over his belt. It was hard to believe he had been the star hockey player back in high school.

"Pete!" he said. "Ready for the shindig?"

Jimmy walked down the path to shake Peter's hand, and then to take Kathy from Claire.

Everything about Connie and Jimmy made Claire slightly uneasy, as if she'd caught them in the middle of something private. They both exuded a sexuality she wasn't used to. Connie always wearing low-cut blouses and too much makeup, and Jimmy with his T-shirts and hairy chest. Even now, following Jimmy up the stairs, she caught a smell of sweat and something male and unfamiliar. Peter smelled clean, of Ivory soap and Old Spice. Sometimes she caught a whiff of shoe polish on his hands. Claire used to like watching him polish his black wingtips, the way he spread newspaper carefully on the floor, buffed them with a chamois cloth, shook the bottle of black polish before spreading it in quick even strokes across his shoes. Such a simple thing, but it had seemed so masculine and sexy.

The door at the top of the stairs opened and Birdy stood there, beaming in her best Chanel suit and rope of pearls. The pearls, Claire knew, were real, a gift from a long-ago lover. The suit she suspected was a copy. But still, her mother-in-law looked lovely, her silver hair piled on top of her head, her green eyes sparkling.

She opened her arms and Peter rushed into her hug.

"Darling," Birdy said to him. "You feel thin."

"I don't want to get a paunch like this guy," Peter said, indicating Jimmy who had come in beside them.

Birdy smiled. "I've heard of fathers who gain weight in sympathy with their pregnant wives."

She seemed to notice Claire for the first time.

"Darling," she said, kissing Claire on each cheek. "Apparently my son is not one of those men."

"No," Claire said, avoiding Peter's eyes. Her husband believed this baby was his, and she worried that with one look he would know he was wrong.

"I've got to go downstairs and get beautiful," Jimmy was saying.

"Good luck with that," Peter teased as Jimmy bounded noisily down the stairs.

"Well, let's not stand here," Birdy said. "I have a bit of champagne waiting for us in the parlor."

"I'll be right there," Peter told her. "I'm going to get Kathy settled with Connie's babysitter."

Claire followed her mother-in-law into what she called the parlor, a formal room filled with old-fashioned furniture, all velvet and beaded and stiff.

"I'm so sorry we didn't make it here for Christmas this year," Claire said as soon as she sat down.

"I missed seeing you all, of course," Birdy said, leveling her gaze right at Claire. "But I worried that something was wrong."

"The baby," Claire said vaguely, hoping the old woman would not question her further.

"A difficult pregnancy then?"

Claire nodded.

The truth was that she and Peter were barely able to be civil to each other at Christmas, he still wounded by her affair and Claire too upset over ending it. They had both been angry, and untethered. She'd never bothered to ask what excuse he had given his mother for their absence. The thought that perhaps he had told her the truth struck Claire, but she quickly dismissed it. Peter would never divulge that to his mother. Or to anyone, she suspected. It was too humiliating.

"Actually," Birdy said, "Peter indicated that you two were . . . well, going through a bit of a rough patch."

"He did?" Claire said, her throat suddenly dry.

"It happens, of course," Birdy said, offering a silver bowl of cashews to Claire, who took a couple only to be polite, holding them in her palm rather than eating them. "Lord knows, Peter's father and I had our moments."

"I just don't feel comfortable with him discussing it with anyone," Claire managed.

"He didn't give me the details," Birdy said.

Claire could feel Birdy's eyes on her, but she didn't look up.

"Oh," Claire said, remembering that she'd put her mother-in-law's Christmas present in her purse. She unclasped it, and took out the slender gift, wrapped in the red and white paper with silver ribbon.

"Merry Christmas," Claire said. "I'm sorry it's so late."

Birdy opened the gift, carefully sliding the ribbon off and being sure not to tear the paper.

"Frost," she said. "How thoughtful."

"I know how much you like poetry," Claire said, "and since he's reading one at the inauguration tomorrow . . ."

"Do you know 'Master Speed'?" Birdy asked.

She didn't wait for Claire to answer.

"A sonnet," she continued. " 'Two such as you with a master speed, Cannot be parted nor be swept away, From one another once you are agreed, That life is only life forevermore, Together wing to wing and oar to oar.' " She smiled. "I think I've got that right. At my age, I'm not always so sure."

"It's beautiful," Claire said.

"I believe that's on his wife's grave," Birdy said.

"Well, I hope you enjoy these poems," Claire said. "It's the latest collection."

"I'm sure I will." She placed the book on the small table beside her chair.

Relieved, Claire heard Peter coming back inside.

"What?" he said when he entered the room. "You haven't opened the champagne yet?"

"We couldn't toast without you," Birdy said.

Peter picked up the bottle and placed the white napkin over it.

"Eighty years old, Birdy," he said as he turned the cork. "And still the prettiest mother on the block."

"Well, still the oldest anyway," she said, obviously pleased.

To Claire she added, "Poor Peter. All the other mothers would be outside organizing games of tag and jumping rope, and his mother was inside cooking or knitting or—"

"I won't hear it," Peter said. "You were fine. The best."

The cork opened with a small sigh, and Peter filled the three glasses.

"To my lovely mother," he said, holding up his glass. "Happy eightieth birthday, Birdy."

They all clinked and sipped, and then Claire excused herself to get ready for the party.

Up in Peter's old room, she sat on the edge of his bed and began to cry. *Wing to wing and oar to oar.* Was her mother-in-law telling her that Claire needed to understand that? Did Birdy know about Miles? Claire wished she had the courage to ask her mother-in-law these questions directly. But the old woman intimidated her.

Sighing, Claire found herself for the second time today wanting to call her old roommate. Rose had told Claire once that men had affairs to stay married, and women had affairs to get out of their marriages. Rose should know. She had always dated married men. In fact, her husband had been married when Rose started seeing him. Before him, a married doctor named Monty bought her Chanel No.5 and silk stockings. An actor took her dancing at the Copacabana and for steaks at Peter Luger. The Italian businessman gave her a tennis bracelet, a thin circle of gold studded with glittering diamonds. At the time, Claire had been slightly horrified at Rose's behavior. *Don't you think about their wives?* she'd asked. *Don't you worry about . . . I don't know, your soul?* Rose had laughed at her. She'd stood back and held out her slender wrist with the diamond bracelet shining on it and said, *No, Claire. I don't.*

Vivien stretched out on top of the twin bed. The bedspread was ivory chenille, with some faded pattern on it, now just a few curlicues of color. A mobile of the solar system hung from the ceiling, the planets moving ever so slightly in the drafty room. Each planet was a different color and different-sized sphere, and Claire tried to remember which was which. She used to know a mnemonic saying to help her remember their correct order. My very excited mother just . . . Just what? Ordered pizzas? But no, there wasn't a planet that started with *O.*

Peter had told her how he and his mother spent all day one Saturday painting these Styrofoam balls, making sure they were sized right and then hanging them on wire in the proper order. They'd use a coat hanger to make Saturn's ring, he'd told Claire. That was what his mother liked best when he was a boy—spending the day with him, just the two of them. Other boys would be outside playing street hockey or basketball, and Peter would want to join them. But the way his mother looked—*so happy,* he'd said—when they did projects like this used to keep him inside with her. They'd built the solar system, a replica of the *Titanic* out of matchsticks, a skateboard from an old piece of wood attached to one of his old roller skates.

Claire reached up and touched Mars, painted a faded red.

Peter could point to each sphere and name it and tell her their names. In fact, he had done that very thing the first time she'd come with him to visit his mother. This was before they got married, when she thought he was the most remarkable person she'd ever known. While his mother slept down the hall, Peter had snuck in here and they'd made love, each squeak of a bedspring stopping them for a moment, each sigh choked on. Afterwards, he had stood naked right there below the mobile and set those planets spinning. *Mercury, Venus, Earth, Mars . . .*

"Jupiter, Saturn, Uranus, Neptune," Claire said into the empty room, remembering.

She paused.

"Pluto," she said finally. She smiled to herself. That was the pizza part.

"Almost ready?" Peter called up to her.

"Almost," she called back.


Claire had found a pewter maternity sheath dress like one she'd seen Jackie wear last year. It had pockets at the side, and flared gracefully from the waist. She'd started wearing her hair in a bouffant like Jackie's too. Everyone had. And standing in front of the mirror now, Claire was satisfied with how she looked tonight.

"Claire!" Peter was calling. "We have the guest of honor waiting."

She could hear the strain in his voice and wondered if his mother heard it too. Again, she wondered what Birdy knew. But there was no time to worry about that now. Claire touched up her hair, lifting the top slightly and spritzing Aqua Net on it, then spraying a bit more on the curled-up tips.

"Coming!" she said, and hurried down the stairs.

"Worth waiting for," Birdy said, even though she was already in her coat and hat. "You look lovely."

"I'm sorry," Claire said, and she saw Peter flinch slightly.

"Women are slow," he said. "Pregnant women even slower."

He had Claire's coat held up, ready for her, and she slipped into it.

As the three of them headed down the stairs and out to the car, Claire vowed to have a good night. Tonight she would be the wife her husband wanted her to be. The daughter-in-law she should be to Birdy. She would be gracious. She would smile. She would not apologize for who, she feared, she might be becoming.

The Hope Club sat on the corner of Benefit and Benevolent Streets on the East Side of Providence. A four-story brick Victorian house, it had been a private club since 1875, and it was, Claire knew, the kind of place that Birdy always wanted to belong to. As a young woman, she had lived a privileged life in San Francisco, with club memberships like this one, and private schooling. Peter had told Claire this when he'd explained his mother's struggles to her. She'd married a laborer, and come East reluctantly. His mother dreamed of living in one of the Victorian houses that lined College Hill in this part of Providence, and used to take Peter for drives past them, pointing out their architectural details, their gingerbread trim, the towers and turrets and rounded porches.

But they never could afford to buy a house like that. Apparently, she had accepted that stoically, never showing his father her disappointment, but Peter saw it in her face, in the way she would park on Bowen Street or Lloyd Avenue and stare up at the painted ladies there. *Someday, I'm going to buy you one of those houses,* Peter had promised her when he was ten or eleven. *No, no,* she told him, *then I would have to clean all those windows.* He told Claire these stories with a mixture of sadness and pride.

To have her eightieth birthday party at this venerable club was a point of pride for Birdy. As she walked in, her cheeks flushed with excitement.

Claire watched her, and saw that her whole demeanor changed when she stepped inside. She had not given much thought to her mother-in-law's past—Peter had told her that she'd been a teacher long ago—but seeing her as she gave her coat to the butler and took a glass of champagne from the tuxedoed waiter, Claire saw that Birdy had once been a very different woman. Or perhaps still was that woman, somewhere deep inside.

There were hors d'oeuvres passed, shrimp paste on triangles of toast and smoked salmon with capers and dill. Claire let Peter keep one hand on the small of her back as he introduced her to the guests. The snow had not kept anyone away, and a small crowd soon gathered in the dining room, looking for their place cards, their names written in calligraphy on heavy white paper.

Claire's mind drifted to Jackie and JFK. What were they doing tonight, on the eve of the inauguration? she wondered. What must it be like to be them, their future stretching gloriously ahead of them?

The night swirled on, Claire drinking too much champagne with dinner.

Before the toasts began, she excused herself and went to the ladies' room to freshen up. She was slightly drunk, she realized. Or maybe more than slightly.

Peter was waiting for her when she came out.

"I didn't want you to get lost," he said.

"I am," she said softly, but he didn't hear her.

He was guiding her backwards, his hands on her shoulders. She almost lost her balance, but he held her tight, urging her into the cloakroom. Inside, it smelled of wet fur and wool, and mothballs.

"You look so beautiful," Peter whispered.

He took her face in his hands and kissed her hard on the lips, parting her lips and pushing his tongue inside to meet hers.

Claire let him kiss her like that, wishing she could feel what she used to.

Peter pressed her between the coats, his hand reaching under her dress.

"Peter," she said, surprised. "Anyone could walk in."

He took a step back. "Why can't you be like this again?" he asked her.

"I don't know what you mean."

"Like you are tonight. Happy. Like a good wife. Like you're mine," he said, his voice cracking.

"I'm trying," she said.

But even as she said it, she imagined years and years of this, of smiling and nodding and pretending to like his kisses. Of pretending to love him.

"I want to forgive you," he said. "God help me, I do."

She was afraid if she tried to speak, she might scream, so she just nodded and gulped back this thing rising in her throat.

"I want to have this baby and make it work."

Claire was nodding and nodding, choking.

"But I'm not sure I can ever look at you without picturing—"

This was too much. She quieted him by kissing him again, by letting him kiss her and grow hard against her.

"Tell me you love me," he whispered.

"I love you," she said, the lie coming easily because this life she was living, all of it, had become such a lie.

Peter stepped back.

"The toasts," he said.

"I just have to put on lipstick," Claire said.

"I'll wait."

He would never trust her again, not even here in this strange city. Obediently, Claire went into the ladies' room, reapplied her lipstick and powdered her cheeks, then went out where her husband waited for her.

Back home after the party, Birdy still beamed.

"It was worth living this long just to have that party," she said.

"It was a wonderful party," Claire said agreeably.

Her ankles were swollen, and she'd removed her shoes. She wanted nothing more than to go to bed. But here they were, the three of them sipping cognac, and recollecting the details of the evening.

Finally Claire excused herself.

"Of course, darling," Birdy said, perhaps eager to have Claire leave. "You need your rest."

Claire didn't even bother to hang her beautiful dress. She pulled on her nightgown and slid in between the cool stiff sheets. Her mother-in-law ironed her sheets, and her napkins, Claire remembered. She was more sober now, and thinking of the party at Dot's that she would miss tomorrow.

The door creaked open and Peter appeared, backlit from the hall light.

"Checking up on me?" Claire said.

"Coming to bed," he said.

He closed the door and she heard him undressing.

"You can stay up with Birdy," Claire told him. "You should."

"She wanted to turn in. Besides," he continued, coming to

the twin bed where she lay, "ever since those kisses in the cloakroom . . ."

He didn't need to finish. Claire understood. She made room
for him in the narrow bed, and almost immediately he was on
top of her, pushing inside, his lips brushing her cheek.

When he was finished, he smoothed her hair back.

"You're getting too big for this way," he whispered.

"I need to sleep," Claire said, kissing him lightly, hoping he
would go.

He did. But Claire couldn't fall asleep.

As she lay there trying, she heard a bang from somewhere
down the hall. And then a faint voice.

Claire sat up, straining to hear.

Yes, someone was calling out there.

Quickly, Claire got up and hurried out of the room.

At the end of the long hallway, Birdy lay crumpled, still in
her Chanel suit and pearls. Her skin was a strange gray, and
from here it looked like she wasn't breathing.

"Peter!" Claire yelled as she rushed to her mother-in-law.

# 6

## Because I Could Not Stop for Death

### VIVIEN, 1919

The Western Union man stood on Vivien's doorstep. She could see him there, waiting.

He banged on the door again.

"Western Union," he said in a voice that let Vivien know he had said those words too many times in his life.

"Yes," she called to him. "I'm on my way."

She smoothed her skirt and patted her hair in place, primping as if for a date. Ridiculous, she thought, taking a deep breath and finally moving toward the door.

"Telegram," the man said.

Vivien nodded, but didn't hold out her hand to take it from him. He was sweating in his rough brown wool jacket with a WU pin on its collar.

"For Vivien Lowe," he said impatiently, shaking the telegram at her.

When this didn't seem to do the trick, he added, "From Denver, Colorado."

"Thank you," Vivien managed.

She accepted the telegram, but did not open it or go back inside. Instead, she stood and watched him straighten the bicycle he had leaned against the house, jump on it, and ride off down the street. A young man in a black suit passed the Western Union man, his head dropped, his eyes on the street.

"Watch it!" the Western Union man shouted, swerving.

But the young man did not look up. He kept moving steadily down the street. When he reached Vivien's door, he stopped and checked a piece of wrinkled paper clutched in his hands. Then he raised his eyes, not seeming to notice that Vivien stood there, and checked the number above the door.

She immediately recognized the grief on his face. The flat eyes rimmed in red. The face blotchy from tears.

"Are you the obituary writer?" the man asked in a voice hoarse from crying.

"Vivien Lowe," Vivien said, extending her hand.

But the man did not offer his. He took a step back, and opened his arms wide as if to indicate the size, the enormity of what had brought him to Vivien's door.

"They're dead," he said. "Both of them."

Vivien walked over to him, taking his arm and gently guiding him toward her. Grief paralyzed you. She knew this. It prevented you from getting out of bed, from moving at all. It prevented you from even taking a few steps forward.

"You found your way here," she told him softly. "That is quite an accomplishment."

He let her bring him inside. He let her slide his heavy black coat from him and lead him to the sofa. With her fingertips on his shoulders, Vivien gently pushed him down so that he was sitting.

"Both of them," he said again.

Vivien sat in the chair across from him. His hands, folded as if in prayer, were creased with dark red. Blood, she realized, swallowing hard.

"Who, darling?" she asked. "Who has died?"

His Adam's apple bobbed up and down as he tried to speak.

"It's all right," Vivien said, patting his knee. "I'm going to make you some hot tea. And some toast. I bet you haven't eaten anything in hours."

He shook his head, as if the very idea of eating was impossible to comprehend.

"You sit right here," Vivien said.

She poured him a glass of water for his dry throat, and placed it in his hands. When he didn't take a sip, she wrapped her hands around his and lifted the glass to his cracked lips. The man began to drink, greedily, water spilling down his stubbled chin and onto his white shirt, which Vivien saw also had dark rust spots splattered across it. He finished the water and held out the glass for more. Three times Vivien refilled it for him.

After the last glass, the man stood, clutching his stomach.

"I'm going to be sick," he said.

Vivien brought him into the bathroom, holding his damp head while he vomited into the toilet.

"There, there," she said as he retched.

Finally, he collapsed onto the floor, pressing his body against the wall. He was a big man, well over six feet tall, with broad shoulders and long legs. His dark blond curls were flattened with sweat, and he gave off the iron smell of blood.

He looked up at her, shaking his head as he spoke.

"Everything seemed to be going fine," he said, his voice filled with disbelief. "She was doing fine."

Vivien kneeled beside him.

"Who?" she asked.

"My Jane." Saying the name out loud made him choke on it. "And our daughter." His eyes shined with tears. "We were going to name her Hazel. Hazel Jane."

The grief-stricken want to hear the names of those they've lost. To not say the name out loud denies that person's existence. People seeking to comfort mourners often err this way. They lower their eyes at the sound of the dead's name. They refuse to utter it themselves.

"But you have," Vivien said, beginning to understand what had happened. "You have named her Hazel. She's Hazel Jane."

"Hazel Jane," he said softly.

Vivien stood and opened the small cabinet above the sink. She took out some baking soda and some lavender water.

"You'll freshen up now," she said. "I'll make your tea and toast while you freshen up."

He got awkwardly to his feet.

"Then we'll sit down and talk and I will write something beautiful for Jane and Hazel," Vivien said.

"Thank you," he said. "Thank you."

"You're welcome . . . ?"

"Benjamin."

"Benjamin," Vivien repeated.


As Vivien sliced two pieces of sourdough bread from the loaf, Emily Dickinson, that strange reclusive poet from Massachusetts, came to her. She had read both of her collections, *Poems* and *Poems: Second Series*, and been struck by the simplicity and power of the writing. That combination seemed to speak to the grief of the young man in her parlor too.

The teakettle whistled and Vivien poured the boiling water over the tea leaves waiting in the cup.

*Because I could not stop for death, He kindly stopped for me,* Vivien thought.

No, that one wasn't quite right. It didn't capture the permanence of this double loss. Wife and infant daughter. Gone.

The smell of toasted bread filled the room. Perhaps the most comforting smell in the world, Vivien believed. It soothed the sick and the grieving equally, this simple nourishment. Vivien removed the toast from the small slot beside the oven, and spread it thickly with sweet butter. She cut each slice into four triangles, and arranged them all on a pale blue plate. She considered adding a ramekin of marmalade. Lotte had sent her home on Sunday with jars of Meyer lemon and orange marmalade. More than one person could ever eat. Vivien took a jar from the shelf, the pale orange jelly thick with rinds.

But then she changed her mind. Simple toast with butter. A cup of tea. That was what was needed here. She returned the marmalade to the shelf, placed the cup and the plate on a tray, and went back into the parlor.

Benjamin sat on the sofa, hunched forward, his face buried in his hands. She saw that he had scrubbed most of the blood from them. Even so, some remained beneath the fingernails.

"Here," Vivien said.

Slowly, he lifted his face and looked at her with an expression of utter disbelief.

"Tell me about Jane," Vivien said, holding the tea out to him.

He took the cup, but put it right back down.

"She's beautiful," he said. "You've never seen a more beautiful girl."

Vivien waited.

"And healthy," he said, his eyes growing wild with disbelief again. "Never sick! During the Spanish influenza, she nursed me and her parents and never got sick herself."

"There's no explanation for what happens," Vivien said. "Or why."

Benjamin picked up a piece of toast and carefully tore it into tiny bits.

"Nine months," he said. "And fine. Just fine. Never even had morning sickness."

He picked up another piece and tore that one too.

"I've never seen so much blood," he said. "I was in France, at Somme, and I've never seen so much blood."

Vivien watched him start on a third piece.

"I saw the life go out of her eyes. One minute she was looking at me, scared, you know? Puzzled. And then she was gone. I saw her go." He said this last with something like amazement.

Was there ultimately some relief in witnessing death? Vivien wondered. If she had been with David that day, if she had watched him die, today her life would be different. Wouldn't it?

"The baby," he was saying, "came out with the cord around her neck. She never took one breath. Not one. The midwife whisked her away so Jane didn't see. And then the bleeding wouldn't stop. We couldn't stop it," he said. "How can that be? We win wars and we stop flooding and . . . and we can't stop a twenty-two-year-old girl from bleeding to death? We can't save her baby?"

*All but Death, can be Adjusted,* Vivien thought. The perfect Dickinson poem for Jane and Hazel's obituary.

*Dynasties repaired — Systems — settled in their Sockets —*
*Citadels       dissolved . . .*

"Don't worry, Benjamin. I will write them a beautiful obituary," Vivien said.

After Benjamin Harwood left, Vivien sat at the small cherrywood desk looking out over the street. She filled her pen with ink, and took a sheet of heavy vellum paper from the single drawer. Lotte teased her about her reluctance to invest in a typewriter. But Vivien had tried to use one and only grew frustrated by the way the keys kept sticking.

A few months ago, Lotte had shown Vivien the new one she'd bought. "Look, darling," Lotte had said, demonstrating, "This shift key makes it all so easy."

"But why go to all the trouble of learning this when I can simply write on a piece of paper?"

Lotte shook her head. "You are stuck in the nineteenth century, Viv."

"I'm not," Vivien insisted, knowing that perhaps Lotte was right.

Sighing, Vivien stared at the blank paper in front of her now. How to capture a life that never had a chance to blossom? Or one cut so abruptly short? Benjamin Harwood had sat in her parlor for most of the afternoon, talking about his Jane. Vivien resisted the urge to take him into her arms and comfort him. His grief was palpable, like a living thing in the room with them. Listening to him, Vivien felt in some way he was articulating her loss too.

She put the pen down.

The telegram. What had she done with the telegram?

Benjamin's appearance at her door had completely undone her. She'd had the telegram in her hand when he arrived. Vivien began to search for it, carefully at first, but then more frantically. How could she have been so careless with something so important?

It wasn't in the kitchen or the bathroom. She looked under the sofa and the chair and the table in the parlor. She went outside to see if it was on the doorstep, or if it had blown into the street. But it seemed to have vanished completely.

Back inside, Vivien opened drawers, knowing that of course she wouldn't find the telegram there. She turned her pockets inside out, and lifted the corners of the rug.

In her heart she believed that the man in Denver was David. Perhaps she would just go, now, to the train station and buy a ticket to Denver. To hell with the telegram. After so much time, she didn't need anything but to find him and take him home.

Trembling, Vivien collapsed onto the sofa. She could almost feel his lips on hers that long-ago April morning when he left her in bed. How many times had she imagined his journey away from her, as if it held a clue to his fate? He had walked down the street, turned the corner, and either hopped on the trolley or continued on foot to Market Street. If he'd gone by trolley, then he would have been in his office when the earthquake hit. His partner would have already been there, waiting for him and their meeting. But Duncan had died that morning, crushed by the collapse of the building. They'd found his body there, buried. Vivien had no one to ask if David had ever arrived. She imagined him dazed, wounded, wandering from the rubble. Wandering all the way to Denver, perhaps.

Something caught her eye, peeking out from beneath the tray of tea and toast. A white edge of paper. Vivien pushed the tray away so hard that the half-full cup of tea toppled and spilled. There was the telegram, waiting to be found.

Her hands still trembled, with relief now, as she ripped it open.

ROOM NUMBER WORN AWAY. STOP. MAN HAS SCAR ON
FOREHEAD INDICATING HEAD INJURY. STOP. IN GOOD HEALTH
EXCEPT SEVERE AMNESIA. STOP. EYES BLUE. STOP. HAIR GRAY.
STOP. HEIGHT 6'1". STOP. COME TO DENVER IMMEDIATELY TO
POSSIBLY CONFIRM IDENTITY. STOP.

Vivien read it once, twice. A third time. Yes, David's hair
would have grayed after all this time and trauma. But she could
see his blue eyes still. She could remember gazing up the length
of him to meet those blue eyes with her own. The possibility that
this man in Denver was David now seemed even more likely.

She needed to go there as soon as possible. Immediately, the
telegram said. This would require packing. Purchasing a ticket.
Finishing the obituaries for Benjamin Harwood's wife and newborn daughter. It would require taking a train for several days,
getting off in Denver, Colorado, and walking into a hospital to
reclaim her life. Finally.


Vivien stayed up until well after midnight composing the obituaries. She knew that her words comforted people in grief. It was a
responsibility she took seriously. Even those people who believed
that David had died on April 18, 1906, still did not know what to
say to Vivien. Grief made people awkward. It made them afraid
and hesitant. But an obituary writer could not be awkward or
tentative. An obituary writer had to be assertive and honest,
kind and insightful.

She included the Dickinson in Jane's. She wrote about
how as a young woman Jane had nursed her own parents and
future husband when they had the Spanish influenza; how she

held Benjamin in her arms at night when nightmares about the war woke him and he trembled, remembering; how her cheeks flushed in the sun; how she liked to knit on cold nights, the yarn tumbling from her lap like a waterfall.

But to write for Hazel, who never got a chance to see the world or to know her father's love, the way it felt to be in her mother's arms, was more difficult. Vivien stood, her neck and shoulders tight from having sat so long bent over the paper. A light rain had begun to fall; she could smell it in the air. David used to love the smell of spring rain. He would wake her if the rain came late at night, as it had now, and make her get dressed to stand in it with him.

She would stand in it now, Vivien decided. She made a cup of chamomile tea, spooned some honey into it, and brought it outside. The rain was so light it was almost mist, dampening her nightgown and hair. Her hair would curl from the moisture, and thinking this she lifted her hand to smooth it. She should have put on slippers before she went out. But she hadn't, so she stood barefoot, sipping her tea, watching the clouds moving across the dark sky. A crescent moon could just be seen through a circle of rain. *That's our moon,* David had said that first night at the Majestic Hotel. Vivien had gone to look out the window, and he had joined her there, standing behind her with his arms around her waist and his chin resting on her shoulder, both of them still naked, sore from a night of making love. He had pointed to the sliver of moon and said, *That's our moon. Whenever you see it, you will always think of me.*

Was it a sign? Vivien wondered. A sign that the man in Denver was indeed David? She knew what Lotte would say. There are no signs or omens. A moon is just the moon. Practical Lotte. Did she ever stand outside barefoot in the rain and stare at the moon? Probably not, Vivien thought, smiling at the idea. Even as girls together Lotte had been the one to worry about danger, the one to take care of them both. She wouldn't have followed David into that restaurant that day, or agreed to go to the Majestic Hotel with him for the night.

Vivien went back inside, catching a glimpse of herself in the hall mirror as she passed. Yes, her hair had wound into moist curls, as she expected. Rubbing it dry with a tea towel, words from Shakespeare's *The Tempest* came to her: *We are such stuff As dreams are made on, and our little life Is rounded with a sleep.* Oh, Vivien thought, letting the towel fall as she walked quickly back to the desk and picked up her pen. That was perfect for little Hazel.

The rain fell harder as she wrote about the dreams Benjamin and Jane had for Hazel. She wrote the story that Benjamin had told her about how they each wrote a hope they had for their child on a slip of paper every morning, and then sent the papers into the wind when Jane's labor began. Where are those hopes and dreams now? Vivien wrote. The quote from *The Tempest* followed this story naturally. Vivien read the obituary over again. It was a good one. An obituary that honored Hazel and her parents.

The next morning, Vivien dressed in her good navy blue suit. She pinned the cameo David had bought her in Italy to the collar and wore her short-brimmed straw hat with the navy velvet band around it. This was an outfit for taking charge, for going to the train station and buying a ticket to Denver.

Walking down Main Street, the sun hot on her cheeks, Vivien felt alive. The air smelled of dust and horses and sweet flowers. All around her, people moved through their day, oblivious to her. Yet she seemed to belong among them, a feeling she did not usually have. When she heard someone call her name, Vivien turned expectantly and found Lotte hurrying toward her with Pamela by the hand.

It was so unusual to see Lotte and Pamela off the ranch that for an instant, Vivien didn't respond. But when they reached her, and Pamela wrapped her thin arms around Vivien's knees, Vivien brought her friend into a hug.

"What a surprise," she said. "You should have let me know you were coming."

"Well, if you ever get a telephone, I might just do that," Lotte said.

Although she was smiling, she had small worry lines around her eyes and mouth.

"Vivvie," Pamela said, her voice hoarse, "can we come to your house? And have a tea party?"

Pamela loved sipping tea out of one of Vivien's china teacups, and eating tiny cucumber sandwiches with lots of butter and the special lavender shortbread Vivien made just for her.

"No tea parties for you today," Lotte said to Pamela.

"Next time, darling," Vivien told her.

"Where are you going?" Lotte asked. "All dressed up like that."

Without answering, Vivien unclasped her purse and handed Lotte the telegram.

"I have to go to Denver," Vivien said. "Surely you see that."

Lotte shook her head. "It reeks of a wild-goose chase. A key. Blue eyes."

"And six feet one," Vivien said, pointing to the telegram. "With a scar on his head."

"Gray hair," Lotte said.

"It's been a dozen years!" Vivien said, unable to hide her frustration.

"I know, Viv. I am sorry but—"

"But the key," Vivien said softly.

"Mama," Pamela said, leaning into her mother. "I'm getting so tired."

Vivien frowned. "You haven't even told me what you two are doing in town."

"The doctor," Lotte said, twisting a strand of Pamela's fine hair in her fingers. "This one has had a fever and a terrible cough—"

As if on cue, Pamela gave a phlegmy cough.

"Almost a week now," Lotte added.

"I shouldn't keep you then," Vivien said. "You need to get her home into bed with a good eucalyptus oil rubdown."

Lotte gave a little laugh. "I suppose I should hang an onion by her bed too?"

"Don't tease me," Vivien said, pretending to be wounded.

"Do you know what I heard?" Lotte said. She lifted Pamela up and held her, the girl's head on her shoulders.

Vivien saw that Pamela had dark circles under her eyes, and her cheeks did look gaunt.

"Poor Pammy," Vivien murmured.

"I've heard that there's a blue mold in Europe that might someday cure all kinds of diseases."

"Blue mold?" Vivien said, laughing.

"You laugh," Lotte said, "but I believe scientists are capable of taking anything, even mold, and figuring out a scientific use for it."

While Vivien had lost herself in novels and poetry, Lotte had spent her time gazing under microscopes and doing scientific experiments.

Pamela gave a little moan, and Lotte's face grew worried.

"I think we will head back," Lotte said.

The two women hugged, and Vivien could feel a new heat emanating from Pamela.

"Go now," Vivien said.

Lotte hesitated, as if she wanted to say something more.

"Let me know if you do go to Denver," she said finally.

"I wish you could come with me," Vivien admitted.

"You know I would if I could, Viv," she said. Again she seemed to hesitate, but this time she indeed set off, Pamela still in her arms.

Vivien watched Lotte walk down the street. Before she turned the corner, her friend lifted her hand in a halfhearted wave.

The sight of San Francisco, her beautiful city, broke Vivien's heart. How well she knew these streets, the hills she and Lotte used to roller-skate down as children, the North Beach corner where they would go for Italian ice. Vivien always got lemon, enjoying the way it made her mouth pucker, the tartness both painful and pleasant at the same time. Lotte liked the sweet fruity ones, strawberry or peach. If she closed her eyes, her own personal map of the city appeared on the back of her lids. The house where she lived so briefly as a child with her parents before they died, just a day apart, from the Russian flu when she was a child.

Of that house, and that couple, Vivien only had the blurriest memories: a swing tied to a tree branch in the yard, being lifted by her father's strong hands, the rustle of her mother's skirts, a Douglas fir so tall that Vivien had to crane her neck to see all the way to the top, where a foil star perched. Her mother had hand-sewn an entire wardrobe of clothes for a doll Vivien had named Melody. She vaguely remembered sitting on a rug in a parlor with her mother, carefully dressing Melody in her new clothes. The doll's porcelain face and soft blond hair remained clearer to Vivien than the face of her mother.

But of course Melody had been with her longer. When Vivien's aunt took her to live with her in the big house in Pacific

Heights, Vivien first dressed Melody in the forest green coat with the black buttons her mother had made just a few weeks earlier. Even as a teenager, Vivien had kept Melody on a shelf in her bedroom, a reminder of some elusive time she could not quite recall. Standing here now on Market Street, Vivien clearly saw that room where she grew up. The high four-poster bed with the hand-tatted bedcovers and pillows; the tall windows that opened out onto the city; the fainting chair covered in pale gold silk where Vivien would sit, a blanket over her lap, and read on rainy afternoons.

Her city.

Vivien opened her eyes to see that she was standing almost exactly where she first met David on the day she bought the ridiculous blue hat. There, just ahead, was the restaurant where he took her. Vivien watched as a streetcar came to a stop, its doors heaving open. She should run to catch it, but the weight of her trunk combined with the weight of her memories kept her in place, unable to move forward.

She did not like being here. She did not like seeing the ghost of her own self everywhere she looked. But the train to Denver left in the morning, requiring that Vivien spend the night in the city. All these years, she had avoided coming back. After those weeks of searching for David in the rubble, at hospitals, on the streets, she had taken Lotte up on her offer to stay in Napa with her and Robert for a while, until she felt stronger. A while had turned into months, and those months into years. Oh, she'd left the vineyard that summer, and moved into her apartment.

At first she would sit by the window and watch the world pass in front of her. People who walked with purpose, who seemed to have somewhere to go. Mothers pushing prams, adjusting their babies' blankets, beaming down at them or fretting over them. Boys on bicycles. Couples holding hands. An entire population of people who continued living their lives even though Vivien's had come to such a sudden halt. They seemed audacious to her, those people with plans and appointments and futures. How could they parade in front of her? How could the world, in fact, keep spinning?

One day, a man knocked on her door. Short and squat, dressed in a bright red jacket, he stood nervously twirling a straw hat in his hands.

"Is this the newspaper office?" he asked her.

Vivien shook her head. She wasn't even sure where the newspaper office was in town. By this time it was late autumn, but she only ventured into the grocer's and the pharmacy, the places where she could get necessities and then return home.

"Could you please direct me to the obituary writer?" the man said as if he really did stand on the doorstep of the newspaper office.

"This is a private home," Vivien said. "I'm sorry."

She began to close the door, but the man stopped her.

"I need the obituary writer. It's for my wife."

At the word *wife* his voice cracked. Eventually, Vivien grew accustomed to that, the way a word, a name, could break a grieving person. But that day, she felt embarrassed by the man's emotion. She recognized herself in that instant, remembering how often she'd cried as she repeated David's name to Lotte. At times, those two syllables seemed to carry all of her grief.

"But I'm just a woman who lives here," Vivien said.

"My wife," the man continued, "is a baker. She came from Austria-Hungary as a teenager. Her family moved to Chicago where her father worked in the stockyards. Disgusting work, for a man who once owned his own haberdashery shop right in downtown Budapest. Her mother took in sewing, and she would stay up all night working in the dim light, beading wedding dresses, hemming gowns, making layettes for babies. My wife, my Gyöngyi, just a girl, but she baked pastries and sold them on the streets, to bring home extra money so her mother didn't have to work so hard. *Eszterházy torta* and *rétes* and *krémes*. Do you know *Rákóczi túrós?* Cottage cheese cake? No? My Gyöngyi made this better than anyone. Better than the finest bakers in Budapest."

As the man talked, Vivien realized that he was the first person since she had left San Francisco who understood grief. Despite all of the hugs and words of comfort, unless you have suffered loss you cannot understand the depth of it, the seemingly bottomless pit of despair that goes with grief. But this man in the bright red jacket and straw hat, he knew. He understood.

Vivien took his arm and brought him inside. She sat him down on her sofa and she made him a cup of tea. He talked, and Vivien listened.

Eventually, he stood. By then dusk had fallen. But Vivien did not light a lamp for fear of interrupting him.

He said, "*Gyöngyi* means pearl. Did you know this? No? A pearl is hidden in an oyster. Do you know, Miss Obituary Writer, how pearls get made?"

"No," Vivien admitted, "I don't."

"When a piece of grit or sand or shell gets trapped inside, the oyster, it has to protect itself from this irritation. So it creates a liquid around the particle, which eventually, over time, becomes a pearl."

Alone, Vivien sat at her small desk and wrote about this woman, this stranger. She described the pastries she baked, the flakiness of her crusts, the smoothness of her creams, how she perfectly balanced fruit and nuts and sugar in her strudels. Vivien took the final line of the obituary from Keats. "Asleep! O sleep a little while, white pearl!"

In the morning, she walked into town and found the newspaper office that the man could not find the day before. She
explained her mission, handing the obituary to a skinny man
with a big Adam's apple.

"But this ain't an obit, ma'am," he said. "It don't say when she
was born. It don't say how she died. And it don't have much in
between those two momentous occurrences neither."

Vivien thought of David, of all the things she missed about
him, the things she thought about when she yearned for him.
The little word game they played. *Delicious,* she had said that
last morning. And he had answered, *Intoxicating.* She missed
his scrambled eggs. Such a simple thing, but on lazy mornings
she would wake up to him bringing her breakfast on a tray. He
added a bit of cream and sugar to the eggs, which made them
light and sweet. He always had two pieces of sourdough bread,
toasted and buttered and half a grapefruit that he'd already cut
the small wedges for her so she could pick them up with her fork.
She missed how when they stood together, her head reached his
shoulder in the exact spot where she would rest it later that night
in bed.

"This obituary," Vivien said firmly, "has every important fact
about the deceased. This is the obituary her husband wants."

She didn't know for certain that this last point was true, but
she believed that when he read it, he would agree.

The man scowled. "What's this business about pearls
sleeping?"

But Vivien was done with this newspaperman. She instructed
him to run it that very afternoon, and then she stepped outside
where, for the first time in the six months since David had disappeared in the earthquake, she finally could take a breath without it hurting to still be alive.

.   .   .

Perhaps it was foolish of her, but Vivien booked a room for the night at the Hotel Majestic. She arrived in front of it on Sutter Street, and stared up for what felt like a very long time at its distinctive bay windows, trying to guess which room was number 208. Finally, she gave up, remembering that she had not paused to admire the view that night she and David spent here. Vivien lifted the handle of her trunk and dragged it to the entrance.

A bellhop hurried to take her trunk for her, and Vivien followed the man inside the elegant lobby. Everything seemed both familiar and foreign. How caught up in David she had been that long-ago night! All she could think of was touching him, and having him touch her. The check-in had seemed interminable. The slow ride up the elevator eternal. Had they even bothered to turn on the lights when the key finally opened the door and a bed awaited them? It seemed to Vivien now that their clothes came off right at the door, as soon as they stepped inside.

"Is room 208 available?" she asked the man at the desk.

"208," he said, turning to the row of cubbies behind him that held keys.

Vivien's eyes followed his finger as it danced across the row of second-floor room keys.

"208," he said, his finger stopping abruptly.

He removed the large key hanging from a golden rope.

But when he held it out to Vivien, she found herself refusing it.

"No," she said, "I've made a mistake. I'd rather stay in a different room."

His face did not belie any frustration or confusion. "A different room then," he said, replacing that key and handing her another one.

Vivien followed the bellhop who was moving her trunk into the elevator. Inside, she pressed her back against one wall, remembering how David had pressed his body against hers that night, perhaps in this very elevator. She closed her eyes, almost feeling his rough face against her own smooth neck.

"Ma'am?" the bellhop asked. "Are you going to faint?"

Vivien opened her eyes and shook her head. What was she thinking coming back here?

"You look like you saw a ghost," the bellhop said. "We got one, you know. Up on four. He fills the bathtub with water and walks up and down the halls."

He paused to measure the effect of his story.

"Some people," Vivien said, "do believe in ghosts."

"They say he's harmless," the bellhop said as the elevator came to a jerky halt. "But anyway, he doesn't come down to the third floor."

Vivien studied the bellhop's earnest face. A ruddy complexion and the sort of nose that came from too much drinking, a road map of veins.

"I wouldn't mind seeing a ghost," Vivien said.

He looked startled, but she didn't explain further. How could she? What was there to say?


The restaurant in the Hotel Majestic was surprisingly empty. Vivien was seated discreetly in the back corner. A woman dining alone always raised eyebrows. Quickly she scanned the large menu. Why, they served crab Louis salad, Vivien read, delighted. She and David used to go to the St. Francis Hotel just for their crab Louis. She hadn't had it since she left the city. When the waiter came, she ordered one.

"Oh," she said as he turned to leave, "and a glass of Chenin Blanc."

"Yes, madame," he said, gratuitously polite.

Vivien knew he found it odd, even disturbing, that she dared come into the dining room without a man, eat her dinner alone, and have the audacity to drink wine as well.

It had been a long time since she'd dressed up and sat in a fine restaurant like this, and she surprised herself when she realized that she missed it. The buttoning and smoothing and primping. The smell of powder and perfume. She missed David's hand on her arm as they entered a restaurant, how he pulled out the chair for her and glided it back into place. The candlelight flickered, casting everyone in the room in a soft glow. Vivien watched the other people eating and drinking—couples with their heads bent close together, men smoking cigars and sipping brandy from crystal snifters. Her gaze settled on a man eating alone, like her, one sleeve of his jacket pinned up. He'd lost the arm in the war, no doubt. She thought briefly of all the obituaries she had written in those months, the Spanish influenza coming right on the heels of the war, the deaths adding up with terrible speed.

The waiter brought her wine, and right behind it came a cart with her dinner. He made a lavish show of tossing the sliced hard-boiled eggs and tomatoes, asparagus and cucumbers with the white crabmeat.

"Shall I add the dressing, madame?" the waiter asked, a small silver ladle poised over the bowl of orange dressing.

Vivien nodded.

*"Bon appétit,"* the waiter said officiously before he walked away.

Vivien picked up the heavy silver fork and took a bite of crab.

The familiar taste brought with it a rush of memories so strong she had to put the fork back down and work hard to swallow. Alone in Napa, her days had taken on such a similarity that she had almost forgotten pleasures like these: good food, good wine, the murmur of conversations. But sitting here tonight, Vivien ached for all of it, and more. How she missed the companionship, the touch, of a man.

She got to her feet quickly, and laid some bills on the table. Before the waiter could make his way to her, Vivien had already hurried out. Was this how she was meant to spend her life? Alone, untouched, unheard? The thought was almost too much to bear. Would someone meeting her now even believe that she had once been like these people, carefree and pretty and loved?


In her room, Vivien unpinned her hair and began to brush it. She still brushed it for one hundred strokes, a habit she'd never given up. She washed her face, first with hot water, then with cold. Her aunt had taught her that this was the best way to keep the pores open and fresh. It had worked too; Vivien always had a clear complexion. Now of course there were small lines around her mouth and eyes, but still her skin was clear and with good color. She rubbed cold cream onto her face in a circular motion, then put all of her toiletries into their small bag and put the small bag back into her trunk. These simple rituals calmed her.

The sheets on the bed felt cool and luxurious. Vivien stretched out, plumping the pillows and trying to block out the memories. As soon as she closed her eyes, hoping to sleep, someone knocked on her door, loud and repeatedly.

"Go away," she called.

But the knocking persisted.

She sat up.

Throwing back the bedclothes, Vivien got out of bed. The knocking was louder, almost frantic now.

"One minute!" she called.

She dug her robe out of her trunk and tied it hastily around her.

At her door, Vivien's eyes rested on the Italian man from Napa. Sebastian, the one who followed her around the library and worked at Robert's vineyard.

"Signora," he said, his face filling with relief at the sight of her. "Oh, signora," he said, his shoulders drooping with some motion she couldn't quite make out.

His name was on the tip of her tongue, though she couldn't recall it.

"Sebastian," he said, all four syllables rolling from his tongue.

"What in the world . . . ?" Vivien began, unable to articulate her surprise and confusion.

"Mrs. Lotte, she say, 'Find Vivien. Try Hotel Majestic.'"

"Lotte sent you?" Vivien said, even more confused.

"Mrs. Vivien," he said, tears streaming down his face. "May I bother you for some water?"

"Yes, of course," Vivien said, holding the door opened wider so he could enter her room.

Embarrassed in her nightclothes, her hair loose, Vivien bent her head as she poured him water from the pitcher by her bedside.

He sipped it, trying to calm himself.

"What is it?" she asked when she thought he was composed.

But at the sound of the question, he began to cry again.

"I don't know how to say it," he said.

"Just say it, that's all," Vivien said.

Sebastian looked at her, right into her eyes.

"The little girl," he said.

"Pamela?"

He nodded. "Pamela, yes. Pamela is dead."

# FOUR

*Among those who come to the house there is sure to be a woman friend of the family whose taste and method of expenditure is similar to theirs.*

—FROM *Etiquette*, BY EMILY POST, 1922

# 7

## We Are All Liars Here

### CLAIRE, 1961

The telephone rang, shrill and piercing. Claire got up slowly, hoping it didn't wake Kathy. She walked down the dark hallway to the small table with the heavy black phone perched on it. Beside the phone sat a yellow legal pad and a blue ballpoint pen as if waiting for important messages.

"Hello," she answered.

"It's me, Clairezy," Peter said.

"How is she?" Claire asked, his use of her old nickname making her feel awkward.

"Not good," he said. "It appears to be a heart attack."

"How terrible," Claire said. "And on her birthday too."

"Strange to see her so . . ." He hesitated. "Vulnerable," he said.

Claire almost said *I'm sorry*, but caught herself.

"How are you?" she said instead.

"There's vending machine coffee," he said. "And a tin of cookies in her room. I don't know who brought them. Those Danish ones? Butter cookies in different shapes?"

"Those are good," Claire said.

"Did you sleep?" Peter asked.

"No."

Silence settled between them.

"I was just in your old room and remembering you telling me how you and your mother made that skateboard out of . . . what was it? An old roller skate and a plank of wood?"

"We called that thing the Tornado," he said. "Painted it purple with a big twister down the middle."

She heard him sigh.

"Maybe I should come to the hospital?" Claire said.

"I'll come and get you first thing," he said. "Try to sleep a bit."

"I wonder if John and Jackie can sleep tonight," she said. As soon as she said it, she realized how foolish it sounded, how inappropriate.

"Maybe not," Peter surprised her by saying. "Maybe they're sitting up thinking they're the luckiest two people on the planet."

She smiled at the idea. "Well," she said, "maybe they are."

"I'm using the phone at the nurses' station," he said.

"Oh. Of course."

"Clairezy," Peter said, his voice low.

"What?"

"I love you," he said. "As much as I hate you, as much as I can't stop thinking about—"

"Ssshhh," she said. "Not now."

They hung up and Claire stood there in the quiet. Her ankles were still swollen and she stood barefoot on her sore feet, the cool wood of the floor beneath her. The heat coming up through the radiators hissed and crackled. She opened and closed her fingers. They were also swollen, and her rings cut into her. She tried to twist first the solitaire diamond, then the gold band below it, but neither would budge.

Claire picked up the heavy receiver again and placed her finger in the small circle marked Operator. She hesitated briefly, then dialed it. When the operator answered in a clipped nasal voice, Claire had to take a breath before she said, "I want to make a long-distance call."

"Do you have the number?" the operator asked, all brusque efficiency.

Did she have the number? Claire almost laughed. She'd memorized it months ago, repeating it over and over as she drove or drifted off to sleep. That number had seemed almost magical. No, it had been magical. Just dialing it had made her shiver with excitement.

"Valley one," she said now, "three nine five nine."

In the space between them, Claire heard pages turning.

"Hold please," the operator said.

Claire realized she was holding her breath as she waited for the phone on the other end to ring. She closed her eyes, imagining Miles asleep in a bed she had never seen, beside a woman she did not know. She knew his hair would be sticking up at funny angles. She knew how he must smell, of his Right Guard deodorant and the pomade he used to try to keep that hair in place. He would taste of Gleem toothpaste and cigarettes and of the Jameson's he liked to sip.

Abruptly, the silence ended and a loud ringing filled the space between him and Claire. He was there, at the other end of that telephone. She imagined it ringing in the dark, waking him. Waking his wife too, no doubt. But he would be the one to rouse himself and answer it. If she said nothing, would he still somehow know that she was the one calling?

Then, just like that, as if no time had passed, his voice was in her ear, rough with sleep.

"Hello?" he said.

Again Claire took a small sharp breath. She thought of all the things she had dreamed of saying to him these past few months. Silly things, like how well the *coq au vin* recipe from the *New York Times* had turned out and how she thought Chet Huntley looked ill like he maybe had cancer and how she had bought the 45 of "Save the Last Dance for Me" and cried whenever she played it.

"Hello," he said again, weary.

And big things. Big things like how she missed him, how she could not bear to remember the blue of his eyes or the way his hand felt on her thigh when they drove together because remembering them broke her heart all over again. Absently, her hand caressed her belly. *Oh, Miles,* she thought.

His voice came through the lines again, softer now. "Claire?" he whispered hopefully.

Claire nodded, unable to speak.

"Please tell me it's you," Miles said, all the pain she had caused him in his voice.

Slowly, Claire lowered the receiver and hung up.

What had she been thinking? Her hands were shaking. She needed a cigarette. *Claire.* He'd said her name. How beautiful it had sounded.


Sitting at the kitchen table, Claire sipped another glass of scotch and smoked a cigarette, her hands still trembling.

When the door opened, she froze, as if she'd been caught doing something wrong.

"Peter?" she said.

But instead, Connie from downstairs walked in.

"I heard footsteps," she said, helping herself to a cigarette from Claire's pack. "Any word?"

"Peter just called," she said. "It appears to be a heart attack."

"Not good at her age," Connie said matter-of-factly.

She sat across from Claire, picked up the bottle of scotch and read the label to herself.

"Michael's got colic," Connie said. "The kid hasn't slept through the night since he was born." She sighed. "Fourteen months. Jimmy's all eager for the next one and I'm like, when that kid sleeps straight through, we can talk about it."

"My neighbor Dot," Claire said, "she put her baby on the dryer and ran it and it worked. It calmed him right down."

"You don't say?" Connie said. "Hmmm."

She got up and retrieved a glass from the cupboard, pouring herself a healthy amount of scotch before sitting back down. In the harsh kitchen light, Claire saw that her eyes looked like someone who needed a good night's sleep—ringed with dark smudges, weary.

"I put some brandy in his bottle sometimes," Connie said. "Just a little. When I'm desperate."

"You should try the thing with the dryer."

Connie nodded. Her eyes traveled over Claire in a way that made her squirm. "When are you due?" she asked, her gaze settling on Claire's stomach.

"Sometime in spring. I don't really know when it happened, so . . ." Claire held up her hands in defeat.

Connie nodded again. Something in the way she looked at Claire, appraising her, made Claire feel like she knew everything about her.

"So sad about Birdy," Connie said, and Claire could see that she really did feel bad.

"What was she like?" Claire asked. "When Peter was young?"

"Glamorous," Connie said. "Exotic. She didn't look like any of the other mothers on the block, I can tell you. But older too, which we found really curious."

"Peter always says she was, I don't know, shy?"

"Maybe," Connie said, frowning. "We all thought she was just kind of fancy, you know? Our mothers were making spaghetti and meatballs for dinner and Birdy was cooking these little bites of chicken and exotic vegetables in a wok. You know what a wok is?"

Vivien admitted she wasn't sure.

"It's like a big steel bowl that you put on the stove and cook food in really fast. We used to all stand around and watch her. And the smells! Ginger and I don't know what." Connie shook her head, remembering. "We all wished she was our mother, in a way."

"So she was fun to be around then?"

"Not fun," Connie said. "Just different from anybody I ever knew before. She was always kind of sad, even when she smiled. My mother said that once and I realized she was right. 'Birdy,' my mother told me, 'has suffered something great and mysterious.' That's what we all thought. But she loves Pete. Whenever he came inside, her face lit up. We could see how pretty she must have been once."

"What color do you think Jackie will wear tomorrow?" Claire asked, suddenly wanting to change the subject.

Connie looked surprised. "Um . . . red?"

"Really?" Claire said politely. Jackie was not going to wear red to the inauguration. Red was too déclassé. "My neighbor Dot is having a little contest—"

"The dryer lady."

"What? Oh. Oh, well, yes. All of the ladies in the neighbor-hood cast a vote on what color Jackie is going to wear and who-ever chooses the right one wins."

"Wins what?" Connie said, frowning.

"It's silly but the winner gets a little party with daiquiris and tea sandwiches and her favorite dessert. Like queen for the day." Dot had even made a tiara out of cardboard, spray painting it gold and covering it in glitter.

"So what color did you pick?"

"Pink," Claire said.

Connie wrinkled her nose in distaste. "She won't wear pink," she said.

"Well, I think she will. With her dark hair, she'd look beauti-ful in pink."

"I think she's homely," Connie said. "Too horsey."

Claire couldn't think what to say. Jackie Kennedy homely? No one thought that. She was beautiful and stylish and sophis-ticated. Everyone Claire knew wanted to be just like Jackie. Dot and Roberta and Trudy had all gotten their hair cut like Jackie's. Trudy read in *Time* magazine that Jackie spoke fluent French, and she went to the library and got French tapes so that she could learn too. She peppered her conversation with French phrases, and ended her sentences by saying, *"n'est-ce pas?"*

"Her jaw," Connie was saying, "is too big." Connie jutted her own jaw and lower teeth forward to demonstrate. Laughing, she poured herself more scotch, and topped off Claire's glass too. "She's from here, you know."

"Well," Claire said, "Newport."

Connie rolled her eyes. "Okay," she said. "That's still Rhode Island. Her father, what do they call him? Black Jack or some-thing? He's a drunk and a gambler and a womanizer. It's true."

"I don't know anything about that," Claire said.

"I don't like womanizers," Connie said. "Thou shalt not commit adultery, right?"

Again Claire got the feeling that Connie knew. She fussed with the buttons that ran down the front of her nightgown, avoiding Connie.

"I told Jimmy if I ever caught him with another woman, I'd cut his balls off."

Claire looked up.

"I would too," Connie said evenly.

"I don't think we can say what we would do in hypothetical situations," Claire said. Her mouth and throat had gone dry. "We just don't know until it happens."

Saying this, she thought of the look on Peter's face that day. She had opened her eyes and caught sight of Peter over her lover's shoulder. He was on top of her and they were naked and Peter stood in the doorway of Kathy's room looking surprised, as if he could not make the details add up.

"Really?" Connie said. "Maybe you don't know what you'd do, *hypothetically*, but I would cut his balls off."

"Well," Claire said.

"Did you ever meet Angie Fiori?"

Claire shook her head.

"Lived down the street. Pete knows her. We all went to high school together. Anyway, you're not going to believe this, but *she* was doing her brother-in-law."

"Really," Claire said, putting her hand up to stop Connie, "I don't want to hear this."

Connie's thin eyebrows lifted. "Her husband beat the crap out of his brother, but I think he should have thrown her out. I mean—"

"I have to try to get some sleep," Claire said, standing up. The scotch had made her dizzy, and she held on to the table for support.

Connie narrowed her eyes.

"How did we ever get on this topic anyway?" Claire said, forcing a chuckle.

"Jackie," Connie said.

"Right." Claire waited for Connie to stand too, to go back downstairs. But she just sat there, waiting. "Will you watch tomorrow?"

"Sure," Connie said. She brightened. "Tell you what. If she wears red, I'll cook you dinner, and if she wears pink, you can cook me dinner."

"Great," Claire said, even though that was a silly idea. Her mother-in-law was probably dying; how could she cook dinner for Connie?

"What would you cook? If you won," Connie said, still not making a move to leave.

"I don't know," Claire said. "Probably *coq au vin*."

"Cocoa what?"

"Chicken. In wine sauce. It's my specialty, kind of."

"Huh," Connie said. "Okay. I'll make you spaghetti and meatballs. I make the best meatballs. Ask Jimmy."

"I really need to go to bed," Claire said. "I'm sorry."

Connie looked surprised. "Sorry? Sorry for what?"

She shrugged and said, "For going to bed, I guess."


The first time she saw Miles was at Trudy's on a Saturday night in May. It was the Saturday right after Dougie Daniels disappeared. Claire and Peter arrived late.

"Babysitter," Peter had explained.

"Regina Knightly," Claire said, which was enough for all the women to nod.

"Enough said," Trudy said, offering a tray of hors d'ouevres.

Regina Knightly was always late, and slow-moving, the last-resort babysitter in the neighborhood. When Cheryl Merckel babysat, she taught the kids her high school cheers, right down to the cartwheels. Beth Piper did elaborate art projects. Diane Carrington wrote plays for them to perform. But Regina Knightly just ate the leftovers and left the dirty dishes in the sink. The women suspected that she rifled through their dresser drawers, spritzed on their perfume, even stole their husbands' condoms. But no one could ever prove any of this.

Peter immediately gravitated toward the men, who stood in a smoky corner arguing about whether Nixon would make a good president.

When the doorbell rang, Claire was relieved. Someone was actually arriving even later.

"Can you get that?" Trudy asked Claire. She was filling another tray with celery stuffed with cream cheese. The way Trudy made those, she always put half an olive on some, some tomato on the others, alternating them neatly. "It's my spare," she added.

"Spare?"

"I needed a fourth guy, to even things out." Trudy tilted her chin in the direction of her husband's sister Polly, who had been widowed recently. Polly had to be invited to every event at Trudy's, leaving Trudy to always be on the lookout for single men. "He's married," Trudy said, "but I was desperate. His wife is in the hospital."

Claire laughed as she headed to the front door. "I hope she didn't just have a baby."

"No. Something silly, like getting her tonsils out. He works with Dick."

Claire walked through the dining room, already set with Trudy's china. The pattern was ornate, a busy cluster of pink flowers in various shapes and shades and the plates themselves scalloped along the edges. The water and wine glasses were pink too. Peter would never have let her choose pink china and crystal. But they did catch the candlelight beautifully.

The doorbell chimed again.

"Claire!" Trudy called. "Did you get lost?"

In the front foyer, a large orange tree bloomed from a golden urn. How did Trudy keep that thing producing oranges, Claire wondered.

She pulled open the heavy front door.

A man peeked at her from behind an enormous bouquet of flowers.

"Trudy?" he asked.

"No, I'm just a neighbor. Trudy is serving the hors d'oeuvres."

They stood awkwardly for a moment, until Claire realized she should take the flowers from him and let him inside.

Weeks later, after she'd walked into Kennedy headquarters and took the seat next to him at a bank of telephones, he would tell her that in that awkward moment, he couldn't catch his breath. *I knew I was in trouble,* he whispered to her. He'd said, *The neighbor,* as she sat down. Claire remembered how he'd listened that night at Trudy's, the way he cocked his head when she told the story about being stuck in Madrid during a rainstorm when she worked for TWA. The story was a funny one, good for a dinner party what with its matador and flooded hotel lobby and tapas. But it wasn't that interesting. Yet he'd listened to her as if every detail mattered, and met her gaze and held it just a moment too long. She remembered that dinner had been roast beef, and about his wife's appendicitis—it wasn't tonsils, after all—and Polly's gruesome description of her husband's slow death. Dessert was chocolate soufflé.

At some point during that first night at Kennedy headquarters, Miles leaned close to her and said, *It's happening again. I can't catch my breath.* Claire had ignored him, but her heart was doing funny things. She could practically hear it pumping her blood and sending it through her veins. In fact, she was getting light-headed. Air, she thought. Fresh air.

It was July, and hot. Claire lit a cigarette and took a deep inhale. She smoked Newports, and they tasted almost minty. The air seemed not to move at all. Rather, it hung heavy and wet, sending sweat trickling down Claire's ribs. She held her light cotton sleeveless blouse out, away from her body, and fanned it, though that did not bring relief.

"Claire."

She turned toward him. He wore a white button-down shirt, sleeves rolled up to his elbows. The lamplight cast a pale blue glow over everything.

"The old era is ending," he said. "The old ways will not do."

"I'm not going to do this," she said, maybe knowing even then what *this* was.

"We can have faith in the future only if we have faith in ourselves," he said, moving closer to her.

"Have you memorized the whole speech?" she said. She could smell her own sweat, and his too, a male musk beneath a layer of lime.

"I have," he said. "But I didn't realize it would relate to me so personally. My old ways. My faith in the future."

Now he stood only inches away from her. A thin line of sweat moved down his cheek.

'You don't even know me," she said.

"Tell me who you are then," he said in a low voice.

"I don't do things like this," she said, laughing softly.

"Neither do I," he said.

"I'm married," she said.

"I know. I met him. Tall handsome guy who doesn't appreciate you."

Claire shivered despite the heat.

"He does," she said, because a wife always defends her husband. But did Peter appreciate her? Did he even really notice her?

"I'm guessing he married a beautiful woman who would give him beautiful children and keep a beautiful house," he said, cocking his head. "He just plugged you into his plan."

"You're fresh," Claire said, starting to walk away.

But he grabbed her arm to stop her.

"I see you," he said softly. "I see something in you."

"I can't parallel-park," Claire told him, unsettled by what he'd said.

"I'll teach you," he said. "You're a smart girl. You'll learn fast."

He thought she was smart? A fast learner? She shook away the image of Peter smiling at her as if she were a child. *Don't even think about that,* he always said, *it's too complicated.* Or: *Don't worry your pretty little head.* About bills or hurricanes or politics or anything at all.

"I'm not a very good cook," Claire continued. "But I try Craig Claiborne's recipe every week. Sometimes it comes out right."

"I make a mean chili," he said. "That and a Craig Claiborne from time to time. The other nights we'll eat out."

"You're out of line," she said unconvincingly.

"What else?" he asked her.

"I don't like *The Red Skelton Show.* I don't think he's funny."

"He's not funny," he said. "Lenny Bruce is funny."

Claire smiled. "Lenny Bruce *is* funny," she said, thinking of how Peter couldn't stand Lenny Bruce. Too crass, he said.

He stood so close to her that she could smell the coffee on his breath.

"I'm a Hoosier," she said. "I was an air hostess for TWA."

"Tell me something that matters."

"My birthday is in June," Claire said. The lights of an Esso station across the street blinked off. "That makes me a Gemini. Do you know anything about that?"

"I think I'm a Libra," he said. "September 28?"

"I think that is a Libra," she said.

"Are we compatible?" he asked. "Libra and Gemini?"

Claire laughed nervously. "I'm married," she said again, wondering which of them she was reminding.

"Do you know what's strange?" he asked, but didn't wait for her to answer. "I love my wife. I do. But there's something here." He waved his hand between them. "I want to stand out here and talk to you all night. I want to, I don't know. I want to get to know you."

Claire wondered about his wife. Was she pretty? What did she do if they didn't have children? What did women without children do all day? Did she work?

"I've always been faithful to my wife," he said quietly. He took her hand then. He pulled her close.

"Tell me more," he said.

"There was this boy in our neighborhood," Claire began. "Dougie Daniels."

He paused. He looked at her in a way that no one had ever looked at her before. Like he was actually seeing her.

"He disappeared. I was in the backyard and the neighborhood boys walked by." She paused, trying to think of how to explain what had happened that day. "He was an ordinary boy," she said finally.

"That was when you knew," he said, his gaze still on her.

"Knew?"

"That no one is safe," he said.

"You'll leave him, of course," he said after the first time they made love.

That was the next week, on an August night so still and hot that the air felt like gauze around them. They were in the parking lot, in his car. Everyone else had gone.

Claire couldn't think of what to say. Women didn't leave their husbands. That wasn't the way it worked. Sometimes a man walked out. He left his wife for his secretary, or an air hostess. Or he lost all his money and went West to look for new opportunities. But women, they stayed.

"I wish I'd met you first," she whispered.

Claire had walked in her house, her legs still trembling. The TV was on. Red Skelton. Peter was laughing.

"How was it?" he asked without looking up when she came in the den.

"Good," she managed to say.

Her eyes moved around the room, taking in all of the things that had once been familiar: the green and gold plaid wallpaper, the curtains that matched perfectly. The Zenith with the rabbit ears on top. The TV trays, metal with scenes of the Old West on them, wagon trains and buffalos. She knew all these things. She did. She'd chosen them. She'd hung the painting above the couch, an oil of orange and gold mums blossoming against a white fence. She'd selected the fabric on the sofa, a soft green tweed flecked with gold and gray. She knew these things, yet nothing looked the same.

Peter finally glanced up at her.

"Can you grab me another one of these?" he said, holding up a bottle of Budweiser.

Claire nodded, but didn't move. Who was this man? Who was this woman? What were they doing here together on this hot summer night, in this room with the suffocating plaid?

"Claire?" he said.

She nodded again, and walked to the kitchen on her shaky legs. She didn't turn on the light. She just stood there in the darkness, inhaling the smell of the spaghetti sauce she'd made for dinner, and of her own Newports, and of another man on her skin.

"Have we the nerve and the will?" Claire said softly. "Can we carry through in an age where we will witness not only new breakthroughs in weapons of destruction, but also a race for mastery of the sky and the rain, the ocean and the tides, the far side of space and the inside of men's minds?"

She took a deep breath. She hadn't told him, but she had memorized Kennedy's acceptance speech too.


Claire did not know how long she'd slept before she felt the weight of Peter sitting on the bed beside her. She opened her eyes.

"You were dreaming," he said.

"Of JFK," Claire said.

He studied her face.

"Is she . . . ?"

Peter shook his head. "Hanging in there. She's medicated, but they said since she pulled through the night, they might be able to ease up on the drugs, so we can talk to her."

"What time is it?"

"Six. Connie's here. She'll take Kathy."

Claire's head felt thick and cloudy. All that scotch. She ran her fingers through her hair, working out the tangles.

She was aware of her sour breath and thick tongue. Her mind drifted to the Kennedys. What were they doing right now? She imagined Jackie in a negligee of French silk. Maybe white. Or ivory. Lace at the throat.

"She doesn't even look sick," Peter was saying. "Just still. Asleep."

Something sour rose in Claire's throat, reminding her that she was pregnant. She swallowed hard, aware now of her heavy breasts. Instinctively, her hand cradled her stomach.

Peter smiled. "How's that little guy?" he said.

"Not so little," Claire said.

In Washington, D.C., at this very moment, bunting was being hung. American flags were being raised. A path to the White House was getting cleared.

"I know what I'm sorry for," Claire said, holding his gaze. "I'm sorry I was with another man."

Her husband's face clouded. The muscles in his arm tightened. For a crazy moment she thought he might hit her.

"I say I'm sorry all the time because I want you to forgive me," Claire said.

Peter didn't hesitate. "I can't," he said. "How could I?"

"Never?" she asked.

"I don't know, Claire."

"Never is a very long time," Claire said as if she could see the endless years of his anger unfolding right there before her.

"Hello?" Connie called from downstairs.

"Okay," Peter called back to her.

He looked at Claire.

"We need to go," he said.

She watched him put on a fresh shirt, rebuckle his belt. She thought about what she was most sorry about: that she'd been caught. If that water main hadn't broken, if Peter hadn't come home that day, everything would be different.

As Claire sat up, a wave of dizziness came over her. Once again, she cradled her stomach protectively. She thought it had happened that first time in the parking lot. Miles had claimed her. He had given her this. The baby moved, pushing against her hand as if to tell her that, yes, she was right.


The snow had stopped. With the temperature hovering somewhere around ten below zero, the tree branches and telephone wires hung heavy, encased in ice.

Shivering as she got into the car, Claire paused. The sun, just coming up, glistened on the frozen world.

"Beautiful," she murmured.

Peter, already in the driver's seat, leaned toward her open door. "What?" he said.

"It looks like a fairyland, doesn't it?"

"I have the heat on," he said. "Come inside and warm up."

It was the kind of cold that settles deep into the bones. Still, Claire took in the sight of all that snow piled high in front of houses and higher still on street corners where plows had dumped it. A mailbox stood almost completely covered, just its rounded blue top poking out from the snow. When Claire spoke, her breath came out in small puffs.

"Get out of the car," she said. She reached her hand inside, across the front seat. "Let's walk in the snow."

He looked up at her, considering. Without turning the car off, Peter stepped outside. She hurried to meet him, placing her gloved hand in his. They used to do things like this, she thought. Once, they had stood in the rain on Lexington Avenue, kissing under his wide umbrella. A gust of wind had lifted the umbrella and turned it inside out. Peter had tossed it aside, and continued kissing her, the rain soaking their hair and faces. As they walked up the street, Claire splashed deliberately in a puddle, and Peter followed her, the two of them laughing and wet. In her apartment later, they'd taken a hot shower together, wrapping themselves afterwards in the thick white robes she'd brought home from hotels in Paris and Rome. Peter ordered Chinese food, General Tso's chicken and pork fried rice that they ate as they watched *Gunsmoke* on the small black-and-white television. Claire remembered thinking that she could live with this man forever, that she could be happy with him.

"Have you ever seen so much snow?" Claire asked Peter.

Now that he'd come out of the car she wasn't sure where to go. They stood on the sidewalk, Peter shifting his feet to keep warm.

"That was some blizzard," he said. In the early morning light, his features softened and made him look younger.

Claire smiled at him, then she held her arms out at her sides and dropped into the snow.

"Claire!" Peter said. "Now you'll be all wet. You'll catch cold."

She lay there for a moment, pushing her body deeper into the snow, making an impression there. The sky above her was a dark blue.

"Claire, really. Get up."

She lifted her arms, and swept them up and down. She had not made a snow angel since she was a child. They were glorious, snow angels. And this one, she thought as she moved her arms through the snow, would have two giant wings, wings that would appear ready to take flight.

"Claire," Peter said again.

Satisfied, she reached her hands toward him. "Help me up." Peter pulled her to her feet.

"What were you thinking?" he said.

But Claire was studying the place where she'd lain, the snow angel she'd made. It looked like nothing, not at all like the beautiful angel she'd thought she'd created. Not like something that might lift from the ground and soar. Ridiculously, hot tears sprang to her eyes. She could feel the cold wet snow seeping through her wool coat now, making her shiver.

"See?" Peter said.

When their eyes met, he looked baffled rather than angry.

Claire got into the car, holding her hands in the wet gloves up to the vents blasting hot stale air.

"You'll catch a cold," Peter said again, turning the heat on higher.

"You don't get a cold from *being* cold," she said softly.

"Really?" Peter said, putting the car into drive. "Where did you hear that?"

She didn't answer him. Instead, she stared out the window, watching the sad triple-deckers go by. The streets were empty this early in the morning. Claire let herself think about how busy Washington, D.C., must be preparing for the inaugural parade. She wondered what Dot would make for the party. If Claire were going she would bring her Hilo hot dogs, franks cooked in a glaze she made out of soy sauce and apricot preserves, cut into bite-sized bits, and speared with toothpicks topped in colorful cellophane spirals. Roberta was supposed to make a cake decorated like an American flag, and Trudy was making her mustard and ham dip that everyone loved so much she had to bring it to every party, even though it was just cream cheese and canned deviled ham with some mustard added to it.

The early morning sun shining on the snow made a strong glare and Claire closed her eyes against it. Peter had turned on the radio and the Shirelles were singing "Will You Still Love Me Tomorrow." Sometimes it seemed like that was the only song they played these days, and Claire had grown to hate it. She tried to think about Dot's party again, but instead she found herself wondering what her lover was doing right now. Was he even awake this early? She imagined him shoveling snow in his driveway, a driveway she could picture too well. Right before Christmas she had driven past his house, hoping to catch a glimpse of him. She had looked up his address in the White Pages and driven to Silver Spring, Maryland, where she asked for directions at a gas station. The house was stunning, white with gabled roofs and turrets, like a house out of a fairy tale. Compared to her own center-hall Colonial, it looked like a house in a magazine, special. The driveway, the one he might be shoveling snow from at this very moment, was long and curved, climbing uphill.

There had been a lot of snow that day too. No lights on that she could see. No cars in sight. Claire parked across the street and studied each detail. The biggest front windows had lace panels instead of draperies. Like everyone in her neighborhood, Claire had hung heavy damask ones. Hers were in a color called Goldenrod. The corner window seemed to have no window treatments at all, and Claire could see dark red walls. The dining room? she wondered. Red walls? The trim around the house and roof had an ornate design. Claire squinted at it, trying to make out the shapes. Animals, she realized. Squirrels and rabbits and chipmunks. The shutters around the windows had the same motif. She decided she hated it, hated the entire house with its woodland animals and lace panels and ugly red walls.

A car turned down the street and panic shot through her. She sunk as far as she could behind the steering wheel, holding her breath until the car passed. Safe, she sat up, glancing once more at the house. Now she saw the shrubs were covered in Christmas lights. Triple strands of them. More Christmas lights than she'd ever seen. How vulgar, she thought. She tried to picture her lover hanging all those lights, wrapping each strand around the hedges. Did his wife stand beside him, guiding him? The thought made Claire sick to her stomach. Quickly, she lurched the car forward, catching a glance of something hanging on the front door. Not a wreath, but something blue and white and complicated-looking. Vulgar, she thought again.

"Here we are," Peter said.

Claire opened her eyes, the large gray hospital looming in front of her.

"I'll park," he said. "Go on inside. Room 401."

The pavement at the front door was slick with ice and Claire walked carefully across it, taking baby steps. Through the revolving door and into the lobby where the hospital smell made her gag, to the bank of elevators. She rode up to the fourth floor, trying not to throw up.

At the nurses' station, Claire stopped and asked for a ginger ale.

"You okay?" the nurse there asked her. "You're pale as a ghost."

Before Claire could answer, the nurse grinned. "Oh, just in

the family way, huh?" She came around the desk and pointed Claire to a row of green chairs. "I'll be right back," she told her.

The nurse looked so young, Claire thought as she sunk onto the scratchy chair. Her white uniform showed off her slender waist and long legs. Her stiff white cap looked almost jaunty above her dark hair. What had she called it? The family way. Claire had never heard that one before. Another wave of nausea spread over her. *Face pale, raise the tail,* she told herself. She pulled a small square table stacked with *Good Housekeeping* magazines in front of her and stretched her legs out on it.

"You going to faint?" the nurse said, appearing in front of her with a small plastic cup of ginger ale.

Claire shook her head.

"Maybe you need a basin?" the nurse asked. Without waiting for an answer, she walked away again, returning with a pea green kidney-shaped dish.

Claire sipped the ginger ale.

"Boys make you throw up," the nurse said matter-of-factly. "Girls give you a nice complexion."

"I think it's passing," Claire said.

"You're carrying like it's a boy," the nurse continued. "All in front."

"I'm not," Claire said. "I've gained so much weight, I'm huge everywhere."

This baby could not be a boy. A boy with another man's eyes? With a nose that turned up slightly at the tip instead of straight and Roman like Peter's?

"I'm never wrong," the nurse said.

She reached behind her neck and unclasped the thin gold chain she wore with a small gold cross dangling from it.

"Hold your hand out," she said.

"Really, I—"

"It's fun," the nurse said. "Hold your hand out."

Reluctantly Claire removed one damp glove and held her hand out in front of her.

The nurse gently tapped the side of Claire's hand three times with the necklace. Then she turned it palm side up.

"Now hold still," she said.

"A necklace is going to predict if I'm having a boy or a girl?" Claire said.

The nurse held the necklace steadily a few inches above Claire's palm. It began to swing back and forth in a straight line. She grinned.

"See? A boy. If it's a girl, it moves in circles."

From behind them the elevator doors groaned open and the heavy sound of a man's footsteps moved across the green and black linoleum.

"Everything all right?" Peter asked, his face creased with worry.

"She thought she might be sick," the nurse told him.

"I'm all right now," Claire said.

"What's this all about?" Peter asked, indicating the necklace that still hung over Claire's hand.

"Foolishness," Claire said, hoping the nurse would let it go at that.

"You her husband?" the nurse asked.

"Yes," Peter said.

"You're going to have a son," the nurse said proudly, as if she'd just delivered the baby herself.

The smile left Peter's face.

"Interesting," he said, his eyes meeting Claire's.

This was what lay between them, the thing neither had dared to bring up. With each day, as Claire grew more pregnant, the question weighed on them even more. Perhaps, Claire sometimes thought, Peter didn't want to know the answer. Perhaps he believed he was the father. He didn't know when the affair had started, couldn't know about that summer night in the parking lot. The night when Claire, who had done the math of it so many times she could recite it by heart, knew she got pregnant.

"Isn't it interesting, Clairezy?" Peter said.

Claire pushed the table away with her feet. "Well," she said, standing, "I think it's a girl. We have a daughter already and this feels exactly the same," she added, lying. It felt completely different, every minute of this pregnancy felt completely different than Kathy.

"My name's Bridget," the nurse said, reclasping her necklace. "When you have that baby boy, you let me know. You call 4 East, ask for Bridget, and say, 'Bridget, you were right.'"

"We'll be sure to do that, Bridget," Peter said. He put his hand on Claire's back, urging her forward.

Claire let him lead her down the corridor, past rooms with sick people and the gurgling sounds of machines. *Claire?* Miles had said. *Is that you?* Why hadn't she said *Yes, it's me?* She could make this right somehow, couldn't she? Couldn't she?


The first time Claire met Peter's mother was five years earlier when they drove to Providence to tell her they were engaged. The night before, Peter had taken Claire to Frankie & Johnnie's, where they'd gone on their first date. When he ordered champagne, something deep inside Claire fluttered. He had spoken of marriage in vague terms over the year they'd dated. He wanted four children, a wife who was a good homemaker and pleasant to be around. "I want my life to be easy. My wife to make everything around me smooth." *I can do that,* Claire had thought. *I want to do that for you.* But as she sat across from him in Frankie & Johnnie's, watching the waiter approach with a bottle of Moet & Chandon and two champagne flutes, Claire found herself wondering if that flutter she felt was cautionary rather than excited. Did she want four children? Did she want to spend her life keeping house and making her husband's life smooth?

The champagne cork popped and in an instant Peter was on one knee. He was opening a small blue box and a square-cut diamond glistened up at her. So handsome, he looked in that moment. His eyes shone brightly, his hand taking the ring from its velvet perch trembled.

Although she didn't hear the actual words, she found herself saying yes, ignoring that strange feeling of doubt. Hadn't Rose agreed that Peter was quite a catch? He had just taken a new job at the Pentagon. His future—*their* future—could only be wonderful. Peter slid the ring onto her finger and pressed her close to him. The other diners broke into applause, and Claire, blushing, smiled out at them.

The next morning they drove to Providence. The entire way there, Peter laid out his plans for them. Claire found herself looking out the window as Connecticut passed by, half listening. As he talked about mutual funds, public schools versus private schools, the benefits of trading in a car every three years, Claire realized that in her life with Peter she wouldn't have to make any decisions.

He patted her knee. "You can choose the names for the girls, and I'll name the boys," he said, grinning.

"Wonderful," she said, her throat suddenly dry.

By the time they got out of the car, the front door of the house had opened and Peter's mother had come onto the porch. She was an older woman—Peter had told Claire that she'd married late in life and thought she was too old to have babies—but beautiful with her high cheekbones and her silver hair pulled back in a French twist, held in place with an antique comb.

Her face lit up when she saw Peter, and she readily opened her arms to him. Claire watched as she closed her eyes in the hug. Peter pulled free first, motioning for Claire to come. As soon as she reached his side, Peter held her hand up for his mother to see.

"Engaged," his mother said. "My, my."

That visit, and all the ones that followed, had a certain rhythm. His mother offered them tea and after she made it in an elaborate ritual of boiling water and choosing tea leaves and then letting it seep for just the right amount of time, she knit as they sat together in the living room. Peter did most of the talking, laying out his plans to her just as he had for Claire. Birdy — right away she had told Claire to call her that, everyone did; and right away Claire had thought it was the worst nickname for the woman in front of her—nodded periodically, or said *My, my.* Sometimes she quoted a poem, as if to make a point.

"Love one another but make not a bond of love: Let it rather be a moving sea between the shores of your souls," she said after Peter described why Claire would be such a good wife.

*"The Prophet,"* Peter explained to Claire, rolling his eyes. "One of her favorites."

"Published in 1923," his mother said without looking up from her knitting, "and it has never gone out of print. That tells you something, doesn't it?"

Later, there would be dinner at the dining room table. Birdy used good china and silverware, crystal goblets and linen napkins. Dinner was lobster salad with Russian dressing on a bed of shredded lettuce. "It's impossible to get crab here," she'd explained.

"So when is this wedding?" she'd asked that first night.

"I always wanted to be a June bride," Claire said.

Birdy's green eyes settled on her at last. "Why is that?" she asked.

"I . . . I don't know," Claire stammered. "It's lucky, I think."

"June is too far off," Peter said. "I was thinking February. My job starts March 1, and of course you'll come with me."

Claire felt more disappointed than his words warranted. She'd always imagined getting married on a warm sunny day, her bridesmaids in pale yellow, clutching bouquets of daisies.

"February is nice," Claire said, trying to sound convinced. June or February, what did it really matter? What mattered was that they start their life together.

Peter's mother looked at her hard.

"When did you get married?" Claire asked Birdy, eager to deflect the attention.

"November."

"One of the girls I fly with had a winter wedding," Claire said. "Her bridesmaids wore green velvet and they carried chrysanthemums. It was lovely."

"Peter's father and I got married in California," Birdy said. "The weather that day was actually quite warm."

Claire nodded. "How nice," she said, picking at her dinner. "You must give me your recipe for this lobster salad."

His mother turned to Peter. "I can see why you want to marry this young woman," she said.

It sounded like a compliment, but Claire always wondered if it was actually an insult.

Birdy lay in the hospital bed with her long silver hair spread out around her like a fan. Claire had never seen her hair unpinned, and it made her seem vulnerable somehow, spilling across the white pillowcase. She did not have the grayish pallor Claire had seen on some sick people. Her cheeks still had a slight pinkish color and her chest rose and fell in the even breaths of someone asleep. That must be a good sign, Claire thought. She'd expected to see a shell, something emptied of the life it had once had. She'd expected machines beeping and solemn faces. But the room was bright, almost cheerful. A calendar on the wall said January 20 in big black letters, as if it were shouting.

"It's inauguration day," Claire said softly as she perched on the edge of the bed. She wondered if her mother-in-law could hear her. "Jack Kennedy is going to be our next president," she continued.

She glanced up at her husband, who was standing by the window gazing out.

"She was so happy he won. Called me up and said that everything would be fine now," Peter said. "Lifelong Democrat. They both were."

It took Claire a moment to realize he meant his parents were both Democrats. He rarely talked about his father, who had died when he was twelve. He'd worked as a foreman in a textile mill and died in an accident involving machinery there. Although Claire didn't know the details, Peter had alluded to how horrendous a death it had been.

She turned her attention back to her mother-in-law. "They say he's wearing a morning suit," Claire said. "Striped trousers, white jacket, silk top hat—"

Behind her, Peter chuckled. "This is what you tell a dying woman?" he asked.

"Well," Claire said, "it's what I'd want to know."

A candy striper with a blond ponytail wheeled a cart stacked with magazines, newspapers, cigarettes, and candy bars into the room.

"Grab a newspaper, would you?" Peter said.

The girl held out a *Providence Morning Journal* to Claire.

"Does she have a *Globe?*" Peter asked.

Embarrassed that he didn't address the girl directly, Claire looked through the papers herself.

"Here's one," she said, plucking a *Boston Globe* from the pile.

On the front page Jackie, dressed in a pearl white satin gown, smiled out at her.

"To think she had a baby just eight weeks ago," Claire said, admiring Jackie's waistline.

"Next thing I know, Clairezy," Peter said, "you're going to insist we name the baby Jackie."

Claire skimmed the article about the celebration the night before, how they'd attended a classical concert by the National Symphony at Constitution Hall, and then drove past the Washington Monument, past bonfires and snow-removal workers with flamethrowers, until they reached the armory itself. She wondered what the concert had been. Something traditional, like Mozart? Or contemporary, like maybe Aaron Copeland? Why didn't the paper give the details? In a couple of hours they could tune into Dave Garroway and maybe see some footage from last night, if there was a television set somewhere.

"It says that Ethel Merman went right up to Jack Kennedy and sang, 'You'll be swell! You'll be great! Gonna have the whole world on the plate!' Isn't that marvelous?"

The list of performers included just about everybody famous: Nat King Cole, Gene Kelly, Harry Belafonte. Claire tried to imagine what it must have been like to be there.

"The party went until one-thirty this morning," she read out loud. "And Frank Sinatra sang, 'that old Jack magic,' instead of *black* magic—"

"Well, I'll be damned," Peter said. "The old bird is interested in all this."

Claire looked up from the paper and saw that the tiniest smile had appeared on her mother-in-law's lips. She took her mother-in-law's hand in her own. It felt small and fragile and dry.

"Isn't it exciting?" Claire said, leaning closer to the old woman.

It appeared to Claire that she gave the slightest nod.

"Did you see that?" Claire said, not taking her eyes from her mother-in-law's face. "Did you see her nod?"

"I'm not sure," Peter said.

"Isn't it exciting, Birdy?" Claire asked again.

She and Peter waited, afraid to breathe too loudly. But nothing more came.

Peter touched Claire's arm. "You can bring the dead back, Clairezy," he said softly.


Dr. Spirito appeared in the doorway, rumpled and yawning. Behind him, Bridget held a stack of folders.

Without having to be asked, Bridget opened the top folder and handed it to Dr. Spirito. He scanned it, yawning again.

"I'm surprised she made it through the night," he said quietly.

He closed the folder and strode into the room, stethoscope swinging. He listened closely, sighed.

"She has such nice color in her cheeks," Claire said hopefully.

"You know what I see time and again?" Dr. Spirito said. "They hover like this, one foot in the here and now and one already moving into the next world, and all of a sudden they sit up and demand ice cream or something. Reminisce. Crack jokes.

Seem to be back. Like they have one last gasp of life in them, you know?"

Bridget nodded as he spoke. "I see that every day."

Peter and Claire studied his mother. She did not seem about to sit up and demand ice cream.

Dr. Spirito made some notes in the file, then snapped the folder shut and handed it back to Bridget.

"She's comfortable," he said, clapping a hand on Peter's shoulder. "She's not suffering at least."

"So we just wait?" Peter asked.

"You just wait," the doctor said.

"Doctor?" Claire said, stopping him before he walked out. "I think she can hear us. I think—"

"Doubtful," the doctor said. "She's somewhere far away, dear."

Claire thought she heard her mother-in-law sigh. She turned, half expecting to find the old woman shaking her head at this. But of course not, Claire thought as she watched the even rise and fall of her mother-in-law's chest.


"I'm going to find us some coffee," Claire said when the big hand on the clock on the wall clicked noisily onto the twelve. Seven o'clock.

"Good idea," Peter said from behind the open *Globe.*

Jackie in her pearl white satin dress smiled out at Claire. Right now, she was getting dressed for the inauguration, Claire thought. They would go first to Holy Trinity Church for mass, then on to coffee with the Eisenhowers at the White House. Claire sighed in frustration. Dot was probably already awake, setting up for the party. Claire could imagine her ironing her white napkins with blue-striped edges, polishing her coffee service pieces.

"Maybe you can rustle up some Danish too?" Peter asked.

"I'll try." Claire grabbed her lipstick from her purse and stood at the small mirror above the sink, carefully applying it. She saw Peter watching her and expected a rebuke. *Why put on lipstick to go to the cafeteria?* Instead, she saw him smile.

"You look nice, Clairezy," he said.

"Thank you," she said, twisting her hair into a chignon. "It's so funny," she continued, "Rose keeps popping into my mind."

"I haven't heard anything about her in ages. Married a pilot, right?"

"Yes," Claire said. She sprayed a little Shalimar on her wrists, then turned from the mirror. "Remember their wedding out on Long Island? They danced their first dance to 'Fly Me to the Moon,' remember?"

But he didn't seem to be listening. "You sure you're just going for coffee?" he asked.

Even though he was still smiling, Claire looked away from him. A warm flush ran up her neck and cheeks.

"And Danish," she managed to say before she walked to the door.

"Claire?"

She paused.

"Anything but lemon, okay?"

As if she didn't know he hated lemon.

"Got it," she said.

At the nurses' station, Bridget had been replaced by a chubby red-haired nurse.

"Excuse me," Claire said. "Sorry to bother you."

The nurse had lots of freckles, a round face.

"Is there a phone I can use? I need to make a long-distance call."

"Well, sure," the nurse said. She picked up a heavy black phone and slid it toward Claire. "Just be brief."

"Of course," Claire said, tucking the receiver between her shoulder and ear and dialing the operator.

The nurse watched her closely. Claire turned from her slightly as she asked the operator to connect her, carefully enunciating Dot's phone number.

It seemed to take forever to make the connection. When the phone began to ring, Claire could picture it on the telephone table in the hallway between the living room and the kitchen. Even when Dot answered, Claire could imagine her taking the seat attached to the little table, perhaps dropping the dishrag onto her lap, bending her head to hear better.

"Oh, Dot," Claire said. "It's so good to hear your voice."

"What's wrong, darling?" Dot said, immediately picking up on Claire's tone.

Of course she would. Dot had an uncanny knack for such things. Later on that terrible day when Peter had found her with her lover, Claire ran into Dot at the market. She thought she'd acted perfectly natural. But Dot had taken her hand and pulled her close. *My goodness,* she'd whispered, *what in the world has happened?*

"It's Peter's mother, I'm afraid," Claire said. "Right after the party—"

"Was it grand?" Dot asked, and Claire heard her take a drag on her cigarette.

"Well, yes. Yes, it was."

"Did you wear the pewter sheath?"

"The thing is, when we got back, and this is so odd really, because she seemed fine, but it appears she's had a heart attack—"

"What?"

"They're not sure she's going to make it," Claire said.

"Oh dear," Dot said.

Claire twisted the telephone cord. "I'm sorry to drop this on you while you're getting ready for the party."

"It's going to be so much fun. I think we've got about ten couples coming. Plus Polly, of course."

"Of course," Claire laughed.

"Even the Waterstons are coming," Dot said.

"How did you ever persuade them to come to a party?"

"I think they just want to watch the inauguration in color," Dot said.

Claire could hear the smirk in her voice. Dot had the only RCA color television in the neighborhood, even though a lot of people were talking about getting a set before the show Walt Disney was producing aired in the fall. Apparently it had to be watched in color.

". . . and the Merrills are coming," Dot was saying, "and do you remember the man who was at Trudy's last summer? He works with Dick? His wife was in the hospital with something . . . maybe getting her appendix out? Hello? Claire?"

"I'm here," Claire said.

"I thought we lost the connection," Dot said. "Anyway, he and his wife are coming and—"

"Dot," Claire said, "I have to go, the nurse let me use the phone to call but—"

"Of course," Dot said. "Are you sure you're all right?"

Claire paused, trying to get control of the tears that had come on. Surely, Dot would know immediately that she was crying.

"Do you need me to do anything?" Dot was asking.

"I'll call later," Claire said.

"Darling? Are you crying?"

"Of course not."

She said goodbye quickly and hung up. The nurse was still watching her closely.

"It's an emotional time," the nurse said. "Hormones make you emotional like this."

Claire wiped her eyes with the back of her hand. "I need to find coffee," she said, trying to collect herself. "And some Danish?"

"Are you all right to go on your own?" the nurse said.

Claire nodded.

"Down to the first floor, all the way in the back. There's a little place for coffee and. If you want a more substantial breakfast—"

Claire waved her hand in the air, as if waving away the words. She mumbled a thank you, then walked to the elevator and pressed the down button. Alone in the elevator, she finally let her mind rest on the fact that her lover—and his wife—were going to be at Dot's party. What if she had been there too? The idea of seeing him again made her tremble. Instinctively, her hands went to her stomach. She felt the slow waking-up of the baby inside, the rolling and stretching. If she had been at Dot's party, as she was supposed to be, she would have seen him again. And he would have known.

The elevator doors slid open. The bright fluorescent lighting illuminated everything in front of her and for a moment Claire forgot what she was supposed to do. Then she stepped out of the elevator, just as the doors began to shut, pushing her way out. Down the hall, she saw people with paper cups of coffee and doughnuts in their hands. But she could not move toward them yet. Instead, she stood, her hands resting on the swell of her stomach, imagining first Dot, filling finger rolls with her famous chicken salad (*I add grapes and walnuts,* Dot had explained) and then Jackie dressing for church. What she did not think of was her lover, how he smelled like limes, or how he might look when she walked into Dot's living room, or what he might do to see her like this.

# 8

## *The Obituary*

### VIVIEN, 1919

On the ride back to Napa, Vivien and Sebastian did not speak. The Ford truck he'd borrowed from Robert to come and get Vivien bounced uncomfortably. It was made for farmwork, not for long-distance drives. Vivien was relieved to not have to make conversation. She closed her eyes and leaned her head back against the seat, inhaling the smells of leather and earth that filled the cab. Pamela's face kept floating into her thoughts, startling her into remembering why she was heading north back to Napa instead of asleep at the Hotel Majestic in San Francisco.

Ever since that man had wandered grief-stricken onto her doorstep and launched her into her career as an obituary writer, Vivien had written hundreds of obituaries, too many of them for children. Just last year, when the Spanish influenza hit, not a day passed without a parent falling into Vivien's arms, overwhelmed by grief. Vivien had struggled to honor a person so young that their character had not yet revealed itself. She had sat at her small desk, staring at a blank piece of paper, trying to find the words to capture the child who had just taken her first steps, the boy who had loved his big sister or applesauce or his mother's lullabies. Children who could only say a few words—*Mama*, *doggie*, *bye-bye*; who had learned to wave or jump or kiss good night; children who could recite the alphabet or count to ten or write their names in shaky oversized letters; so many children dead, and Vivien given the task to capture the thousand days or less they had lived.

On April 18, 1906, when that earthquake hit San Francisco and took David from her, Vivien began to speak the language of grief. She understood that grief is not neat and orderly; it does not follow any rules. Time does not heal it. Rather, time insists on passing, and as it does, grief changes but does not go away. Sometimes she could actually visualize her grief. It was a wave, a tsunami that came unexpectedly and swept her away. She could see it, a wall of pain that had grabbed hold of her and pulled her under. Some days, she could reach the air and breathe in huge comforting gulps. Some days she barely broke the surface, and still, after all this time, some days it consumed her and she wondered if there was any way free of it.

She knew the things that brought comfort: hot tea, clear broth, a blanket on one's lap, the sound of one's loved one's name said out loud, someone to listen, a hug. But even these things could not comfort a parent who has watched their child die, who has sat helplessly by their child's bedside. The parents of dead children wail. They pull at their clothes and their hair as if they need to leave their bodies, shed their skin, disappear. Vivien had come to recognize the blank stare in their eyes, the grief robbing them of any other emotion but it.

And now Pamela was dead, and Lotte had entered this world. Vivien remembered a mother who had come to her last winter, her face bloated with grief. The woman had been unable to sit still, and instead paced relentlessly around Vivien's parlor. She had lost not one but two children, within hours, and she kept repeating the events of that morning as if by mere repetition they would change. Vivien had seen this often. Mourners needed to tell their stories. Not once or twice, but endlessly, to whoever would listen.

"They were playing together at my feet," the woman said. "I even remarked on how cheerful they both were, how happy. I remember thinking that I had been doubly blessed. Two beautiful happy children. And then first Amelia got sick, right in front of me. I rushed her off to my bedroom, to get her away from Louisa. This influenza is highly contagious. I know this. And by the time Amelia was gone, Louisa was already sick, already dying too. The doctor never even made it to our house. When he arrived it was too late. He said, 'So many children gone. Too many.' And I screamed at him. 'But not mine! Not mine!'"

She walked and told the story again and again, stopping only to stare at Vivien in disbelief.

Finally she said, "The Twenty-third Psalm. I keep saying it to myself. But the words have stopped making sense."

That was when Vivien realized that in fact those particular words made too much sense.

"The psalm says, 'Yea, though I walk through the valley of the shadow of death, I will fear no evil: for thou art with me; thy rod and thy staff they comfort me," the woman said. "But God isn't comforting me. I hate him! He is cruel, not loving."

How the grief-stricken hated God! Vivien thought. She could hear her own voice cursing him, could feel her own heart hating him.

She wrapped her arms around the woman, and said softly, "Darling, the psalm tells us that we must walk through the valley. We cannot walk around it, I'm afraid."

The woman's voice against Vivien's shoulder was muffled. "I don't want to," she cried. "I don't want to be there. I want my babies back."

Vivien used the Twenty-third Psalm in Amelia and Louisa's obituaries. *Thou preparest a table before me in the presence of mine enemies: thou anointest my head with oil; my cup runneth over.* Their mother's cup had runneth over with joy and with sorrow, all in a matter of hours.

"Yes," she had told Vivien later that afternoon, when exhausted from pacing and crying and the business of death. "Yes, that is the perfect thing to express this grief, for which there are truly no words."

The touch of a hand on her knee jolted Vivien. Lost in the world of grief, she had forgotten that she was in this truck with someone else.

"You're crying," Sebastian said softly. He held out a white handkerchief to her.

"Am I?" Vivien said.

Light was just beginning to break in the distance. Vivien took the handkerchief and wiped her eyes and cheeks.

"It is a sad day," Sebastian said.

"Yes," Vivien said.

She wondered, not for the first time, how the sun dared to show itself on a day such as this one. But it would. It would shine brightly down on all of them. Flowers would blossom, trees would bear fruit, women would give birth, and the world, as if ignorant of what had happened here, would continue to spin.


"We should arrive in another hour," Sebastian said.

The sky had turned the particular shade of violet that it did as the sun prepared to rise, a color Vivien had seen too often during sleepless nights wracked by grief. Although that condition of her grief had passed some time ago, she recognized this color, this sky too well.

"How do you call this color?" Sebastian said, pointing one finger upward without moving his hands from the steering wheel.

"Violet," Vivien said.

"Like the small flower? But the color is not the same."

"It's also a female name," she said.

"Violet," Sebastian repeated under his breath. *Vee-oh-letta.*

"Do you have this name in Italian?" Vivien asked him.

"We have Viola. Like in Shakespeare's *Twelfth Night.*"

Vivien glanced at him quickly, as if she had never laid eyes on him before. Maybe Lotte had been right about this man.

"You like Shakespeare?" Vivien asked him.

Sebastian sighed. "Like is too weak a word for how he makes me feel."

Vivien nodded. "I know what you mean."

"Yes, I see you in the library. The way you love the books."

"How did you land in Napa, California?" Vivien asked him, feeling a genuine tug of interest.

"You see, my father, he was a soldier for the king. But when there was no more king, he had no work. He tried farming, but he was not a good farmer. I learned, though. About soil and crops, the rain and the seasons. How to nurture things."

"So you came here," Vivien said.

"My sisters came to America first and they got jobs in New Jersey, in the factories. But I didn't want to be inside all day. I couldn't be. My friend Michele, he told me they were looking for workers for vineyards in California. He went to work for Gallo, and he sent for me. And here I am now."

Despite herself, she felt her heart softening toward him. It was grief making her so vulnerable, she thought. The news of Pamela's death, what waited for her at the end of this trip.

Sebastian reached across the seat and took her hand in his rough, callused one.

"I nurture you," he said.

It was the wrong word, Vivien knew. But she didn't pull her hand away. She let it rest there, in his.

Sebastian kept his eyes on the road ahead as the sky turned from violet to lavender, lightening with the sun.

When the truck passed under the arch with the words *Simone Vineyards* carved into it, Vivien reminded herself why she was back here instead of at the ferry terminal boarding her train to Denver. *Pamela is dead.* She repeated the words, as if by saying them over and over they might make sense. But as Sebastian parked and Pamela didn't appear to greet Vivien, the words made even less sense. Pamela dead? The little girl's tanned face, with her bright blue eyes and tangle of blond curls floated in front of Vivien, alive and vibrant.

Her eyes darted to the house. White crepe streamers and violets hung on the door. Lights blazed in every room. The shadows of people moving about the kitchen were silhouetted in the windows.

"I don't want to go in," Vivien said.

Sebastian, who had already opened his door to get out, closed it quietly.

"Then we sit until you are ready," he said.

Didn't he understand? She would never be ready. Her friend was in there crazy with grief. Vivien, so familiar with the landscape of death, for once did not know what to do or say.

"As long as I'm out here," Vivien said after a moment, "then nothing has happened. Once I step inside that house, Pamela will really be dead."

"Vivien," Sebastian said softly. "Pamela really is dead. I saw her myself. The dottore, he came, but it was too late. The influenza is not as strong this time, but it still can kill. The lungs fill up—"

"Stop!" she said harshly. "Shut up."

"I stop," he said.

Vivien tried to sort out what he had told her. Pamela had influenza. The strain was less virulent this time around, yet it had turned to pneumonia anyway and killed her.

"You saw her," Vivien said.

"I did."

The kitchen door opened and a man and a woman stepped outside. It was light enough now to see that they were the couple from the neighboring vineyard, the ones who raised goats and made the cheese. The woman looked dazed, her face creased from crying. The man kept his head down, until they neared the truck. Then he looked up and, recognizing Vivien, stopped at her window.

She rolled it down, reaching her arms out toward him.

"She's been asking for you," he said, grasping her hands.

His wife's eyes were wild. "Pamela's dead," she said, and there was awe in her voice. "Dead," she repeated.

Sebastian got out of the truck and came around to the passenger side.

"Sebastian," the man said. "I know they'll be grateful you found Miss Lowe and brought her here safely."

He let go of Vivien's hands to reach into his coat pocket.

"I'm sure they intend to compensate you, but they're not themselves. You understand." He took out a fat roll of bills and began counting them.

But Sebastian stopped him. "I will not take money for helping," he said.

"I insist," the man said.

"It is my honor to do this for them," Sebastian said. "For
Pamela."

But the man kept thrusting the bills at him.

"He said he doesn't want to be paid for this," Vivien said
sharply.

At the sound of Vivien's words, the man shoved the money
back in his pocket, mumbling an apology.

Sebastian put his arm around Vivien protectively. She
turned her face away from what the woman was saying and into
his scratchy wool coat. She could hear his heart beating beneath
it, and smell his sweat.

"Thank you," Sebastian said. "I take her inside now."

He steered her away from the couple, his grip on Vivien
strong and steady.

"I'm sorry for that," she said.

"Stupid people," he muttered.

The kitchen door loomed in front of them. Vivien had to pull
herself together before she saw Lotte.

"Can we sit a minute?" she asked.

Without answering, he led her to the picnic table where just
a short time ago she had sat eating chicken and beans, drinking
wine with Pamela on her lap. He guided her down to the bench,
and he sat close beside her.

Vivien breathed in the morning air.

"You can do this," Sebastian said.

He took her face in both of his rough hands. It had been so
long since she'd been touched by a man in this way that Vivien
felt her knees actually tremble. Then Sebastian pulled her face
toward his, and kissed her on the lips. His lips were chapped,

rough like his hands. The kiss was not passionate or long. Before she could think what to do, it was over and he was helping her to her feet.

"Lotte needs you," he said gruffly.

"Don't ever do that again," Vivien told him.

She took another deep breath, then walked ahead of him into her friend's kitchen.

The silence surprised her. Someone stood at the stove making coffee and scrambling eggs. People sat, stunned, at the kitchen table. Even the dogs, two German shepherds, lay quietly in the corner, staring out at everyone.

"Where is she?" Vivien asked. "Where's Lotte?"

The woman at the stove said, "With Pamela. In the parlor."

Vivien thanked her and moved across the kitchen, through the narrow hallway lined with muddy boots and dusty hats and jackets. Pamela's were there with the others, as if she would come to claim them at any moment. Vivien paused, and pressed the girl's jacket to her nose, inhaling. The jacket smelled of the outdoors, and faintly of Pamela.

The night she was born, Vivien had sat in that kitchen, making tea for Robert and warming milk for Bo, who was still a toddler. She had run upstairs when she heard Lotte's screams, and arrived by her side in time to see the baby's head crowning. Lotte had grabbed her hand and squeezed hard as the midwife ordered her to keep pushing. Vivien watched Pamela arrive in one fluid motion, all of her sliding from her mother and into the midwife's waiting hands.

"A girl!" Vivien had shouted.

"Really?" Lotte said, lifting her head to see for herself. "Oh, Vivvie, the fun we'll have with her."

Vivien hadn't been there for either of the boys' births. But she had watched Pamela come into the world. She had sat by her friend's side, counting her perfect toes and fingers. *Look how long they are,* Lotte had said. *We'll teach her piano, Viv.* They had rubbed the soft down on her bald head, deciding she would be blond and stay blond, unlike Lotte whose fair hair had darkened over the years.

*She's a keeper,* Vivien had said.

And now she was dead. Vivien stood in the doorway of the parlor and took in the scene before her. Lotte kneeling by her dead daughter, holding her hand. Pamela lay, dressed in the one dress she owned, a green velvet one Lotte had bought her in San Francisco last year. *She has to wear dresses too,* Lotte had explained when she showed Vivien the ruffly dress with its smocked bodice and lace-trimmed sleeves and neck. Her hair was too flat and her face was bloated. She hardly looked like Pamela at all.

Perhaps hearing Vivien there, Lotte glanced up. At the sight of her friend, she jumped to her feet and began to keen, wailing and rocking and screaming Pamela's name.

This was grief, as raw as it could be. Vivien recognized it. She knew what to do.

Vivien stepped forward, and opened her arms.


This was how to help a family who just lost their child. Wash the clothes. Make soup. Don't ask them what they need. Bring them what they need. Keep them warm. Listen to them rant and cry and tell their story over and over. Vivien did these things during the days that followed Pamela's death. When friends came in to pay their respects, she took their coats and hung them up. She led them into the parlor, and when Lotte looked up into their faces, confused and ravaged by grief, Vivien softly said their names for her. *Adelaide and Thomas are here. Pamela's friend Catherine. The Martinellis. The O'Briens.* Dutifully, she recorded the flowers that arrived: white lilacs, Easter lilies, white roses. She offered the guests tea and shortbread that she baked fresh each morning. She swept the floors and opened the curtains to let light inside.

Every morning, Vivien watched Robert go out into the vineyards. He needed the comfort of his work, and she didn't question that. In her years as an obituary writer, she had seen men argue cases in court or put new roofs on houses hours after they'd lost a loved one. From the kitchen window, Vivien saw Robert methodically mowing down the crimson clover. Bo and Johnny helped their father, walking behind him and collecting what he cut down. In the late afternoon, when the work was done, they washed their hands and drank big glasses of buttermilk. Then they went outside and played mumblety-peg or marbles in the dirt until it turned too dark for them to see. Back inside, Bo avoided his mother and the parlor where she sat with his dead sister. Instead, he sat at the big wooden table in the kitchen and drew pictures of horses that he signed and handed to Vivien. Johnny, though, would go in the parlor and stand by his mother, staring down at Pamela in disbelief. His father had to lead him out of there, yanking on him as if he were uprooting vines from the earth.

But Lotte wouldn't leave Pamela's side. She held her dead daughter's hand and spoke to her as if the girl could hear. She told her she was sorry. *I should have called the doctor sooner,* she said. She told her who had come by the house and how warm it had become. Sometimes she called the girl's name, her voice rising in panic. *Pamela! Pamela!* This broke Vivien's heart, a mother's voice calling out to her dead child. Lotte would never again see those bright blue eyes or hear Pamela's slightly husky voice saying Mama. When she needed to, Vivien wrapped her arms around her friend. She washed her face with one of the cloths Lotte knit by the dozens. She combed Lotte's hair and sprinkled lavender water on her to hide the sour smell of grief that rose from her. At night, she tucked a pillow beneath Lotte's head and covered her with a soft blanket.

The night before the funeral, the house grew quiet in its grief. The sobs that had filled it on and off for three days were temporarily silenced. Vivien stood in the semidark kitchen, setting a freshly baked pound cake on a plate. She whisked lemon juice and powdered sugar together until they were smooth. With a knitting needle she poked holes in the cake, then poured the sticky glaze on it. Tomorrow, the house would be full of mourners. Vivien needed to feed them. Oh, she knew they would come with baked casseroles, and pots of beans and soup. But she wanted to make the things she believed would bring comfort to Lotte and her family. This bitter cake. The chicken soup warming on the stove. The bread rising for the second time in the large enamel bowl. She would get up early and bake that bread so that it would be warm for them after they buried Pamela.

Vivien looked around the kitchen. It smelled of yeast and lemons. Everything was clean and polished. She wiped her hands on the apron of Lotte's that she'd been wearing all day, a white one with a print of large red apples. The apron seemed almost happy, and therefore out of place in this house. She untied it and slipped it off, hanging it on its hook by the sink.

She needed air, she decided. She reached for one of Lotte's hand-knit sweaters, an oatmeal-colored one with a straight neck. The sleeves were too long, and she pushed them up to her elbows before heading outside into the night.

So many stars, Vivien thought as soon as she stepped outside.

Those stars and the chilly air stopped her immediately. She pulled the sleeves back down, and wrapped her arms around herself.

"It doesn't seem right," a voice said.

Vivien recognized it. Sebastian. In the busyness and sorrow of these past few days, she had completely forgotten about him.

"That is what you are thinking, no?" he said.

He was sitting at one of the long picnic tables, smoking a cigarette. Vivien walked over to him and sat beside him.

"Yes," she said. "The stars shouldn't be so bright. Nothing should look this beautiful."

He held out his cigarette to her, and she shook her head.

"Everything should mourn the little girl," he said.

They sat in silence for a few minutes, Sebastian smoking and Vivien gazing upward. She saw Orion's Belt and the Little Dipper, and the sight of those constellations made her cry. Just a few months ago, she and Pamela had lain on their backs in the field and Vivien had pointed out these very stars. The hunter. The large bear. The Little Dipper. The Milky Way.

"Let's take a walk, hmm?" Sebastian said.

Vivien followed him across the yard, into the vineyards.

"The crimson clover, it a cover crop," he explained, as if it mattered. "It add . . ." He paused, searching. "Nu-tri-ent?"

Vivien nodded.

"To the soil, you see? Robert, he mowed it down so it will self-seed and come back again in September. For the harvest."

When they stopped walking. Vivien dared to glance upward again, this time seeing the moon, with thin clouds passing across it.

"It's waning," Vivien said.

Sebastian looked up too.

"The reverse of a waxing moon is called a waning moon," she continued. "When the moon is decreasing in brightness."

"I think this moon is appropriate then," Sebastian said softly. He was looking at her, not the moon. Vivien met his gaze. She let him take a step closer to her. And then another.

"Vivien," he said. But nothing more.

She did not consider stopping him. To do this, Vivien thought as his lips kissed her lips, was to be alive. To do this, she thought as his lips moved down her throat and to her collarbone, was to fight back at death. It had been so long since a man had touched her that Vivien felt off-balance when desire spread through her. Sebastian steadied her, holding her in his arms, which were strong from working in these fields.

Sebastian did not taste like David. He did not feel like him. His skin was rough, his mouth full of the taste of tobacco and red wine. Later, Vivien would think that she lowered to the ground first. She dropped to the damp dirt and lifted Lotte's sweater over her head. She unbuttoned her dress, and watched as Sebastian cupped her breast, slipping it from her corset. The waning moon illuminated their naked skin as clothes dropped off each of them.

When he entered her, it was as if something she had lost was returned to her. She half sat up, surprised by that feeling.

"I remember," she said out loud.

Sebastian paused in his movements. He lifted her so that she was sitting facing him. The shift in position sent a thrill through Vivien, and she heard herself moan.

He kissed her hard on the lips.

"Are you mine?" he whispered. But then he chuckled and shook his head. "This is not what I mean," he said.

She told him to stop talking.

For a while that night before the funeral, Vivien remembered how it was to be alive. But when morning came and she saw Lotte's face, the grief etched there perhaps forever, Vivien felt only shame at what she had done.

Lotte had managed to dress in an old black dress that was too tight for her more ample body.

"Vivvie," she said at the sight of her friend putting two loaves of bread into the oven to bake. "You need to write it."

Vivien felt flushed from the heat of the oven, and from her own guilty conscience.

"Write it?" she said.

People were approaching the house. Robert and the boys would carry the small wooden coffin up the hill to the family cemetery. Already, Robert was out there, digging Pamela's grave.

"Pamela's obituary," Lotte said, her voice hoarse from crying.

"Oh, Lotte," Vivien said. "I can't. I only do that for people I don't know. People I don't love."

The door opened and Sebastian walked in to the kitchen. Vivien could feel his eyes on her, but she refused to meet his gaze.

"But you have to," Lotte said. "Tell the world about my Pamela, Viv. Tell them how she is, what she's like, so no one forgets."

"No one will forget," Vivien said.

How she wished this man would go away. But he stood there, waiting. Her cheeks burned.

"You have to," Lotte said again.

Vivien knew that grief made people unreasonable. Selfish. It was unrelenting and illogical.

She put her arm around her friend.

"Of course," she said. "I will write the obituary."

# FIVE

*If you see acquaintances of yours in deepest mourning, it does not occur to you to go up to them and babble trivial topics or ask them to a dance or dinner. If you pass close to them, irresistible sympathy compels you merely to stop and press their hand and pass on.*

—FROM *Etiquette*, BY EMILY POST, 1922

# 9

## *What Her Mother Taught Her*

CLAIRE, 1961

Claire came from a generation of women who did not question things. A generation raised by women who didn't question. Before her mother died, during the sixteen years when they got to be mother and daughter, she'd taught Claire the things she believed a woman needed to know: always wear a hat to keep the sun off your face so you don't get wrinkles; moisturize every day; never go to bed with your makeup on; if you put Vaseline on your hands and a pair of white cotton gloves over them and go to bed like that, your hands will always be soft; a man likes soft hands; always get up before your husband so that you can do your own morning routine in private, make yourself look pretty, and have his breakfast ready when he wakes up; keep up on current events; agree with your husband's opinion, even if you think he's a horse's ass for believing that; buy lard fresh from the butcher and use it in fried chicken, piecrusts, and seven-minute frosting; the key to a perfect dinner is to serve meat with a starch and a vegetable and to always have candlelight; everything tastes better when eaten by candlelight;

know how to sew a hem, darn a sock, replace a button—these skills help to make you indispensable; never go to bed with dirty dishes in the sink or cigarette butts in the ashtray; never refuse your husband's sexual desires; get your hair done every week; when asked to bring something to a dinner party, bring it on a plate that you leave as a gift; always let the man drive; men take out the trash and mow the lawn; always wait for the man to open a door for you and light your cigarette; a woman needs to know how to swim, skate, and ride a bike; never swear in front of a man; and Claire, *honey*, love goes out the window when there's no money. A woman knows how to live on a budget, to stretch a dollar, to cook hamburger meat at least six different ways, in patties and Salisbury steak and chili and poor man's beef Stroganoff and Sloppy Joes and meatloaf.

Her mother spoke, and Claire listened.

"At thirty cents a pound," her mother would say, shaping hamburger with chopped onion and Worcestershire sauce into perfect patties, "I can make four of these. One for you, one for me, two for Daddy."

Claire watched her mother, always in a dress covered with an apron, always in high heels and earrings, move around the kitchen like it was a dance floor. The wallpaper was yellow with a pattern of red and blue teapots. The stove and refrigerator matched, both a shade of yellow that even now, when Claire saw something that color, made her think of her mother. If she closed her eyes she could even smell her mother's L'Air du Temps and Aqua Net.

"Why does Daddy get two?" Claire asked. She sat perched on the sink with its blue plastic drainer, neat stack of Brillo pads, gold container of Borax, and the ceramic frog whose gaping mouth held sponges.

"Number one," her mother said without breaking stride,

slicing tomatoes and shredding iceberg lettuce, "because he's worked all day, and number two because women have to watch their weight."

On warm nights, Claire and her mother sat together on the glider on the screened-in porch and listened to the crickets. In the distance, where the houses stopped and the fields began, they could sometimes see fireflies. As a little girl, she would join other neighborhood children and collect them in an empty mayonnaise jar. Her mother poked holes in the lid so they could at least live a few hours.

"Watch," her mother said. "They flash for six seconds, then go dark for six seconds."

Claire watched and counted. Six seconds of flashing. Six seconds of darkness.

"Like Morse code," her mother said.

From the basement came the sound of her father's electric saw.

"What message are they sending?" Claire asked.

"The males are calling the females, I think. Look at me! Look at me!"

Claire smiled, but her mother looked serious, staring off at the light show.

"Are you happy?" Claire blurted, surprising herself. She had never considered such a thing before, if her mother was happy or not.

"Don't be silly," her mother said softly.

"What is love?" Claire used to ask her mother as they sat together at the kitchen table waiting for their nails to dry, blowing on them and waving them in the air. China Doll Red or Bermuda Pink or Coral Reef, the shiny colors glistened and her mother always answered the same way.

"You just know."

Such an unsatisfying answer. Claire would scowl and try to figure out what her mother meant. Was love so unique, so special, that when it happened it made itself absolutely known? The way Gloria Delray performed her cheers every Saturday at football games. She shook her pompoms and shouted *Give me a W* as if no one could possibly be a better cheerleader, a prettier girl. She jumped the highest and did the most cartwheels and smiled the widest brightest smile.

"Sometimes," Claire said softly, "I hate Gloria Delray."

"Don't say hate," her mother said, predictably.

"Well then," Claire said, blowing on her nails again, "I dislike her tremendously."

Her mother tried to hide a smile, but Claire glimpsed it.

"What's so bad about Gloria Delray?" her mother said. She was debating whether or not it was safe to apply the next coat of polish.

"She thinks she's so great," Claire said.

"Is she?"

Claire glared at her mother.

"Is she great?" her mother asked.

"Well, she's a good cheerleader," Claire said, reluctantly.

"So are you," her mother said, pointing a perfect finger at her.

"Not as good as her," Claire admitted.

"Then work harder at it. Practice more."

"How did you know you loved Daddy?" Claire asked as her mother took her hand in her own soft one and carefully applied the final coat of polish to each of her short square nails.

This time her mother didn't hide her smile. "He walked in that dance and I saw him and I thought *That is the man I'm going to marry.*"

Claire sighed in frustration.

"But how could you know that?" she asked.

"Don't wiggle," her mother said. She seemed to be considering Claire's question carefully. "He had confidence. Broad shoulders and a certain way of entering a room that told me he would be a good husband. A man who would get things done. Take care of things."

Claire watched the lovely top of her mother's ash blonde hair as she slowly moved the brush from bottle to nail.

"This was before the world went crazy, of course," her mother said finally. "The stock market hadn't crashed. People hadn't lost all their money. Banks hadn't closed." She shook her head, remembering. "People were . . . I don't know . . . hopeful. Black Friday and the war took away all that hope, I'm afraid."

"You knew you loved him because you felt hopeful?" Claire persisted.

Her mother laughed. "Maybe. Yes. Back then, you could take a look at a man and believe the two of you were going to fall in love and live happily ever after."

"I feel hopeful," Claire said even though she wasn't sure she did feel hopeful. Or even understand what her mother was talking about.

Her mother kissed the palm of Claire's hand.

"That's good, sweetheart. Don't ever lose that. Love goes out the window when there's no money, you know. A woman has to stay strong. Men aren't really very strong at all."

"They aren't?" Claire said. She thought about Danny Jones, the quarterback who went out with Gloria Delray, the boy every girl including Claire longed to have notice her. Danny Jones looked very strong. Once, Claire had seen him pick Gloria up by the waist as if she were weightless.

"At the first sign of trouble, a man falls apart. That's why women have to work so hard to stay optimistic and upbeat, to be frugal and understanding. To not question everything," her mother added.

Later, when her mother came in to kiss her good night, Claire asked her if love felt like ginger ale bubbles.

"What you want," her mother said, "is someone who can take care of you. A man who can provide for you and your children. Someone steady. Someone predictable. If you want to feel ginger ale bubbles, Claire, drink a glass of ginger ale."

All of that, the cooking together and watching the fireflies and talking about love, happened a year or so before her mother died, when Claire first got breasts, when boys started to notice her. In the time that had passed since those afternoons at the kitchen table, painting their nails or playing Crazy Eights or making Waldorf salad—Claire carefully mixing the apples and nuts her mother had chopped into the mayonnaise and sour cream— Claire wondered what advice her mother would give her now. Would she have said Claire should marry Peter, a good provider, a man who was indeed steady but who could not show warmth or share intimacies? What would she think of Claire now, pregnant with someone else's baby? Living in shame every time her husband even glanced at her? *Fuck me*, Claire used to whisper to Miles. Hadn't her mother told her that a woman never swears in front of a man? She could still hear her mother saying "H–E– double hockey sticks!" when her cake came out of the oven too dry or her gravy lumped up. *Fuck me*, Claire would beg him.

Sometimes, driving home from meeting Miles, her thighs sticky and her skin flushed pink, Claire got a clear picture of her mother, as clear as if she had seen her just yesterday: wearing a soft green dress cinched at the waist with a yellow ruffled apron over it and beige high-heeled pumps, bent over the oven, her back straight, a dish towel she had knit herself, off-white with even red stripes, in her hands, as she pulled out a cake pan. She touched the top of the cake with her fingertip, able to tell its doneness by the way it sprang back. "H-E-double hockey sticks," she said, her voice so full of disappointment that Claire's heart broke remembering. "It's only a cake," Claire's father told her. Her mother looked at him, "George," she said, "It's not just a cake. This is what I do."

Standing at the nurses' station in that hospital where her mother-in-law lay dying down the hall, Claire's mind raced with these memories, strange fragments she thought she had forgotten. She thought of Gloria Delray, who had gone to college, to the University of Indiana in Bloomington.

"What are you studying there?" Claire had asked her that first winter after they'd graduated from high school and Gloria had come home for the holidays. The two girls ran into each other at the five-and-dime on a cold afternoon just before Christmas. Outside the wind howled. The sky was gray with snow-filled clouds. Gloria had her long dark hair pulled back in a ponytail and she wore a red and white University of Indiana jacket over a red turtleneck and dark blue dungarees. She smiled at Claire as if Claire didn't know anything about anything.

"I'm going to get my MRS," Gloria said in the same sure way she used to order a crowd of hundreds to give her a W.

At first, Claire didn't understand what Gloria meant. By the time she did, Gloria was already heading toward the door, clutching her bag of last-minute presents: a bottle of Jean Naté and a tin of cherry pipe tobacco and a matchbox car.

"Oh!" Claire said, thinking that Gloria was clever. "Your MRS! But what about Danny?"

Gloria laughed. "Danny isn't going anywhere, Claire."

If her mother had been alive that day, Claire would have asked her what she thought about that. Danny Jones was working in his family's supermarket. He would be a good provider, Claire thought. Her father had some saying about how the cobbler's son always had shoes. Danny's children would always have food, wouldn't they? Where exactly did Gloria want to go with her MRS?

"Are you lost?" an orderly pushing a mop asked Claire.

*Yes,* Claire wanted to say, but she shook her head and thanked him.

Slowly she made her way back to Birdy's room where nothing had changed. The old woman lay in the bed, unmoving. Peter was gone, probably getting more coffee. The room seemed vacant, even though someone was in it.

Claire went to the window and adjusted the blinds, letting in the early morning sun. She paused to admire the way the ice-covered branches glistened.

When she turned back around, she was surprised to see her mother-in-law's eyes open.

Claire smiled at her, but the old woman's face was crossed with confusion.

"Who are you?" she asked.

"Claire. I'm Claire." Claire wondered if she should go and get someone, a nurse or even the doctor.

The old woman stared at her hard. Then her face softened and she shook her head sadly. "I thought you were someone else," she said, and closed her eyes.

"No," Claire said.

She waited, but her mother-in-law did not speak or open her eyes again.

When Peter came in, he stopped as soon as he saw the look on Claire's face.

"What's wrong?" he asked.

"Your mother," Claire said. "She talked to me."

His eyes shifted from Claire's face to his mother's. "Claire," he said as if he were speaking to Kathy.

"She opened her eyes and asked who I was and when I told her she got disappointed and said she thought I was someone else. Then she went back to sleep."

"She knows you," Peter said. "Don't be silly."

Claire didn't respond. The man is always right, even when he's wrong. Wasn't that what her mother had told her?

"I'm feeling quite irritable," Claire said.

"Are you feeling sick again?"

"Irritable," Claire said gruffly.

"I believe you," Peter chuckled.

They stared at his mother, Claire half expecting her eyes to fly open and for her to say something else. But she didn't. The big hand on the clock moved noisily into place.

"I should have brought my knitting," Claire said, although she didn't really want to tackle that difficult sweater.

"Why don't you go back to the house and get it?" Peter said.

The idea of getting fresh air, of being free of all this and driving through the snowy city suddenly seemed like exactly what she needed.

"Would you mind?"

Peter dropped into one of the hard chairs and picked up the *Globe*. "No need for you to be bored to tears," he said.

"I'll get it and come right back," Claire said.

But Peter didn't answer. He already appeared involved in a news article.

She put on her coat and still–damp gloves.

"I'll need the keys," she said.

"They're in my pocket," he said, indicating his jacket hanging behind the door.

"Well then," she said after she'd collected them and picked up her purse.

"Drive slow," he said. "It's icy."

Of course it was icy. Hadn't they just had a huge blizzard? But she told him she would be extra careful.

"By the way," Peter said. "I found a TV, up in what they call the solarium. We can watch the inauguration."

"Oh, good," Claire said.

"Hurry back," Peter said as she moved toward the door.


As soon as she emerged from the car, Claire heard Kathy crying. Moving as fast as she could up the narrow path Jimmy had shoveled, she climbed the steps, finding the front door unlocked. That smell of oil heat and yesterday's supper hit her as soon as she walked into the small foyer, and Claire swallowed back the bile that rose in her throat.

The steps that led up to her mother-in-law's apartment stretched invitingly in front of her. The thought of climbing back into bed appealed to Claire much more than dealing with Connie and Jimmy and all of their children. But Kathy's crying did not seem to be letting up. Claire took a few deep breaths, then pushed the door to the downstairs apartment open. Cartoons blared from the television, and a trail of toy soldiers and crushed Frosted Flakes led to the kitchen. Claire hardly noticed the little boy in the big wet diaper chewing on one of the soldiers.

"Darling," she said, lifting Kathy from the high chair where she sat, red-faced from screaming.

"Who the hell is Mimi?" Connie said. She was sitting on a stool at the breakfast counter, still in her nightgown, smoking a cigarette.

"Her stuffed animal," Claire said, smoothing Kathy's tangled hair. "I forgot it," she admitted softly.

To Kathy she murmured, "Mimi's waiting for you at home." This only made Kathy scream louder.

Connie, unfazed, got up and poured herself more coffee, holding the percolator up as if it were asking Claire if she wanted some.

"Yes, thank you," Claire said.

She patted Kathy's back, taking in the chaos of the kitchen. In a second high chair, Cindy—a girl with lots of dark curls and her father's green bulging eyes—played in milk that had spilled from her cereal onto the tray, humming as she splashed. The baby slept splayed in a playpen in the middle of the floor. Dirty dishes crowded the counter and the sink and that Shirelles song blasted from the radio.

"God, I hate that song," Claire muttered.

Kathy's sobs had turned to hiccups, and Claire sunk onto one of the stools, still patting her daughter's back.

"Sugar? Milk?" Connie asked, holding the bottle of milk over the cup.

"Black," Claire said.

Connie slid the cup to Claire, somehow finding a path amid the mail and kids' drawings and crumbs that littered the counter.

"How's Birdy?"

"You're not going to believe this but she opened her eyes and spoke to me," Claire said.

"Right before they die, they do that," Connie said knowingly.

Claire decided that Connie reminded her of Gloria Delray. She had that same confidence in everything she said.

"It's true," Connie continued. "My *nonna* did it. At death's door, then all of a sudden she asked us to sing 'Oh, My Papa.' She loved that song. You know it?" Without waiting for an answer, Connie said, "She sang right along too. And I asked her how to make gnocchi, why mine always came out like lead, and she told me the secret."

Kathy had quieted and was sucking her thumb, her eyes on the cartoons.

"Don't overknead the dough," Connie said.

"Hmm," Claire murmured politely. "Well, I better get back. I'm just going to get my knitting."

"You knit? I crochet. Mostly just afghans."

"The women in my neighborhood have a little knitting circle," Claire said. "It's something to do. You know."

"These the ones with the contest?"

Claire frowned.

"The Jackie thing," Connie said. "What color will she wear today."

"Oh, yes," Claire said. "The same ones."

"Teresa down the street, she crochets these cute little men that you put your extra toilet paper rolls inside. They have long legs and funny hats. Cute. She said she's going to teach me."

"That's nice," Claire said. She'd noticed a toilet paper roll dressed in one of these crocheted outfits in Connie's bathroom earlier when she'd changed Kathy's diaper. It looked hideous with its long crocheted legs dangling over the bowl.

"I'll send you the pattern," Connie said.

Claire smiled and nodded politely, then carried Kathy into the living room where Little Jimmy, the oldest, had managed to chew the heads off an army of Redcoats. He grinned up at Claire, his mouth circled in red. Claire hesitated, then scooped up all of the soldiers—Roman gladiators and Civil War Confederates and doughboys and Redcoats. Most of them were headless, she realized as she dropped them onto the top of the television.

"Thanks for watching her," Claire called as she left, relieved to be out of the apartment's old food and dirty diaper smell.

Upstairs she grabbed her knitting quickly and then got back into the car, feeling guilty that Kathy would no doubt spend the morning in front of that television set, ignored.

Still, as she drove back to the hospital, a peace settled over her. She liked being alone, away from Peter and his dying mother. Away from Connie's dirty apartment and her mother-in-law's empty one. She fiddled with the radio until she heard Elvis Presley singing "Are You Lonesome Tonight?" Singing along softly, she let herself miss her lover. She imagined driving to Dot's instead of to the hospital, showing up at the party. His wife wouldn't be there after all, and somehow seeing each other again would solve everything.

Even as she thought it, she reprimanded herself for being so foolish.

Elvis sang, "Does your memory stray . . ."

Tears sprang to Claire's eyes. She changed the station, twirling the knob without caring where it landed.

The hospital appeared in front of her, gray and hulking. It looked like a place people went to die, Claire thought. The parking lot was full, and she had to drive around and around to find a space. For a moment, she considered leaving again. But to go where? Back to that house? She imagined picking up Kathy, combing her hair and washing her face and the two of them boldly driving away. They could stop at Rose's in New London, Connecticut, make a getaway plan. They could drive all the way to Washington, D.C., and get a glimpse of JFK and Jackie, on their way to an inaugural party.

Across the parking lot, an elderly couple made their slow way to their car. Claire sighed, and drove in their direction. As she waited—eternally, she thought—for the man to unlock the door and then open it for his wife and then help her inside—it hit Claire that she might never have what those old people had: a marriage that lasted for all those years, a man who, bent and frail himself, would still pause to tenderly take her elbow, to look at her with love.

And then an even stranger thought came to her. Maybe she didn't need someone to take her elbow, to lead her around.

Claire shook her head, as if shaking the thought away.

The man's shiny green Valiant finally backed out of the parking space and she turned the car into it. Last night, Peter had liked her pretending, playing the good wife again, a role she knew too well. *Agree with your husband's opinion, even if you think he's a horse's ass for believing that,* her mother had told her. She could bite her tongue when she disagreed. She could try to learn to parallel-park, touch her hair less, stop apologizing. Didn't all of the women she knew do this? Didn't Dot learn how to play golf because her husband wanted her to? Didn't Trudy take every vacation on the Outer Banks because her husband liked to go fishing there? She spent her time in Duck cleaning the rented cottage, cooking three meals a day, and watching her three kids. *Someday,* Trudy always said when she came back, her nose peeling and her chest freckled from the sun, *I might actually go on a real vacation.* Hadn't Roberta voted for Nixon because her husband was a Republican?

*What you want,* her mother had told her, *is someone who can take care of you. A man who can provide for you and your children. Someone steady. Someone predictable.* That described Peter. It did. His pants were always perfectly creased, his tie tied in a Windsor knot, his shoes polished. He gave her a big budget, let her buy what she wanted for herself, let her redecorate when she got bored with the wallpaper or the carpeting. At the Pentagon, he got his promotions right on schedule. He did the right thing.

Her lover came crashing into her mind, asking her what she wanted. *From you?* she'd asked Miles, confused. *From life,* he'd said. No one had ever asked her that and Claire had not known how to answer. He always wanted to know what she thought, and why. What she felt, and why. These questions made her feel off-kilter, like the world had tilted and she wasn't certain how to regain her balance. How could she ever explain to anyone that although the sex was important—necessary, even—that it was the talking between them that mattered. It had never occurred to Claire until she met him that a man and a woman could be so similar, that a man might want to know her so well.

Miles had made her buoyant. Without him, she had deflated. She would find herself walking around the house, drinking glass after glass of water, needing to be filled up. She started to talk to herself, sharing her thoughts and feelings with the empty rooms. One day, frustrated, she'd pulled all of the fluffy bath towels from the linen closet and thrown them out in a frenzy, screaming as the mauve and aqua terrycloth fluttered around her. She wanted to go to the china cupboard and smash her wedding china, take the heavy crystal glasses and fling them at the walls. Break mirrors and tables and the French doors that led to the patio. All of these simple domestic things, so benign for so long, had become parts of a cage to Claire. They trapped her in that house, in that marriage.

Now that a man had listened to her, had seen her for who she was, Claire refused to be submerged again. But she had to. To walk away from Peter was to risk losing her home, her daughter—and thinking of her life without Kathy in it every day made Claire shake. If her mother-in-law hadn't begun to die, Claire would have stuck with her plan and decided what to do. But now she just had to walk carefully across the large icy expanse of asphalt. She just had to go into that hospital and be Peter's wife. At Dot's, her lover and his wife were arriving. He was taking off his hat and handing it to Dot at the door. He had his hand on the small of his wife's back.

*If you want to feel ginger ale bubbles, Claire, drink a glass of ginger ale,* her mother had told her.

Claire entered the revolving door and stepped into the hotel lobby. The air buzzed with excitement. Nurses and doctors, orderlies and candy stripers, visitors and staff, all moving toward the solarium to watch the inauguration. John F. Kennedy would step up to the podium. He would raise his hand and take the oath of office, with Jackie watching. With the world watching. And, Claire realized as she pressed the up button for the elevator, they were watching with hope. For the first time in a long time, people were allowing themselves to be hopeful again.

The elevator came. Claire stepped inside with a large group of people.

"This is our country's finest hour," a man with a buzz cut and square glasses said. He looked like he'd been crying.

"I wonder what Jackie will wear?" one of the nurses said.

Claire smiled at her. "I think pink," she said. "She looks beautiful in pink."

"She looks beautiful in everything," an older woman with her hair in curlers said.

The elevator arrived at Claire's floor, and she squeezed out.

Her mother had told her that it was hope that had let her believe in her future. Maybe this sense of hope surging through the country today would give Claire that same ability.

The nurses' station was empty. The hallway too felt deserted. At the door to her mother-in-law's room, Claire held up her knitting bag for Peter to see.

He got to his feet. "Just in time," he said. "Everyone's gone to the solarium already."

It seemed wrong to leave all the patients, Claire thought. She glanced over at her mother-in-law. What if what Connie and the doctor had said was true? What if she died alone while they were upstairs watching the inauguration?

"Do you think it's all right to leave her?" Claire asked Peter softly.

He was slipping his shoes back on, tying the laces.

"I do," he said. "It's not going to change anything one way or the other."

Claire, who had been lingering in the doorway, came into the room. She took her mother-in-law's hand in hers.

"We're going to watch John Kennedy get inaugurated," she said. "The entire country will be watching," she added. That felt wrong, so she said, "I'll tell you all about it when we get back."

Behind her, Peter chuckled. "I bet she can't wait."

Claire let go of the old woman's hand and turned to her husband. "Stop," she said. "Don't be that way."

He frowned slightly. "That's the way I am, Clairezy. You should know that by now."

Peter took her arm and nudged her along.

They were almost out the door when it happened. A rustling of the bedclothes. The bed creaking. They stopped and looked back.

Peter's mother was struggling to sit up, staring wildly at something neither of them could see.

"Mom?" Peter said, his face so full of surprise that he looked to Claire like a little boy.

The old woman turned toward his voice, that wild look still in her eyes.

"Mom," Peter said.

His mother's face relaxed. She almost smiled. She reached her arms out as if to hug him, her fingers reaching toward him and Peter hurrying to meet them.

Then she opened her mouth and said one word.

"David," she said. "David."

"Mom?" Peter said.

The old woman looked at her son without any sign of recognition.

"Mom," he said again, sitting beside her on the bed, her eyes closely following his movements. "It's Peter."

When she didn't respond, he added, "Your son."

Claire heard footsteps hurrying down the hall and stepped back into the corridor. A very young nurse was rushing past, her hair shaken loose from beneath her cap. A name tag pinned to her breast said, STUDENT NURSE, and beneath it her name, PENNY.

"Excuse me," Claire said to her. "Penny? I'm sorry to stop you but we need someone in here, fast."

The girl's eyes widened. "I only just started my rotation here," she said. "Is it a real emergency?" Her cheeks turned pink beneath the freckles that blanketed her face.

"I think so," Claire told her.

Penny looked frightened. "I only just started," she said again.

"Could you run to get someone who can help?"

She nodded, relieved, and ran off in the direction of the nurses' station.

Claire stepped back into the room where Peter was speaking softly to his mother.

"And here's Claire," he said. "My wife Claire."

Birdy turned a slow steady gaze on Claire.

"You're in the hospital," Peter told her.

"I can see that," she said, her voice a dry croak.

Peter smiled at that, a glimmer of his mother coming back.

Claire poured her a glass of water and held it to the old woman's lips.

"Who's David?" Peter asked when she'd finished sipping.

Birdy looked at him, surprised.

"What do you know about that?" she asked.

"You just called for him," Peter said.

His mother smiled sadly. "So," she said, "at the end of my life, I call for David."

"No one said it's the end of your life," Claire said quickly.

"Darling," Birdy said, resting her head back on the pillow and closing her eyes, "I'm saying it."

She was quiet for a moment, then she said softly, "I dreamed of Lotte."

Claire glanced at Peter, but he just shrugged.

"I dreamed I was at her farm, at one of her dinners, and Pamela was there and everyone looked so healthy. So happy. Even me," she added.

Again Claire glanced at Peter.

"You've got a whole cast of characters who I don't even know," Peter said, stroking his mother's hand.

Birdy sighed. "It was all so long ago," she said wearily.

Penny poked her head in, her face redder and her eyes more frightened.

"Jeez," she said, "everyone's gone to the solarium to watch the inauguration. That's where I was headed when you stopped me. They almost canceled it, you know. The inauguration. On account of the snow. I heard it's only twenty-two degrees out there and with the wind and all it feels more like seven degrees."

"Well, you need to forget about that and go find a doctor," Peter said sharply.

"But I looked," Penny insisted.

"Maybe you could go up to the solarium?" Claire suggested. "If they're all there?"

The girl nodded. "I'll do that," she said, happy to leave the room.

Claire wondered how she would ever make it as a nurse.

"Why don't you go with her?" Peter said to Claire. "That one might forget to come back."

"All right," Claire said.

She too was relieved to go. She would find a doctor, but she would also get to watch a tiny bit of the inauguration. Maybe she would even get to glimpse Jackie.

Walking quickly, she caught up with Penny at the elevator.

"What's the emergency anyway?" Penny said when she recognized Claire beside her.

"My mother-in-law," Claire said. "She had a severe heart attack last night and the doctor said she wouldn't pull through. But now she's talking to us. Gibberish, but just the same."

Penny's eyes glazed, as if she had no interest in the events at all.

The elevator arrived and after they stepped in and the doors slid shut, Penny said, "I'm only doing this to marry a doctor. All the sick people and stuff aren't exactly my cup of tea."

Surprised at the girl's honesty, and her motivation, Claire couldn't even think of a response.

"If you marry a doctor," Penny continued, "your life is so easy. I bet I'll have a built-in swimming pool and wall-to-wall carpeting and everything."

"But life isn't about things like that," Claire said.

Now Penny looked surprised. "Oh, isn't it? It doesn't look like you did too bad for yourself. That husband of yours is kind of dreamy, and you're both dressed like you're not hurting for anything."

"Yes, but I meant to say that you should fall in love for love's sake, not—"

Penny interrupted her with a sharp laugh. "It's just as easy to fall in love with a rich man as it is a poor man, I say."

The elevator stopped and the doors slowly opened. Claire immediately saw the solarium at the end of the hall, with a crowd of people spilling from it.

"How did you meet your husband?" Penny asked Claire.

"On an airplane. To Paris," Claire said.

"Paris," Penny said, impressed.

"I was an air hostess and—"

"Aha!" Penny said, pointing a finger at Claire. "That's another way to meet rich guys."

Claire struggled to respond. How could she tell this girl that marrying for security, for the wrong things, would not make her happy?

But Penny did not want to talk. She walked into the solarium ahead of Claire, who watched her survey the room before going to stand by a tall young doctor with glasses like Buddy Holly used to wear. Penny planted herself beside him. When the doctor spoke to her, she looked up at him without raising her head, just by lifting her eyes slowly upward.

On the television, the presidential motorcade moved slowly up Pennsylvania Avenue. Claire saw the car with JFK and Jackie come into view. He wore a silk top hat. Jackie wore a hat too, a seamless wool felt one in taupe. Taupe? Claire thought. She strained to see if she could tell what color Jackie's outfit was yet.

But she couldn't make out anything but their beautiful faces smiling out beneath their hats. Roberta had thought Jackie wouldn't wear a hat at all, even though all of the other women had insisted that protocol demanded it. And here she was in a hat tipped to the back of her head rather than sitting straight on top. Claire smiled to herself. Now they would all have to start wearing their hats that way.

"She's hanging in there still," the man beside her said.

At first Claire didn't recognize him, but then she realized this was the doctor they'd spoken to earlier.

"Doctor!" she blurted. "My goodness, I almost forgot. I came here to get you."

He glanced at the television, and then back at Claire.

"She spoke to us," Claire said. "She sat up and spoke."

Once again, the doctor glanced at the TV.

Then he sighed. "Let's go take a look," he said.


As Claire and Dr. Spirito walked down the hallway, Claire begged off, pointing to the ladies' room.

"Of course, of course," Dr. Spirito said, continuing on his way.

But instead of going into the ladies' room, Claire ducked into one of the phone booths that lined the wall. Inside, she sat on the small stool and emptied her change purse. Almost five dollars in nickels and dimes. Surely that would be enough to call Rose. The idea had struck her as soon as she saw the bank of phone booths, their wooden doors lined up in a neat row. Rose had popped into her mind so frequently since they'd left yesterday that Claire decided to call her old roommate.

The operator found Rose's number in New London and told Claire how much money to deposit. Like magic, there was a brief pause, then the shrill ring of the phone in her ear.

"Hello," Rose answered, her voice the same husky one Claire used to envy.

"Rose, it's Claire Fontaine," Claire said, returning to her maiden name easily.

"Claire!" Rose shrieked.

Then, away from the receiver, she called, "Honey, it's Claire Fontaine on the line," and Claire heard Ed exclaiming what a wonderful surprise this was and how the hell was old Claire?

Claire had stood up for Rose and Ed at their wedding, and Rose had done the same for hers six months later. That was the last time they'd seen each other. Ed wrote Christmas letters, long funny ones about his layovers with TWA and what Rose had redecorated that year and which exotic location they'd hiked or biked, Ireland and Argentina and Greece. At first, Claire had sent Christmas cards, beautiful paper cuts of snowflakes or winter scenes, a quick note written inside, a photo of Kathy in a baby Santa suit trimmed in white fake fur one year, the next a snapshot of her in the snow in her red snowsuit. But nothing this past Christmas. Claire had been too overwhelmed by everything that had happened to pretend they were still a happy family.

"It is so funny that you're calling today," Rose was saying. "Ed and I were just talking about you after the news last night."

"News?"

"Aren't you still down in Alexandria, Virginia?" Rose asked. "We didn't get a card from you at Christmas—"

"I know," Claire said, remembering how in his Christmas letter this last time, Ed had actually written in rhyme. "I'm sorry. Life has been—"

"Well, then you know about that boy who was kidnapped down there," Rose said.

"Dougie Daniels? Oh, Rose, it was just awful. He lived two streets away from us. In fact, I saw the car that afternoon."

"She saw the car that took that boy," Rose said, away from the phone again.

"No shit," Claire heard Ed say.

"But you didn't hear that they caught the man?" Rose said to Claire.

"What? They did?" Claire said. Odd that Dot hadn't mentioned that when they'd spoken earlier.

"He lived in . . . where did he live, Ed?" Ed's reply was muffled. But then Rose said, "He lived in Arlington. The Shirley Park Apartments. Do you know them?"

"No."

"Apparently he was some kind of a handyman there. Franklin Smythe. Not Smith. Smythe."

Claire shook her head. "Such news," she said.

"His picture's been plastered all over the newspapers. And they showed him on *Huntley-Brinkley* last night. Gorgeous."

"What?"

"He's gorgeous," Rose said. "Looks like a movie star. Like that young actor. Ed?" she called again away from the phone. "Who's that actor I like so much? The young guy?"

"Robert Wagner?" Ed said.

"No, not Robert Wagner. I'll think of it as soon as I hang up," Rose said, back to Claire now. "Gorgeous," she said again.

"Wait until Peter hears."

"Is Peter there?" Rose asked.

"That's the thing. We're at the hospital in Rhode Island. His mother," she added.

"As I remember," Rose said, "I didn't much care for her. Kind of stuck-up. Pretty, but kept to herself."

"I just thought that since we were so close, I should call," Claire said.

"Did you have to drive in that blizzard?"

"We did. And I'm pregnant. Fat and swollen and uncomfortable," Claire said.

"Again?" Rose laughed. "Do you two know what's causing them?"

Claire laughed along with Rose. But the laughter seemed to strangle her, and she coughed to clear her throat and before she knew it she was crying.

"What's the matter?" Rose was asking, but Claire couldn't find her voice.

"Can I do anything?" Rose asked.

Claire shook her head, as if Rose could actually see her. Claire thought of all of Rose's flippant advice, delivered so matter-of-factly, about affairs and blow jobs and men and life. She tried to think of the question she needed an answer to, something that Rose might be able to know how to handle. An affair, yes. But getting caught like that. Being pregnant now.

"Oh," Claire said finally, "it's all such a mess."

"Did he cheat on you?" Rose said quietly, and Claire could imagine her friend stretching the cord of the phone as far as she could so that Ed wouldn't hear. "Is that it? I know some women get pregnant when they catch their husbands. It's a way to keep him, they think."

Claire laughed.

"What?" Rose said.

"Rosie," Claire said, still laughing, "the thing is, *I* had the affair—"

"What?"

"—and he found us together and now I'm pregnant—"

"Claire," Rose said, "I don't know what to say."

"You always said it was all right. That affairs were all right."

"That was before I got married, I guess," Rose said, her tone no longer warm and caring.

"But, Rose—"

"I think you'd better get ahold of yourself," Rose said. "Jesus, Claire. You're Peter's wife. You're a mother."

Claire rested her head against the wall. Bored people had carved their initials in the wood. Someone had written HELP!!!! in pen. The hot, airless phone booth reeked of perfume and sweat mixed with the hospital odors. She tried to picture Rose on the other end of the phone, in her home in Connecticut. Hadn't she told Claire once that she could see the ocean from her living room window? Is that where she stood now, her face creased with judgment, Ed looming somewhere in the background?

"This baby," Rose began, but she stopped herself.

"Rose," Claire said, breathing in the strange phone booth smells. "Maybe I could come and visit you. I would like that."

There was a silence that seemed to go on forever.

"Rose?" Claire said.

"That would be swell. But Ed's got a flight to Rome and I think I'm going to go along."

"Oh."

"Remember that crazy place where we used to get Chanel bags? Down that alley?"

"I should hang up," Claire said.

"I can get you one, if you want," Rose said. A peace offering. "Nothing cheers a girl up like a new bag."

"Thanks," Claire said.

After she hung up, Claire sat in the phone booth, her head pressed against that wall, taking slow deep breaths.

She didn't know how long she stayed there before the accordion door opened.

"Oops," a man said. "I didn't know you were in here." He was holding a jar of dimes.

"I'm finished," Claire said.

"You sure?"

"Yes," she said, standing.

Her pregnant belly made it hard for her to squeeze past him. For an awkward moment they stood wedged half in and half out. Then the man angled his body, making room for Claire to leave.

Dr. Spirito and Peter stood in the hallway outside her mother-in-law's room.

"I can't be optimistic at this point," the doctor was saying when Claire approached them.

"But she sat up," Peter said, and the desperateness in his voice made Claire want to go to him and wrap him in her arms.

Peter looked at Claire and said, "She just asked for a cup of Darjeeling tea and some cinnamon toast."

"I don't have a crystal ball," Dr. Spirito said. "I wish I did. The damage to her heart is substantial."

"I'm sorry," Claire told the doctor.

Peter turned to her, his eyes hard. "Why are *you* sorry?"

"I just meant . . ." Claire began. But what did she mean?

"Look," the doctor said, "why don't you both just come upstairs, watch the inauguration. Then go home and rest up. See where we are tomorrow."

"That's a good idea," Claire said. "We don't want to miss his speech."

"Fine," Peter said.

He hesitated. "Is it all right to just leave her?"

"She's a bit confused," the doctor said. "Not really dementia, but more like temporary amnesia. The nurse will keep her company, try to get her back to 1961. She talked about some poor kid who died of the Spanish flu, and taking the train to Denver, and all sorts of things from the past."

"Are you sure it's temporary?" Claire asked.

"I've seen it go both ways with old folks."

Amnesia, Claire thought. It didn't sound like a bad thing to her.


Crowded into that hospital solarium, everyone's eyes fixed on the television that hung in a corner of the room, Claire imagined Dot's party. She could picture the couples squeezed onto the Colonial sofas and armchairs, so many that people probably perched on the armrests. Some men, polite, would stand, hands on their wives' shoulders. Then she imagined all of the living rooms across the country, every citizen watching this very same moment, and imagining it, Claire shivered.

Peter rubbed her arm. "Cold?" he asked her.

She couldn't think of how to describe this feeling overcoming her, this sense of unity, of hope. Hadn't her mother described the years before the Great Depression this way? *There was hope then*, she'd said. Hope that made people fall in love and feel optimistic. Hope for a bright future.

Uncharacteristically, Peter wrapped his arms around her, and rested his chin lightly on the top of her head.

John Kennedy was raising his hand now. He was taking the oath of office.

"He's not wearing his hat," someone in the room said.

"There go hats," another person said. "Out of style as of 12:52 p.m., January 20."

Disappointed, Claire saw Jackie in a taupe wool dress with a matching coat. The coat had a sable fur collar and a matching muff, her hands tucked inside it. And that pillbox hat, tipped jauntily back on her head.

Taupe. No one would ever guess taupe.

When Kennedy began his inaugural speech, the solarium went still. Behind him, LBJ sat frowning, his oversized ears practically moving with the wind. Claire listened, trying to keep her mind from going to her lover, standing perhaps this very minute in Dot's living room, his hands on his wife's shoulders, listening to these very same words.

"So let us begin anew," JFK was saying, "remembering on both sides that civility is not a sign of weakness, and sincerity is always subject to proof. Let us never negotiate out of fear. But let us never fear to negotiate."

Claire felt Peter step away from her, ever so slightly. She resisted turning around to look up at him.

"Let both sides explore what problems unite us," Kennedy continued, "instead of belaboring those problems which divide us."

At this, Claire did turn to glimpse her husband, who stood with his jaw set hard, his hands shoved into his pockets.

She focused again on the new president's speech, and when he finished, she applauded hard along with everyone else in the room.

"It's truly a new beginning," an elderly woman standing beside Claire said in an Eastern European accent. She said it as if she were speaking directly to Claire.

"It feels that way," Claire said, wondering why she had this lump in her throat, why she felt so empty.

"No, no, it is. That boy, he's going to change the world." The woman pointed to the television. "You watch."

"I hope so," Claire said.

Nurses and doctors were pushing their way out now. The hallway outside the solarium came alive with calls over the PA for Doctor this and Doctor that.

The whole hospital had held its breath for this moment, Claire thought.

She touched Peter's arm lightly. "I'm going to call Dot," she said. "Then I'll meet you downstairs?"

He nodded, and joined the stream of people exiting. Claire couldn't read his expression. Was he unable to stop belaboring what had divided them? She left with the stragglers, wondering if she was able to stop.

Back in the phone booth, the operator connected her to Dot, reversing the charges.

"Taupe!" Claire said as soon as Dot accepted. "Can you believe it?"

"I picked cornflower blue," Dot said. "Wouldn't she have looked beautiful in cornflower blue and that black hair of hers?"

"I didn't even hear who designed it."

"Cassini," Dot said. "And the hat was someone named Halston. Apparently he does hats for Bergdorf Goodman in New York."

"I wish I was there with all of you," Claire said.

"We missed you, darling. You did get to hear the speech, didn't you?"

"Every word," Claire said.

"Magnificent, wasn't it?"

Claire could hear the voices of Dot's guests raised in excitement. She strained, trying to hear one above them all. But they remained a blur.

"I should get back," Claire said.

"I hope she doesn't die today," Dot said. "It's not a day to die. Not at all."

"Dot? I almost forgot to ask. Did anyone pick taupe?" Claire was already laughing at how ridiculous a question she'd asked.

"Yes!" Dot said.

"What? Taupe? Don't tell me Trudy won?"

"Not Trudy, no. The wife with the appendix. Peggy. She actually guessed taupe. Not beige or camel or ecru. Taupe."

"How could she?" Claire managed to say.

"She's brilliant, that's all," Dot said. "Hurry home, you hear?"

Peggy. His wife's name was Peggy. And she was brilliant.

The baby inside Claire kicked hard. Claire put one hand lightly on her stomach, feeling the little foot banging there, kicking, as if she were trying to get out.

# 10

# The Man in Denver

## VIVIEN, 1919

"Tell me about Pamela," Vivien said to Lotte.

Lotte looked at her with vacant eyes, eyes that made Vivien want to look away. She had seen eyes such as these before, of course. Many of the people who showed up on her doorstep asking her to write an obituary had this very look, as if the life had been extinguished from them. Lotte, like all the others, vacillated between this vacant dead stare and a wild, out-of-control one in which her eyes blazed and jumped around, only landing briefly on people and things as if they were searching for something they could not find.

"You know her," Lotte said, her voice as flat as her gaze. "You know all about her."

They sat together on the long sofa where Lotte had spent most of her time since the funeral two days earlier. Vivien had a stack of thick paper on her lap and held a fountain pen. The two women's knees touched. Vivien couldn't help but remember the afternoons they had sat close like this as girls, each lost in a book, the slight pressure of Lotte's knee on hers the only reminder of the world outside the novel. Perhaps that was why Lotte had settled so close to Vivien now, to keep her centered, to remind her that there was a world outside the one of grief that she now inhabited.

Vivien laid her hand on Lotte's leg. "Of course I do," she said. "But I find that when I write a . . . a . . ."

She stopped. For some reason, she couldn't say the word *obituary*. It was as if by saying it out loud, Pamela would be more dead somehow.

Lotte turned that awful gaze on Vivien.

"An obituary," Lotte said without emotion. "Pamela's obituary. Because she's dead she needs an obituary."

Vivien found she held her breath as Lotte spoke, afraid at any moment the other grieving mother would appear, the one that thrashed and scratched at herself, and wailed. Yesterday, Lotte had screamed, *I want to get out of my skin! I want it off!* She was wearing her grief, Vivien realized. If she could take off her skin, she might be able to inhabit the right one.

"The way I proceed," Vivien began, hating the formality in her voice but unable to speak otherwise, "is to ask you to tell me about . . ."

Again she faltered.

She took a breath. "About Pamela," she said, "and while you talk I write down the things that strike me."

"Strike you how?" Lotte said.

*Oh, Lotte,* Vivien thought as she looked into her friend's flat eyes, *are you in there somewhere?*

"I can't explain it really," Vivien said. "Something just clicks and I know what to write."

Lotte nodded absently. Her fingers kept working the hem of her dress. It was the dress she'd worn to the funeral, and she refused to take it off. *I'll wear it forever,* she'd yelled at Robert when he tried to unbutton it and replace it with a clean blue one. *I'll wear it so I'll never forget the day they put my baby in the ground.*

"I should have taken her to the doctor sooner," Lotte said. She said this a dozen times a day, maybe more.

"It wouldn't have mattered," Vivien said. It was what she always said in response.

Lotte nodded again.

"Did you think David would die that day?" she said softly.

"I don't think he died, Lotte," Vivien said.

"You think he's in Denver," Lotte said.

"Maybe."

"Because you believe that if had died, you would know somehow. You would feel it."

"Yes," Vivien admitted.

"You see, that's why I can't believe Pamela died. I didn't feel like she was sick enough to die. I didn't feel anything out of the ordinary."

Lotte's fingers worried her hem, twisting it and turning it over and over in her hands.

"Do the people who come to you know ahead of time? Do they have some kind of sign, some intuition that I lack?" she asked.

"No, no," Vivien said.

"What kind of mother doesn't realize her daughter is dying?" Lotte said, and now her eyes were filling with fear and confusion. Her hands worried that hem, and her body began to tremble.

"What kind of mother doesn't know?" she said, her voice growing louder.

"No one knows these things," Vivien said.

Bo's head popped around the corner. He saw where his mother was going and he quickly disappeared again.

"A mother should know," Lotte insisted. She was on her feet now, pacing.

She rubbed her arms vigorously. "I could jump out of my skin," she said. "I want out. I want out of here."

Vivien got up and tried to stop Lotte, but her friend pulled away from her.

"Take me with you," Lotte said, turning abruptly to face Vivien. Her cheeks were flushed, and her eyes shining.

"Where, darling?" Vivien asked.

"To Denver," Lotte said, impatient.

"You can't leave your children," Vivien said. "Not now."

Without warning, Lotte broke into a run. She ran out of the living room, past Bo and a neighbor boy at the kitchen table, and out the door. Vivien followed, trying to keep pace with her. Through the yard, across the vineyard, and beyond to the hill where the small family cemetery sat. There, on Pamela's grave with the freshly dug earth, Lotte flung herself down. Like an animal, she clawed at the dirt, crying and calling Pamela's name.

Out of breath, Vivien bent and tugged her friend upward. She wrapped Lotte in her arms, and led her out of the cemetery. Lotte resisted, but Vivien held firm. Dirt streaked Lotte's worn face, and a small clump tangled in her hair. She smelled of sweat and earth. She smelled of heartbreak.

As they made their slow way back to the house, Lotte trying to break free every few feet, Vivien caught sight of Sebastian working in the field. Yesterday he had cornered her. *You will come back to me?* he'd asked. *Maybe,* Vivien had said.


"She was just a little girl," Lotte told Vivien.

Hours had passed. Vivien had managed to finally bathe her

friend, to comb the tangles from her hair and scrub the dirt off her hands and face. The sky was violet as dusk settled over the vineyard. The women sat at one of the long wooden tables outside, a salad of fresh tomatoes and cucumbers on a platter in front of them. Vivien opened a bottle of wine, and filled two glasses for them. Then she asked Lotte again: *Tell me about Pamela.*

"She was such a good rider for her age," Lotte said, her gaze focused on some distant point beyond Vivien. "Bareback. Western."

She continued, shaking her head. "I worried she'd have a fall, that she'd get hurt. How foolish of me. Instead some germ got her. Something I couldn't even see."

"I liked watching her ride that horse," Vivien said. "The brown one with the white markings on his face."

"Happy," Lotte said. "She named him Happy."

They sat in silence for a few minutes, sipping their wine. Crickets chirped. Out in the fields, fireflies blinked on and off.

"She loved Robert Louis Stevenson," Lotte said. "You were reading her *Treasure Island* just a few weeks ago."

"Pamela did love books," Vivien said.

"Adventure stories. She would get mad if the boys could do something that she couldn't. Like climb that apple tree over there."

Lotte kept talking, in fits and starts. Remembering how as a toddler Pamela would chase her brothers, put her hands on her hips, and order them to stop being boys. How if they were too rough with her and made her cry, Lotte would make them tell her they were sorry and Pamela would shout: *Sorry isn't good enough.* Vivien listened, glad that Lotte was finally talking and eating a little. She would write the obituary later that night, and then she would try again to leave for Denver.

The obituary was already taking shape, the words to capture

the little girl who wanted to have adventures, who dreamed of fighting pirates and racing horses.

Robert Louis Stevenson, Vivien thought. She remembered reading Pamela his *Child's Garden of Verses* last summer. "The Land of Counterpane." *When I was sick and lay a-bed, I had two pillows at my head, And all my toys beside me lay, To keep me happy all the day.*

Pamela had said, "Auntie Viv, wouldn't it be terrible to be so sick that you had to stay in bed all day every day?"

And Vivien had pointed out the last line of the poem, how the land of counterpane is called pleasant in it.

"Well, I don't think it would be pleasant at all," Pamela had said. "Imagine not being able to run outside?"

"I think Stevenson was a sick child himself," Vivien explained. "But he grew up to be quite an adventurer."

"What did he do?" Pamela demanded, unconvinced.

"He chartered a yacht named *Casco* and set sail from San Francisco."

Vivien remembered when Stevenson set sail that summer day in 1888. The newspaper had covered his departure, and Vivien could still see the photograph of Stevenson with his wild long hair and bohemian clothes, standing at the prow of *Casco*.

"Where did he go, Auntie Viv?" Pamela asked, her curiosity getting the better of her.

"For nearly three years he wandered the Pacific. Tahiti and Samoa and the Hawaiian Islands. He became a good friend of King Kalākaua."

Pamela's eyes were shining with excitement. "A real-life king? That's what I want to do, sail the Pacific and meet kings and savages."

Vivien stroked Pamela's soft blond hair. "I have no doubt you will do all that and more," she'd said.

·   ·   ·

Vivien had never seen mountains before. When she stepped off the train in Denver later that week, the sight of them made her weak. The Rocky Mountains loomed above the city, topped with snow even in spring, and appearing almost purple in the early morning light.

"Pretty, aren't they?" a woman standing beside her said.

Pretty wasn't the adjective that Vivien would use. Magnificent. Majestic. But she nodded to be polite.

"I came West in 1900, from Boston," the woman continued. "To teach school. And I still remember stepping off the train here and seeing the Rockies. How they took my breath away."

"You live here then?" Vivien said. The woman had dark hair coming loose from beneath her wide hat, and a long horsey face.

"I don't anymore," she said. "I left ten years ago for Oregon. You ever been to Oregon?"

Vivien shook her head.

"Now that's God's country," she said. "We've got mountains too. And Douglas fir and redwoods and the Pacific. God's country for sure."

"I need to find the hospital."

The woman grinned. "But I'm going to the hospital myself. We can share a taxi?" the woman continued. She was one of those people who didn't require responses, Vivien thought.

Vivien followed her off the platform and into Union Station. In front of it sleek black cars were lined up, waiting for passengers.

"The Mizpah Arch," the woman said, pointing to the beautiful stone arch that welcomed people to Denver.

"I didn't expect such a sophisticated city," Vivien admitted as they got into a taxi.

"We hosted the Democratic National Convention in '08," the woman said

Her face had taken on a sadness Vivien took for nostalgia.

"The Mint," the woman said, pointing out the window. "The Cathedral Basilica of the Immaculate Conception." She sighed and settled deeper into the seat.

"So many trees," Vivien said.

"One hundred and ten thousand to be exact," the woman said. "Mayor Speer had them planted in his City Beautiful movement. That's Speer's Civic Center," she added as they passed a large park.

"It sounds like you love it here," Vivien said.

The woman nodded absently.

Vivien wondered why the woman had moved from this city that clearly moved her so much, but she was too polite to ask. She had left San Francisco because it was too painful to stay. People had their private reasons.

They turned onto West Colfax, a paved street lined with beautiful buildings and well-dressed men and women. Vivien shook her head. She had been imagining cowboys and cattle.

"Do you teach school in Oregon too?" Vivien asked.

"I cook in a lumber camp there," the woman said.

"You're quite an adventurer," Vivien said, her voice catching on the word. She thought of Pamela, poor Pamela.

"I lived a dull life in Boston until I was twenty-five years old. When no one seemed to want to marry us, my girlfriend and I decided to head West. The land of opportunity, we thought."

"Was it?" Vivien said.

"Abby died here, in childbirth. The man I married drowned, and they never recovered his body. So . . ."

"How terrible," Vivien said. "I'm sorry."

To her surprise, the woman smiled.

"But that's why I've come back," she said. From her purse she pulled out a folded newspaper clipping and handed it to Vivien. "See?"

Vivien recognized it as soon as she unfolded it. The man with amnesia.

"I think it's my Jeremiah," the woman said. "The description sounds just like him."

"But what about the hotel key?" Vivien asked, her throat dry.

The woman shrugged. "Ten years of wandering around, lost. Maybe he went to San Francisco. Maybe he stayed at that hotel."

Carefully, Vivien refolded the clipping.

She could feel the woman's eyes on her.

"That's why you're here, isn't it?" the woman said.

"Yes."

Their eyes met.

"Well," the woman said finally. She put the clipping back in her purse and looked out the window.

For the rest of the ride to the hospital, neither of them spoke.


Vivien had not expected the sophisticated city of Denver, and she had not expected that she would be one of almost a dozen women who had come to identify the man with amnesia. But she found herself sitting in a waiting room off the lobby of the hospital with other women, all clutching that same newspaper clipping. They had come from Chicago and Wyoming and Ohio. One woman had come all the way from Philadelphia. There was a nervous energy in the room, the woman from Philadelphia's leg jumping up and down, up and down, and one of the women from Chicago tapping on the table in a rapid pattern. No one spoke. What was there to say? Every one of them wanted that man to be their husband or son or father.

The door opened and a tall, thin older woman walked in, twisting a white handkerchief in her fist.

"He's not my Simon," she said. She looked around the room, surprised. "My Simon, he went to the war. And he vanished. The government can't find him. No one saw him get injured. Or worse. He just vanished."

The women all looked down at their laps, ashamed to show their relief, their hope. If the man wasn't her Simon, he could still be Mark or Reginald or Jonathan.

Or David, Vivien thought as she too avoided the woman's face. She heard the woman collecting her things and shuffling out of the room.

A woman holding a clipboard entered. She wore a honey-colored tweed jacket with a matching skirt and gold wire-rimmed eyeglasses.

In a loud, crisp voice she announced, "Martha Vale."

From beneath downcast eyes, everyone peeked as the woman from the train station got up, smoothed her skirt and patted her hair into place, straightened her shoulders and walked out the door toward the man who had forgotten who he was.

It seemed that the entire room held its breath after Martha left. The woman from Philadelphia's leg jumped restlessly. The woman from Chicago tapped, tapped, tapped on the table. The smells of lavender and violet water and lilies choked Vivien. There seemed to be no air in the room, all of it consumed by the hope and fear of the women. Beside Vivien, a woman had started to knit, and the clacking of her needles added to the other nervous sounds.

"This is torture," the knitter said in a thick Irish brogue. "My Paddy would want me to find him, to bring him home. That's the only thing keeping me here."

Vivien glanced up. The knitter had steel gray hair pulled back in a messy bun and the red hands of someone who had worked with them all her life. She was knitting a sweater with thick oatmeal yarn.

"This will be the ninth sweater I've knit for him," she said to Vivien. "I knit them and put them in his drawer with cedar, to protect them, you know?"

"Of course," Vivien said.

The woman went back to her knitting.

Just when Vivien thought she might lose her mind, the door opened. Martha stood there, not moving until the woman with the clipboard nudged her forward.

Seeing the tears on Martha's cheeks, Vivien got up and went to her. But when she touched Martha's shoulder, the woman shrugged her off.

"What was I thinking?" Martha said as she angrily picked up her valise and her coat. "Everyone saw him go under that day. They saw him disappear in that river. Why would I put myself through this?"

"I'm sorry," Vivien said softly.

Martha spun around.

"No you're not. You want this to be your man. You hope everyone in this room gets disappointed so that he just might be yours."

The vehemence with which she spoke forced Vivien backward, away from her.

Martha leveled her gaze on the rest of the women.

"The same goes for all of you," she said.

They watched her leave, pushing past the woman with the clipboard as she did.

"She's right, of course," the woman from Philadelphia said.

"Vivien Lowe," the woman with the clipboard announced in her clear, crisp voice.

Vivien wished she'd thought to put some color on her lips, to wear her good silver comb, the one David had bought her one Christmas. She wished she looked younger, more beautiful.

"Vivien Lowe?" the woman said.

"I'm Vivien Lowe," Vivien said, surprised by how tremulous her voice sounded.

The woman held the door open. And Vivien walked through it.

The woman with the clipboard remained cold and efficient as she led Vivien down a corridor, around a corner, down another corridor where she stopped in front of a room with its door closed. There, she hesitated. Her face softened and she touched Vivien's arm.

"Over one hundred people have come here," she said. "All women. All hoping this man is the man they've lost. Maybe it's the war that's done it, made us all so desperate. Maybe it's the Spanish influenza. So much loss these past years. We're all walking around brokenhearted, filled with grief. Lost."

As she spoke, Vivien thought of the obituaries she'd written. So many of them! Thousands of words, all of them trying to capture grief, to show the world what had been lost.

"Yes," Vivien said softly. "I understand."

"How I wish that the man in that room is your husband," the woman said. "But as weeks pass, it seems less likely that he belongs to anyone."

The woman shook her head. She looked at her clipboard, taking the pen she kept tucked behind her ear and preparing to write.

"Your husband's name?" she asked.

"David. David Gardner," Vivien said.

The woman wrote the name down. "San Francisco, California?" she said.

"Yes."

"I'll come in the room with you. I have to," the woman said. "It's hospital policy. If I didn't, you could tell me that he recognized you even if he didn't and we could release him to the wrong person. We're not doubting your integrity—"

"You're just recognizing our desperation," Vivien interrupted.

"Well," the woman said.

"May we go inside now?" Vivien asked.

"Of course."

She put her hand on the doorknob, but hesitated. "We call him John Doe," she said. "For obvious reasons."

Vivien nodded and the woman opened the door at last.

The room looked very much like the waiting room where Vivien and the other women had been. Loveseats and chairs lined up against the walls. A hooked rug on the floor and a window looking out at the city.

Sitting on one of those chairs, reading a book, was the man.

When Vivien saw that the book was Jack London's *The Call of the Wild*, hope fluttered weakly in her chest. David would be reading Jack London.

"John," the woman said. "Here's our next guest."

The man lowered the book and looked wearily at the woman and Vivien.

He had blue eyes, gray hair that needed to be trimmed. A scar on his forehead. Could he be David? Vivien wondered, moving closer to him. It had been thirteen years. A lifetime. Still. Wouldn't she know him right away?

"I'm Vivien Lowe," Vivien said, watching for some flicker of recognition on the man's face and seeing none.

He smiled sadly.

"I wish I could tell you that means something to me," he said.

His voice reminded Vivien of parchment paper, of something old that hadn't been used in a long time. Once she had seen someone pull an old letter from her purse and it had turned to dust when she opened it. His voice was like that. David's had been strong, deep.

"I see you're reading Jack London," Vivien said. "I used to see him at a restaurant in San Francisco. Coppa's," she added hopefully.

Again she waited for a reaction. Again she got none.

"It was sitting over there," the man said, motioning to a bookshelf in the far corner of the room. "I just picked it up."

Vivien read the titles on the shelf: the Complete Works of Shakespeare and Henry David Thoreau's *Walden* and *The Scarlet Letter.* Did it mean something that of all those books, he had chosen *The Call of the Wild?* Or was it just happenstance, like so many other things in life? She remembered the man who had come to her to write an obituary for his wife who had died suddenly. They had finished dinner and she sat down to her sewing and when he looked over at her she was dead. "The only thing we can count on in life," he had told Vivien, "is unpredictability."

"May I sit?" Vivien asked the woman with the clipboard.

When she nodded, Vivien sat across from John Doe so that she could see him better. If David were older and thinner, if he had gone through terrible things for all these years, might he be the man before her now?

"Do you know him?" the man was asking. He held up the book. "Jack London?"

"Oh, no. He just frequented a restaurant where we used to go," she said. "He died a few years ago," she added.

"Did you go there, to that restaurant, with the man you're looking for?" he asked.

Vivien looked into his eyes. They were dull and vacant, as if the life had been knocked out of them.

"You have a hotel key," she began.

"Mrs. Lowe," he said, "I don't remember why I have that key or how I ended up in Denver. Nothing. My mind is completely blank."

"I see," she said.

Over all these years she had read so much about amnesia, but nothing had explained what was in an amnesiac's mind, only what wasn't there.

The woman with the clipboard stood. "Last week, a Miss Minnie Nash came from Cheyenne and she could not be certain if John Doe was her fiancé or not. She went back to Wyoming to retrieve some documents. Photographs, that sort of thing. If you can't be certain, you can do the same."

"David had a scar," Vivien said. "Under his chin."

Even as she said this, Vivien knew it was pointless. This man was not David. This was not the face she had stared at as he slept, the mouth she had kissed with such youthful passion.

The woman turned to John Doe.

"I do have a lot of scars," John Doe said. "Apparently I'm quite accident-prone."

"This one is a bit ragged, and right here," Vivien said, touching the spot on her own chin.

The man shook his head, his face registering neither disappointment nor relief.

As if on cue, they all stood. Vivien shook the man's hand and wished him luck. Then she followed the woman out of the room and down the maze of corridors. Neither of them spoke. The only sound came from their heels tapping against the floor as they walked.

When they returned to the waiting room, the women still there looked up as they entered. Vivien avoided eye contact with any of them. Quickly, she gathered her trunk and coat, her hands trembling. She hurried out of there. From behind her came the woman's voice, calling the next poor woman: "Dorothea Kane."

Outside of the hospital at last, Vivien stood on the street. Passersby pushed past her. The Rocky Mountains rose beautifully in the distance. She willed her body to be still. She closed her eyes and took a deep breath. Then another. The air here was so crisp. She let it fill her lungs and then she opened her eyes.

# SIX

*If any women are to be present and the interment is to be in the ground, some one should order the grave lined with boughs and green branches—to lessen the impression of bare earth.*

—FROM *Etiquette*, BY EMILY POST, 1922

# 11

## *Arabella*

### CLAIRE, 1961

They left the hospital to rest for a bit. In the car, Claire told Peter someone had guessed taupe. "Can you believe that?" she muttered.

Peter laughed. "I can't believe that you girls even had a contest about it." He reached across the seat and touched her hair. "Silly," he said.

Claire looked out the window at all the snow.

"Maybe we can take Kathy sledding," she said.

"In your condition?"

"The baby's not going to fall out or anything," she teased.

"Still," he said.

"Do you think there's a sled somewhere?" Claire asked.

"Maybe. I bet Jimmy and Connie have a couple."

"I suppose we could take Little Jimmy. Connie's had Kathy all morning. It would only be fair."

She could tell that Peter still wasn't sold on the idea, but she didn't care. She would take the kids by herself if he didn't want to come. Claire could practically feel it, how the wind whipped at your cheeks as you went downhill. How your stomach almost hurt from the speed and the bumps, like a roller coaster in a way. Of course she would have to find some warm clothes, for herself and for Kathy. They'd left in such a hurry that Kathy only had her toggle coat and a hat. No snow pants or mittens.

"Maybe they have a snowsuit that Kathy can wear," she said.

"I thought you were exhausted."

"I am. But getting some fresh air would be nice."

"And where exactly is this sledding going to take place?" Peter said.

"You tell me. Where did you go sledding when you were a boy?"

"Roger Williams Park, I guess."

"Then that's where we'll go," Claire said.

Peter sighed his exasperated sigh.

"We'll go if you want. But you have to be a spectator. Okay?"

It wasn't okay, Claire thought. Pregnant women rode horses and swam and did all kinds of things. Why, Dot had gone skiing at twenty-eight weeks and Bill had seemed absolutely proud over it. *She's a tough one*, he'd said, beaming.

But Claire said, "Whatever you want," then pressed her forehead against the window.

She wanted to point out how the ice covering the trees and telephone wires glittered, giving everything an almost magical look. She wanted to say how pretty it was. But surely Peter would have something to say about that too, so she just kept staring out the window, watching Providence slide past her.

"Someone called for you," Connie said as soon as Claire and Peter walked in the house.

It was as if she had been standing in that hall waiting for them, Claire thought.

"For me?" Claire said.

Peter was frowning.

"Who in the world—" Claire began, but Connie was unfolding a piece of lined yellow paper and getting ready to read from it.

"2:20 p.m.," Connie said.

"You just missed your mystery caller," Peter said.

"Dot called and said—"

"See?" Claire said to him. "It's just Dot, that's all."

"She apologizes for bothering you, what with Peter's mother and all, and she says it's silly but she thought you would want to vote now for what color Jackie is going to wear tonight, to the ball."

"Jesus," Peter said under his breath.

"She says," Connie continued, "winner gets a dinner party in her honor. Couples."

"How fun!" Claire said.

Connie folded the paper again and handed it to Claire.

"She says she voted midnight blue," Connie added.

"That's exactly what I was thinking," Claire said. "Now I'll have to come up with a different color."

"I still say red," Connie said, lighting a cigarette.

The smell brought a wave of nausea to Claire, and she thought again of finding some sleds and going outside in the cold fresh air.

"I mean, who wears tan? Did you get a load of her today? Tan," Connie said.

"Well, taupe," Claire said.

Connie narrowed her eyes.

"Technically she wore taupe," Claire said.

She hadn't noticed that Jimmy was standing in the doorway of his apartment, wearing a white sleeveless T-shirt that didn't cover all of the hair that spread like grass across his chest and arms.

"Taupe?" he mimicked. "What the hell is that?"

"It's . . ." Claire struggled to describe it. "Sort of beige—"

"Tan," Connie said, smirking.

"Fine," Claire said, wanting to get out of there. She was actually having trouble catching her breath.

"You okay?" Jimmy asked. "You're a little green around the edges."

"I need some fresh air," she said. "I was thinking I could take Little Jimmy and Kathy sledding. At the park?"

"Sure," Connie said. "The sleds are down in the basement."

Claire had her hand on the door that led outside.

"I'm just going to step out for a minute," she said.

As she was closing the door behind her, she heard Jimmy saying, "She's kind of delicate, ain't she? Connie just pops kids out."

"Nine months," Connie said, "and I don't even burp."

Claire sat on the cold stoop and leaned her head against the front door.

*Think about Jackie,* she told herself. She closed her eyes and took in big mouthfuls of air. So lucky, Jackie was. The first lady. With that handsome husband and those children and the White House and all that Newport money and horses and speaking French. Like someone in a fairy tale.

Claire opened her eyes. White. Jackie would wear white tonight. Not cream or winter white but fairy-tale white. Maybe with sparkling beads. She was certain of it. She could almost see it, Jackie in a glittering white gown, dancing with her husband the president.

Smiling, Claire went back inside and up the stairs to her mother-in-law's to call Dot.

. . .

Claire had forgotten how long it took to get children in their
snowsuits and mittens, the squirming as the layers piled up, the
forcing of their little feet into boots and their sweaty hands into
mittens. By the time they had been zipped and snapped, Claire
was exhausted. A few weeks ago, after a big snow, she had wres-
tled Kathy into her snow gear only to have the girl crying and
cold within minutes, ready to go back inside. Today, at least, all
of the work getting Little Jimmy and Kathy ready to go sledding
would pay off with an hour or two bumping down the snowy
hills at the park.

On the way there, the children ate Cheerios in the backseat and looked at *The Poky Little Puppy* together. Claire could
almost imagine a future with two children, Kathy and this new
baby sitting back there, playing and talking, growing up under
her supervision. For these twenty minutes, as they drove past
snowdrifts and cars stuck off the roads, Claire could let herself
forget.

But then, just as suddenly as a sense of ease had come over
her, Claire remembered what Rose had told her.

Claire glanced at the children to be sure they were still occu-
pied before she said in a low voice, "They arrested the man who
took Dougie Daniels."

"They caught him?" Peter said.

"You hadn't heard?"

He shook his head. "I'll be damned."

"What kind of person would do such a thing?" Claire said.

She didn't expect an answer, but Peter said, "A sick bastard,
that's for sure."

At the word *bastard* she looked to be sure the children hadn't heard. Kathy was holding the book and pretending to read it out loud, and Little Jimmy listened, rapt.

"It's over finally," Claire said, trying to imagine Gladys Daniels receiving the news. It would never be over for her.

Up ahead the park came into sight. All of the hills were dotted with sledders, bright splashes of red and green and blue against the white snow. The sky had turned from pewter to a clear royal blue. Cloudless, it seemed to stretch forever. Claire smiled to herself, pleased with her idea to do this. She leaned across the seat and kissed Peter lightly on the cheek. Surprised, he put his hand to his cheek, as if she had branded him.

"Thank you," she said anyway.

"The things I do for you, Clairezy," he said, his hand still resting on the spot her lips had touched.

Was he trying to erase it? Claire wondered. Or preserve it?

She didn't linger in the car. Instead, she stepped into the cold air and helped the children out of the car. Gripping one child with each of her hands, she moved across the crowded parking lot. Behind her came the sound of the sleds scraping across the icy asphalt as Peter dragged them along. Connie and Jimmy had a trove of sleds down in that basement, and Claire had selected a small one with a high back and two medium-sized sleds.

But when they finally reached the place where everyone was sledding, Kathy was cranky, already too tired to want to climb the hill at all. No amount of cajoling could change her mind. Little Jimmy, on the other hand, tried desperately to drag one of the bigger sleds up, undeterred by the slipping backward that kept him more or less in place.

"Look at Sisyphus," Peter said.

"He's the one who—"

"The boulder," Peter said.

"Right."

He loved those Greek myths. Persephone and Hermes and Aphrodite. Claire couldn't keep them straight. For Christmas he gave Claire an elaborately illustrated book on Greek mythology, written by a Swiss couple. The wife had made the drawings with woodblocks, or some such. It was pretty enough, and she made a big show of how impressive she found it, but really she thought it was a gift for him. At night, he read to Kathy from it, when all the girl wanted was her Little Golden Books, *The Poky Little Puppy* and *The Little Red Hen*, with their simple stories and bright illustrations.

By this time Kathy was having a full-blown tantrum, screaming as loud as she could, demanding Mimi and stomping her feet.

"I'll take him up," Peter finally said.

"And leave me with her?" Claire said.

"This was your bright idea," Peter said, taking the rope from the sled Little Jimmy had been trying to get up the hill. "Come on, buddy." He took Little Jimmy's hand.

Claire watched him walk steadily up the hill.

"Kathy, stop that now. Sledding is the most fun you can imagine," Claire said in her most soothing voice.

But the tantrum had taken over completely, and there was no talking to Kathy.

Claire knew she should pick up her daughter, even though Kathy would make her body go rigid and just scream louder. She could see Peter and Little Jimmy almost at the top now. Jimmy practically ran the rest of the way, jumping up and down as he waited for Peter to reach him there.

"Here comes Daddy and Jimmy," Claire said, pointing.

Kathy quieted for an instant, but it was just to catch her breath before starting another round of screaming.

"Be quiet," Claire said through gritted teeth.

All she had wanted was some time outside, the feeling of the fresh air on her cheeks and the wind in her hair. How had she managed to get stuck down here with an unmanageable toddler while Peter—who hadn't even wanted to come—was flying down the hill, grinning?

The sight of him made her so angry that she sat Kathy down on the baby sled and picked up the rope to the second sled.

"Stay here," she told her daughter.

"Mama!" Kathy yelled.

Claire didn't turn around. She walked up the hill, taking big gulps of air. She could feel her heart beating hard against her ribs, feel the baby inside her kicking.

Kathy's now-distant voice yelled again: "Mama!"

Claire had reached the top. She waited for a group of four or five teenagers crammed onto a shiny toboggan to position themselves at the crest before she sat on her sled. She would have preferred to lie down across it, but her stomach was too large for that, so she sat up, stretching her legs and holding on to the rope to steer. At the bottom of the hill, Kathy was a small faceless dot in a red snowsuit. From here, Claire could not hear her cries. She only heard the whoosh of the wind and the chatter of other sledders. The tobogganers were squealing as they zigzagged downward.

Exhaustion washed over her again. What was she thinking coming here? Peter had been right. She should have stayed inside and taken a nap.

Squinting against the glare of the sun, Claire tried to pick out Kathy in the crowd at the bottom of the hill. She saw green and blue and pink snowsuits, but not the red one Kathy wore. She shielded her eyes with her hand, trying to stay calm. But no. She could not find Kathy there. Claire thought about Dougie Daniels and that man, Smythe. All of these people, she thought, all of these strangers. Any one of them could be a monster like Smythe. If someone saw Kathy alone there, it would be so easy to snatch her without anybody noticing.

"Kathy! Kathy!" Claire called foolishly. The wind ate her words as soon they left her lips.

Awkwardly, she tried to run down the hill, but sleds veered dangerously close to her and, afraid of being knocked down, she could not make her way through them.

Claire frantically scanned the crowd for sight of Kathy. She had to get down, she decided, sitting clumsily on the sled and pushing off with her feet. The sled started to go immediately and with speed. This was a bad idea too, Claire realized immediately. She needed to slow the sled and jump off. Get to the bottom of the hill and to her daughter's side before anything happened. But when she stuck her foot out to slow down, it forced the sled off its course and sent it in a different direction without slowing at all.

Claire pulled on the rope to steer, but she was moving too fast. The sled had taken on a life of its own. She glanced over her shoulder, and when she looked forward again she saw the sled heading for a giant tree. Digging both of her feet into the snow, Claire stopped the sled finally but not the momentum of her body. She flew off the sled. For a moment, she was airborne, tumbling.

Then she hit the tree. Hard.


When she opened her eyes, Claire was on her back, gazing up at that clear blue sky. Already a crowd had gathered, and a man was bending over her asking something.

Claire blinked. Her hand went instinctively to the back of her head where she felt something warm.

"Do you know what your name is?" the man asked her.

"Claire," she said, her voice sounding like someone else's. The fingers that had touched her head were covered in blood.

"Do you know what year it is?" he asked.

His face was very close to hers, so close that she could see the stubble on his cheeks and chin and smell the cocoa on his breath.

"Do you know who the president is?" the man asked as if her life depended on getting these right.

"Kennedy," Claire said.

"Whoa," someone towering above her said. "That's a lot of blood."

She could feel it, pooling around her head and neck.

"Has anyone called an ambulance?" someone else shouted.

The man peering at her said his wife was doing that very thing.

"Ma'am?" Another man kneeled at her side, his face creased with worry. "Are you pregnant?"

Claire's hands went to her belly.

"She is," the new man said. "She's pregnant."

In the distance Claire could hear a siren.

"What kind of fool would go sledding when she was pregnant?" a woman in the crowd said.

Claire thought about Kathy at the bottom of the hill in that red snowsuit that was too big for her.

"I needed to find my daughter," she said.

She tried to sit up, but as soon as she lifted her head everything around her started to spin.

"Whoa," the first man said, pushing her back down lightly. "Hold on, Claire."

The siren grew nearer.

Peter's voice rose above the others. "Let me through," he was saying. "That's my wife there."

He appeared before her, Kathy tucked under one arm and Little Jimmy under the other. Carefully he set the children down. They stared at her, wide-eyed. Little Jimmy sucked his thumb.

"Jesus, Claire," Peter muttered.

"You have Kathy," Claire managed to say, relief washing over her. "Thank God."

"The ambulance is here!" someone called.

"My head," Claire said, touching it again and feeling fresh blood.

Peter took her bloody hand and held it lightly. Two emergency technicians arrived with a stretcher.

"Do you know your name?" one of them asked.

They both looked about twelve years old. One of them had acne and glasses and skinny arms.

"Claire."

He looked at Peter, who nodded.

"Okay, Claire," the one with acne said, slapping a blood pressure cuff on her, "what day is today?"

"Inauguration day," Claire said.

"BP is sky-high," he said.

"She's pregnant," Peter told him.

Something passed across the technician's eyes. "How's that baby?" he asked Claire.

She closed her eyes, willing the baby to move.

"Still," she said finally.

One of them lifted her head gently and let out a low whistle. "You'll be getting some stitches," he said.

Claire kept her eyes closed.

"On my three," one of them said. He counted to three, then Claire was lifted from the cold snow and onto the stretcher.

"Make way now," the one with acne ordered the crowd.

Like Moses and the Red Sea, the crowd parted. Claire smiled to herself. She might not remember who Sisyphus was, but she knew her Bible stories. Every Sunday as a girl she'd gone to Sunday school in the church basement. They used to draw pictures of Moses as a baby in the basket among the bulrushes, and Noah loading all of the animals two by two onto the ark. Her drawings always had lots of details, rain pelting Noah and the animals, a frog guarding baby Moses.

"Does anything besides your head hurt?" the technician asked her.

"My back," Claire said.

"Do you have a bad back anyway?"

"No."

But she had felt back pain like this. When she went into labor with Kathy, she'd had these same low sharp pains. She remembered being surprised labor hurt there instead of in the front.

The ambulance waited for them, doors opened wide, at the bottom of the hill. The technicians smoothly slid the stretcher into it, and Claire watched as the doors closed, blocking out the faces of her husband and daughter and Little Jimmy. Although Jimmy wore an excited expression, Kathy looked stunned. She hadn't made a sound the entire time. She stared at her mother as if Claire had become someone new. And Peter, Claire thought. Peter's jaw was set hard, his mouth turned down, and his eyes filled with disappointment.

With the doors closed on all of that, Claire finally managed to ask the question that she could not say out loud in front of her family.

"Is my baby all right?"

The technician didn't meet her eyes. He lifted her head gently and placed fresh gauze beneath it.

"I don't know," he said.

The ambulance lurched forward, its siren wailing. To Claire, it sounded like the cries of a newborn, sharp and insistent, demanding your attention.

In the Emergency Room, a doctor stood over Claire frowning.

"How many weeks?" he asked.

"Is my husband here?" Claire asked.

The doctor raised one eyebrow, a talent Claire's lover also had. It was charming, Claire used to think. But now she found it disarming.

"How many weeks?" the doctor repeated.

Claire tried to see over his shoulder, where people were milling about. She couldn't locate Peter there.

"Twenty-six, I think," she said.

That eyebrow again. "Not sure?"

She shook her head.

"How many live births have you had?"

The word *live* made her shiver.

"One," she answered.

Were there un-live births? But she immediately realized that of course there were. She remembered reading that Jackie Kennedy had had a stillborn baby girl before Caroline. But surely this baby, *her* baby would be all right. She willed the baby to move. Claire closed her eyes and thought as hard as she could: *Move.* She pressed on her stomach, trying to initiate a little game she'd played with the baby: she pressed against its foot or elbow until it pressed back. But she couldn't even feel any part of the baby when she pressed now.

"What in the world inspired you to go sledding?" the doctor asked. No eyebrow-raising this time, just a steely stare. "In your condition?"

"I lost sight of my daughter and I was afraid of getting knocked over by all the sleds," Claire said. The words sounded ridiculous, and she stopped talking.

A nurse came in with a tray of equipment.

"We have to sew up your head," the nurse said cheerfully.

"Sew it up?" Claire said, her hand shooting to her head and landing on warm, bloody gauze.

"You've cracked it good," the doctor said.

For some reason, he reminded Claire of Connie, the way they both seemed to see right through her, to know everything she'd done.

"I think I'll give you a little something to relax you," the doctor said.

Within minutes of the shot the nurse gave her, Claire grew woozy and thick-headed. She listened as the doctor explained that he was giving her an injection to numb her wound, and then that he was going to start stitching it. His voice sounded like he was at the opposite end of a tunnel. Claire closed her eyes, giving in to the way her body seemed to float, the way her mind drifted from one thought to another effortlessly. She could feel the tug of the needle and thread on her head, but nothing hurt her. Instead, she felt light and almost happy.

She wondered where Peter had gone to. Probably brought the children back to his mother's house. Then she thought of his mother, upstairs in this very hospital. Was she still alive? Claire wondered, but as soon as she wondered that her mind veered off to a night with her lover. For the first time in a long time, she let herself linger there, remembering his face. He had blue eyes and black hair. Black Irish, he'd called it. Although he wasn't as handsome as her husband, there was something about his face that was more inviting. When he listened to her, he had a way of cocking his head, as if he needed to catch every word.

Claire drifted again, to the afternoon they'd escaped the city heat and gone to the beach in Delaware. It had been a feat, that excursion. To find someone who could take Kathy all day without appearing suspicious. To invent a believable story to tell Peter; she'd landed on telling him she was going on a women's-only full-day tour of the Corcoran Gallery of Art. He liked when she took an interest in things like that. He'd even said, "Bravo, Clairezy," when she'd told him her lie. The truth was, as a girl she'd been the best artist in her class. She'd painted the scenery for all the school plays, and always helped paint the front windows for Christmas. Claire enjoyed wandering that gallery. She especially liked Mary Cassatt's *Young Girl at a Window*. The girl's blue- and lavender-tinged white dress and hat really did look like changing natural light to Claire. And the girl looked so thoughtful Claire couldn't help but wonder what she might be thinking.

But wait. Claire's mind had settled on that painting by Mary Cassatt, but she wanted to remember that day at the beach in Delaware. How they rode waves together and fell heavily onto the blanket, breathing hard. How his wet hand had found hers and held on to it as they lay in the sun. Later, when she'd licked his skin, it tasted salty. His hair was stiff with salt, and his shoulders were bronzed by the sun. They had eaten fried clams and drunk cold beers on the boardwalk.

"Tell him you liked the Remington," he'd said.

"The cowboys?" she'd asked.

"I get the impression he'd like that."

By then they had left the beach and checked into a little motel. The room smelled musty and the sheets were damp, but they hadn't cared. Through the slats of the venetian blinds, Claire could tell that it was getting late. Too soon, they would be in the car heading back to their lives.

*"Off the Range,"* he said. "That's what it's called."

"But I like the Cassatt," Claire said.

"He'll say that of course you do. You're a woman and so you like that painting. The Remington will surprise him."

"Cowboys with pistols," she said dismissively.

"Remington pushed the structural limits of the bronze medium with that one. Apparently he bragged, 'I have six horses' feet on the ground and ten in the air.'"

He had kissed her then, and she had not wanted him to stop.

"Oh, Claire," he whispered, sounding almost desperate.

Later he told her that he loved the Cassatt painting too. "What is she thinking?" he'd said.

Back at home, Claire made pork chops in the oven, and Rice-A-Roni and string beans.

"Did you know the Corcoran was the first public museum to acquire Remington's work?" she said as they ate dinner. "They acquired *Off the Range* in 1905."

Peter looked up, surprised.

"So it was a good day?" he said.

Claire nodded. "A very good day."

He didn't notice her sunburned nose. Or if he did, he didn't bother to mention it, or to wonder how she could have gotten a sunburn inside the Corcoran.


"I guess you really did love that sculpture," Peter said, chuckling.

Claire forced her heavy eyelids open.

"You've been talking about Remington," he said.

She jolted upright, still light-headed.

"Whoa, girl," Peter said gently, pressing her back down onto the bed.

Claire looked around. "I'm not in the ER?" she said.

"They admitted you," he said. "But there's good news. You're right down the hall from my mother. Makes my life easy anyway."

"Peter?" Claire asked tentatively.

He waited.

"Have they said anything about the baby?"

"No one is saying much of anything," Peter said, sighing. He stretched his long legs out.

Outside, the sky had turned dark. Claire wondered how much time had passed. She put her hands on her stomach and pressed, searching for a foot or knee or elbow. Hoping for some response. But all she felt was her tight hard stomach, unyielding.


When a doctor came into her room a while later, Claire was relieved that it wasn't the smarmy one from the ER, with his eyebrow lifting and steely gaze. This doctor had movie-star good looks. To Claire, he bore an uncanny resemblance to that new actor, George Peppard. Just last summer she'd seen George Peppard playing Robert Mitchum's illegitimate son in the movie *Home from the Hill*. Peter had teased her that she had a crush on the character he played, Rafe. Hadn't Dot told her he was starring in some new movie with Audrey Hepburn?

The doctor was frowning beneath his short bangs.

"I'm Dr. Brown," he said to Peter, extending his hand.

The two men shook hands. Dr. Brown had a tan, Claire noticed, even though it was January.

"It looks like we have a bit of a problem here," he told Peter.

Peter was frowning now too. Neither of them paid attention to Claire.

"Have we lost the baby?" Peter said, lowering his voice as if Claire wouldn't be able to hear him if he spoke softer.

"I'm afraid that's how it looks," Dr. Brown said.

Ridiculously, Kathy's birthday party came to her mind. They'd had Stan the Animal Man come with his menagerie of snakes and turtles and bunnies. Stan the Animal Man had produced a hedgehog from one of the cages. He'd held out the small animal and demonstrated how when a hedgehog got frightened it rolled into a perfect anonymous ball for protection. Maybe babies did something similar, keeping still until they knew they were safe again.

"I think she'll come around anytime now," Claire said.

Dr. Brown and Peter both looked over at her, surprised.

"She probably got scared," Claire said. For a moment, she could feel the impact of hitting that tree, the sickening sound her body had made when it thudded to the cold hard snow.

Dr. Brown patted the blanket, somewhere around her knee. The doctor patted again. "Now, now," he said, "you're young. You can have a dozen more babies if you want."

*How many live births have you had?* that other doctor had asked her.

Seeing that she had started to cry, Dr. Brown said it was time to see what's what.

He shook Peter's hand again and told him he would be right back.

"I hate him," Claire said as soon as Dr. Brown had left. "He acts like I'm not even here."

"I thought he was very professional," Peter said.

He was adjusting the blinds, trying to close them. Instead, he pulled the wrong cord, sending them flying upward to reveal the dark sky and the parking lot lights. In their glow, Claire could see snow flurries dancing in the air.

Peter got the blinds to go back down, but when he pulled the cord this time he sent half of them up at a sharp angle.

"It's my baby," Claire said. "And he hardly spoke to me."

When Peter yanked on the cord again, he finally got the blinds back down again, and closed.

Without turning around, he said, "That's the real problem, isn't it, Claire?"

"I don't know what you mean," she said, knowing exactly what he meant.

She saw Peter's shoulders move up and down, and she thought he might be crying. "Oh, that's keen," he said. "Honestly, Claire. You're a terrible liar."

"Actually," she said, wanting to hurt him, "I'm a very good liar. You have no idea—"

"Of how long you were fucking off on me?" he said. "Do you think I haven't been putting the pieces together for months now? Do you think I'm that stupid? Your sudden interest in politics, in campaigning for Kennedy."

"No," Claire said, "I did want him elected. That had nothing to do with it."

"You did it to be with him," Peter said. "You never had any political inclinations."

"You've got it wrong," Claire said, her head throbbing.

Did it matter, she thought, if Peter believed she'd only campaigned for JFK to be near Miles instead of knowing that she'd gone there because she wanted to and found Miles only afterwards, by coincidence?

"Maybe this is the best thing that could happen," Peter was saying. "So we can move forward."

Claire tried to imagine what moving forward could possibly mean. Pretending Peter hadn't walked in that day? Pretending this baby had never existed? Pretending she hadn't loved another man?

"We'll do just what the doctor said. As soon as possible. You'll be pregnant again by spring. I promise."

"You promise?" Claire said in disbelief.

She had never known anyone who'd lost a baby this far along. Miscarriages, sure. But not a baby so close to being born. Her mind raced with questions that she didn't want to have to answer. Would there be a funeral? Would people come to it? They hadn't even chosen a name yet.

Peter sat beside her on the bed.

"We'll have a dozen more if you want, Clairezy. I swear this is a blessing."

"It is not a blessing," she said. "This is my baby. I want her."

Peter studied her carefully for what seemed forever.

"Is it his?" he said finally, his voice so controlled that a chill went up the back of Claire's neck.

Claire's throat tightened. "I think so."

Peter nodded. "Then I hope it's dead. God forgive me, but I hope this baby is dead."

"Don't say that. You don't mean it, Peter. I know you don't."

The clatter of a cart entering the room startled them. A nurse with a solemn face came in, followed closely by Dr. Brown.

"Let's see what's going on here," Dr. Brown said.

He smiled at Claire. "No matter what, this will be over in a couple of hours and you can get on with things."

Claire began to tremble. Her hands clutched her stomach. She had gotten so big with this baby, as if it were superhuman, growing with abandon. How could such a baby be dead?

"Why are you so tanned?" Claire asked the doctor. She wanted a different doctor. One who looked less like George Peppard, less handsome and more serious.

"Skiing," he said.

Claire watched as the doctor walked over to the sink and began to methodically wash his hands.

*Move*, Claire willed her baby. *Move.*

Her hands cradled her big belly.

"Move," she said out loud, though no one seemed to hear her.

"The nurse is going to give your wife an injection, similar to what they gave her down in the ER," Dr. Brown told Peter. "A little Scopolamine for pain. A little Demerol to relax her."

"She's pretty agitated," Peter said.

"We'll send her down to X-ray for a fluoroscopy to see if we can pick up any movement. I'll check her here first with a fetoscope. That should let us know if there's a heartbeat. If things go the way I think they will, we'll shoot her up with some Pitocin to start labor and the whole thing will be over by midnight."

"Labor?" Claire asked. "But I'm only twenty-six weeks along."

The nurse asked her to turn over so she could give her the shot. "To relax you," she said.

"I don't want to be relaxed," Claire said. "I want to understand what's going on."

"You have to deliver that baby if it doesn't have a heartbeat," the doctor said. "That's all."

"That's all?" Claire said, practically shouting.

"Maybe you can give us a hand?" Dr. Brown said to Peter.

Just like that, Claire was on her side, Peter's strong hands keeping her still. She felt the needle go in, and within no time that same floaty feeling filled her. She thought her whole body might lift right off the bed and float away. The idea appealed to her. She could float out that window, through the snow, all the way back to Virginia.

"It's already working," the doctor said, his voice sounding far off in Claire's ears.

"She'll start talking about Remington in no time," Peter said.

"Rifles?" Dr. Brown asked.

"The artist. She likes this sculpture of his . . ."

Claire stopped listening. Her mind was doing that thing, ping-ponging from one thought to another, unable to settle on any one thing. She had been considering naming the baby Caroline, like Caroline Kennedy, if it was a girl. She got to choose the girl names and Peter got to choose the boy names, that's what they'd decided. No. That's what Peter had decided, Claire thought.

Peter was laughing again.

"She's obsessed with the Kennedys," he said.

Had she spoken out loud?

"The whole country is," Dr. Brown said. "I'm a Nixon man myself."

More reason to not like him, Claire decided. A Nixon man.

"Hold still now," the nurse said, her mouth close to Claire's face. "Do you hear me?"

"Yes," Claire answered. Her tongue felt thick, like she had wool in her mouth.

Through half-opened eyes, Claire watched the doctor put a stethoscope around his neck and place the ends in his ears. Unlike a regular stethoscope, this one had a funny little thing attached to it. Somehow her hospital johnny was lifted and Claire saw the beautiful rise of her belly. The doctor had that attachment on it, and he lifted one finger to keep everyone silent.

Claire struggled to keep her eyes open. She tried as hard as she could to focus. When she'd given birth to Kathy, they had knocked her out completely. She'd gone from searing pain to blackness to opening her eyes and a nurse holding up a tiny baby wrapped in a pink blanket. She'd missed the birth altogether. But she wouldn't miss this. She wanted to remember every detail.

Dr. Brown kept moving the little piece, lifting his finger, closing his eyes, and listening hard. Again and again, until he'd covered the entire landscape of Claire's belly. Then he dropped the ends of the stethoscope from his ears and glanced up at Peter.

"We'll send her for the fluoroscopy, just to be sure," he said.

"Sure?" Claire asked.

"By this time tomorrow," Dr. Brown told her gently, "this will all be behind you."

She had to call Miles, Claire thought as two orderlies appeared out of thin air and began to wheel her out of the room and down the corridor. She had to tell him about their baby. He would come and stop them. He wouldn't let this happen.

"Excuse me," Claire said. "I need to make a call."

"Sure you do, honey," one of the orderlies said, not unkindly.

"You see, the father of my baby is in Alexandria, Virginia. At an inauguration party. I have the number."

"She's high as a kite," the orderly said.

"Poor thing," the other one said. "It's better this way."

"Maybe you could make the call for me?" Claire asked them. They were in an elevator, going down.

"703-337-5180. That's my friend Dot's number. She's having the party."

The elevator doors slid open and the gurney bumped out and down another corridor.

"You'll need to ask for Miles Sullivan," she said. "Have you got that?"

"Uh-huh. Miles Sullivan."

Claire's mind drifted again. Were they in the basement? Wasn't that where the morgue was? Had she actually died at some point?

"Am I alive?" she asked.

"You are indeed."

At some point, she must have fallen asleep because when she

managed to open her eyes again, she was back in the elevator going up.

"Did you call Dot? Did you find him?" she asked.

But her words came out garbled. She tried again. But somehow she couldn't speak any clearer.

Back in the room, the nurse was waiting with an IV all set up. Dr. Brown was nowhere in sight.

"It's best not to think about what's happening," the nurse told Claire.

But how could she think about anything else?

The clock on the wall with its white face and big black numbers said nine-thirty. Claire's head hurt from the drugs and from where she'd cracked it. She struggled to keep her eyes opened, focusing on that clock.

Peter dozed in the chair beside her, a newspaper on his lap.

As if she'd spoken, he jumped awake.

"It's done," he said softly.

*A pronoun is a word that takes the place of a noun,* Claire thought, remembering her eighth-grade English teacher, Miss Bailey, with her cat-eye glasses and white hair tinged an odd blue-violet. What was the noun for IT?

"You'll feel better when the medicine wears off," he said.

Claire closed her eyes. She would never be better. Her baby was dead and she would never be over it.

"Don't cry, Clairezy," Peter was saying. "The doctor said it went well. You can get pregnant again, we just have to wait a couple of months."

"Where is she?" Claire managed to ask. "Where's the baby?"

"They took her right away," Peter said. "She's gone."

"I want to see her," Claire said, opening her eyes and trying to get up, to get out of that bed and find her baby.

"They don't do that," he said, holding her in place.

"Did you see her?"

"God. No."

The doctor came in, wearing his inappropriate tan, his stethoscope swaying.

"I want to see my baby," Claire said before he spoke.

"You think you do," he said, "but you don't."

He gently pushed her down into a lying position.

"It was a girl, right?" she asked.

The doctor pressed her stomach. "Tender?" he asked.

"Right?" Claire said, her voice rising.

"A girl, yes," the doctor said, sighing.

"We have to name her," Claire said to Peter. She felt hollow, like she'd been literally emptied out.

"In my experience," the doctor said, "that just makes it worse. Better to move forward."

"Peter?" Claire said.

"Listen to the doctor," Peter said, "He's done this hundreds of times."

"We'll keep her overnight," the doctor told Peter. "But then she's good to go."

Peter extended his hand. "Thank you."

Claire watched the two men shake hands and exchange good-byes, as if nothing had happened here, as if the baby she had felt moving inside her had never existed. Twenty-six weeks. At twenty-six weeks, a baby had a heart and lungs. She was perfectly formed. Claire knew this from her obstetrician back in Washington. At her checkup just a few days ago, the doctor had shown her a poster that explained all of that. *That baby weighs a couple of pounds now*, the doctor had said. *Your job is to eat well and fatten that baby up.* Claire had told him that when certain songs came on the radio, the baby kicked more. *Well maybe you've got a rock-and-roll star in there*, he'd laughed.

Claire realized the doctor had left and she and Peter were alone in the room now.

"Arabella," Claire said.

"Who?"

"That's what I want to name her," Claire said. She didn't tell him that was the name of the baby Jackie Kennedy had lost.

Peter sunk back into the chair.

"It's done," he said again.

After Peter left to go back to his mother's house and get some sleep, Claire did exactly the opposite: she struggled to stay awake. She didn't want to forget even one minute of this: the cramping in her stomach, the darkness of the room, the smell of blood and disinfectant in the air, the hospital sounds on the other side of her closed door—crackling intercoms, soft hurried footsteps, the murmur of voices. *I will remember everything about the night Arabella died*, Claire promised herself and her dead daughter. Even if everyone else pretended that a baby had not been lost here tonight, Claire would not.

She was startled by the ringing of a phone by her bed. Peter had spared no cost, apparently. Here she had a private room, and a telephone.

"Hello?" Claire answered hesitantly, because who knew she was even here?

"Oh, sweetie!" Dot's voice rang out.

At the sound of her friend, Claire began to cry.

"Peter called and told me what happened," Dot was saying. "I don't even know what to say, except that we are all so sorry."

"It was a girl," Claire told Dot. "A little girl."

"He didn't say," Dot said softly.

"Arabella. That's what I named her."

There was an awkward silence. Claire cried into it until Dot said, "Guess what? You won."

"What do you mean?"

"Jackie wore white tonight. To the inaugural ball," Dot said. "She looked gorgeous, Claire. The gown was strapless and embroidered with beads and silver thread, so that it kind of shone, you know? And it had a silk chiffon overblouse that made it sophisticated. Of course she would think of something like that. They said she helped design it."

"Sounds pretty," Claire said.

"And can you picture this? She wore full-length white kidskin gloves."

"That's a special touch," Claire said.

"So when you come home you'll get a little dinner party as a prize," Dot said.

Claire tried to imagine reentering her life after all that had happened. She tried to see herself dressing for a dinner party, sitting at the vanity with the triple mirrors in her bedroom, putting on her makeup and choosing which earrings to wear. But it seemed impossible that soon she would be able to do that: to walk arm in arm with Peter down Huckleberry Lane to Dot's house where there would be cocktails in heavy crystal glasses, warm puffs of cheese on a silver tray, salty mixed nuts; to sit beside someone at Dot's long dining room table and make small talk; to be witty, or even a little charming; to hug everyone at the end of the evening and let Peter help her into her cashmere coat and step out into the cold winter night; and then to thank the babysitter, check on Kathy, get into bed and wait for her husband. All of it impossible.

"I'm sorry, Dot," Claire said, realizing that Dot had been talking. "I didn't catch that."

"I said isn't it wonderful that they caught the man who did that terrible thing to Dougie Daniels? It's finally over and we don't need to think about it again," Dot said with a sigh of finality.

"So much to not think about, isn't there?" Claire said.

"Well, yes," Dot said slowly. "Better to think about what I'll serve for your prize dinner. Maybe beef Wellington? And to think about Jackie's gown and how at this very minute they're twirling on the dance floor at the Armory."

Claire got out of bed, tucking the receiver between her shoulder and cheek and stretching the phone cord so that she could go to the window and open the blinds. Outside, snow had begun to fall again on the half-empty parking lot. The sky looked almost bright with the clouds and snow.

"It's snowing again," she said.

"We missed you today," Dot told her. "Roberta's husband actually got tickets to the ball and they're there right now. She promised to tell us all about it tomorrow. Oh, and that couple? You know the ones who—"

"Yes," Claire said.

"She had a bit too much to drink and got all weepy and chatty. Like the time Trudy drank too many daiquiris last summer and told everyone how she lost her virginity? So embarrassing, remember?"

"Yes."

"Well, it seems they're adopting a baby. A little boy just born a couple of days ago. I'm not sure Bill would ever adopt. Would

Peter?" Then she added quickly, "Not that you would ever need to. I'm sure you can have more babies, right, Claire?"

"Adopt a baby?" Claire repeated. "But why in the world—"

"Mumps," Dot said, lowering her voice. "Apparently the husband had mumps and can't . . ."

Claire pressed her forehead against the cold window, trying to think.

"Dreadful, isn't it? I mean, who knows what the real parents are like? Why, they could be hemophiliacs or Communists or just about anything," Dot was saying.

*Mumps?* Claire thought. The baby, Arabella, was hers and Peter's after all. And now, Miles was about to start a family with his wife. He was moving on without her. As he should, Claire knew. Yet the loss of him, of who she was and who she was with him, made her choke.

"But darling, you need to rest. I'll pick up your newspaper from the steps tomorrow and bring in the mail. You'll be in your own house before you know it."

Claire hung up the phone, sitting on the edge of the bed. She thought of her husband and what he said, that this was for the best. But that was because he believed they would never really know who the father was. One more thing not to think about. One more thing to push away. Had people told Dougie's mother not to think about what had happened? Was the world unwilling to think about men like Smythe and babies who died too soon and women who did not love their husbands?

Well, Claire thought, she wasn't unwilling.

A nurse came in and Claire recognized her as the one who earlier that day had predicted she would have a boy.

"I see you're sitting up," she said. "That's good. You should even take a little walk."

Claire didn't answer.

"Just need to take your temp," the nurse said.

"You don't remember me?" Claire said.

The nurse put the thermometer in Claire's mouth and watched the Timex on her wrist.

"It was a girl," Claire said.

At last the nurse glanced up. She took the thermometer from Claire and read it, carefully recording her temperature in the chart.

"It doesn't matter now," she said when she'd finished. She gave Claire a bright smile. "Water under the bridge."


The hospital corridors were dim and silent. Claire's legs felt heavy and clumsy as she moved along them, reading the room numbers as she passed. It was odd to have this swollen stomach, these large breasts, but to have such emptiness.

She paused at Room 401. Then she opened the door and stepped inside.

Her mother-in-law lay on the bed, asleep. Her color was better, a bit more pink in the cheeks. And someone had combed her hair and pulled it into a long low braid.

"Birdy?" Claire said softly. "It's Claire again."

But she didn't seem to hear her. A monitor sent lines across a screen, a steady row of ups and downs that reminded Claire of the way she drew waves as a child.

She hesitated. "Something bad happened today, Birdy, and I've been thinking about how no one talks about things. Do you know how many people have told me to not think? To move on?"

Claire licked her dry lips.

"I had an accident and the baby died." Claire nodded, as if validating her own statement. "It was a girl," she added.

At this, her mother-in-law's eyes shot open and a look of panic crossed over her.

"Oh, Lotte!" she said, tears falling down her cheeks. "I'm so sorry about Pamela."

"No, no, it's me. Claire," Claire said.

Birdy stared at her hard, then let out a sigh.

"I was confused," she said, more to herself than to Claire. "For a moment I got confused."

"That's all right," Claire said.

"Someone has died?" she asked. "A child?"

"The baby," Claire said. "Our baby."

"Oh, darling," Birdy said, "how awful. If I weren't in this bed, I would make you some tea and toast. Or maybe some broth." She nodded. "I would listen to what you have to say."

"Yes," Claire said softly, a feeling of great affection for this woman filling her. "Yes, that's what I need. Tea and toast and someone to listen to me."

"We all do, darling," Birdy said.

# 12

## The Return

### VIVIEN, 1919

Vivien returned home, tired and weary, from all the travel and from all the disappointment. She made a cup of Darjeeling tea, the kind that Duncan MacGregor had told her was most restorative. Sipping it, she thought of how David would say that Duncan probably made that up, but if the tea restored her, then that was all right. For the first time in over a dozen years, when she thought of David, he seemed far from her, a long-ago memory. This trip to Denver had almost erased possibility for her. Had almost erased hope.

A knock sounded on her door, soft, almost tentative. Vivien waited. For all these years, she had turned her life over to her clients and their grief. Tonight, she thought, she needed to turn to her own grief.

Another knock, firmer this time.

With a sigh, Vivien stood, smoothed her skirt and patted her hair in place. She imagined a person out there, heartbroken, desperate for someone to listen. Funny, she thought as she went to the door, that described her as well.

The woman standing there looked surprisingly like a younger version of Vivien herself. She had the same dark red hair, but with the glimmer of gold streaks that Vivien had had as a young woman. Her skin was smooth and pale, her lips full and pouty, just as Vivien's had been before the lines of grief and age had arrived, before her own lips had grown thin and set. Even the woman's eyes were the same cat-like green of Vivien's.

"Are you the obituary writer?" the woman said immediately. No hellos or how are yous.

"I am," Vivien said. She made allowances for bad behavior. Who knew what had brought this woman here to her doorstep?

Vivien stepped aside to let the woman in, but she didn't move.

"So you're her," she said. "The obituary writer."

Vivien nodded.

"You're famous, you know," she said.

"Well," Vivien said, her cheeks coloring.

It was true that she had gained some fame for her obituaries, but she preferred to stay out of the limelight. Newspapers had offered her money to move—to Chicago or Los Angeles—and be their obituary writer. *Collier's* magazine had wanted to interview her, and *The Saturday Evening Post* had asked if they might run some of her obituaries. But she'd declined all of these offers. She even refused to take an office at the Napa newspaper. She liked to meet people here in her home, to not have to interact with newspapermen and editors.

"No, you are. That's why I want you to write my husband's obituary. It has to be perfect. Special," the woman added.

Vivien nodded. "It will be," she said. "If I write it, it will be special."

The woman peered over Vivien's shoulder, into the parlor.

"Do you want to come inside?" Vivien asked.

The night air was cool, and the woman wore only a thin

blouse in the palest green. Celadon. Like Fu Jing's jade bracelet, the one she never took off.

"What I wonder," the woman said, "is whether you ever write obituaries for people who are still alive?"

"Alive?" Vivien said.

The woman laughed and pointed a finger at Vivien. "That's a good one, right? But that's what I need. An obituary for my husband who is still alive."

For an unsettling moment, Vivian wondered if the woman meant to kill her husband. But she was just a slight thing, and she had the nervousness, the skittish look and darting eyes of someone preparing to face grief.

It was unusual, but not the first time someone had come to prepare the obituary for a person about to die. Usually, the illness had been so long and slow that the wife was ready to be done with the business of dying.

"Your husband is ill then?" Vivien said.

And at the very sound of those words, the woman crumpled, bending in on herself and crying hard.

"There, there," Vivien said, putting her arms around the woman and leading her inside. Her bones felt fragile beneath Vivien's hands.

"Let me make you some tea," Vivien said as she urged the woman onto the loveseat.

This made the woman cry even harder.

Vivien sat beside her, trying to soothe her. "I'll make you some tea and then we'll have a nice talk. I'm sure I can help you."

"Tea?" she said. "Yes, that sounds good. Thank you. Do you have Darjeeling?"

"You want Darjeeling tea?" she said. "So few people know Darjeeling."

The woman studied Vivien's face carefully.

"I've heard it's restorative," Vivien continued.

"How did you come to know such an exotic tea?" the woman asked. Her eyes never left Vivien's face.

"A man I knew in San Francisco," Vivien said. "A long time ago. He had lived in India and was something of an expert."

"I see," the woman said.

"As I said, it was a long time ago," Vivien said again, suddenly uncomfortable.

They sat in silence until Vivien rose. "I'll make us both some nice tea and we can talk," she said.

She felt the woman's eyes on her as she left the sitting room and went into the kitchen. There, she filled the kettle with water. She lit the burner on the stove, watching the blue flame appear. She took one of the porcelain teapots and carefully measured the loose tea into it. Her hands were shaking.

Vivien paused and leaned against the sink, feeling the cold slate against her back. It was as if this woman had come for something else, not for an obituary at all. The way she'd studied Vivien. The business with the tea. Vivien could almost hear Lotte telling her to stop being ridiculous.

The kettle whistled. Vivien filled the pot and placed it on her black lacquer tray with two teacups and a bowl of sugar. She added a few pieces of shortbread on a plate. Sometimes a grieving person craved sweets.

"The tea is ready," Vivien said as she lifted the tray and carried it out of the kitchen, into the sitting room.

She took a step in and stopped.

The woman was gone.


The next morning, Vivien baked: bread, corn muffins, molasses cookies. As she stirred and chopped and measured, the woman kept coming into her mind. But no matter how hard she thought, Vivien could not make any sense of the mysterious visitor. She made a pot of vegetable soup, then put everything in a wicker basket to bring to Lotte. Sebastian had left her a note, offering to pick her up and take her to visit Lotte. And Vivien had accepted, hesitantly. What had happened that night Pamela died was a onetime thing, a mistake made in the throes of grief. Vivien could see that. But could he?

By the time Sebastian arrived, Vivien had talked herself out of any civility she might have offered him. If David was dead, then she was going to mourn him properly. After so many years of helping others grieve, Vivien had to figure out how to do it for herself now.

She met him at the door with the basket already in her hand, her coat on and buttoned.

"Perhaps I could have some coffee?" he asked her. "After the long drive?"

"Of course," Vivien said reluctantly. She couldn't refuse him coffee, not after he had come for her like this.

She held the door wider to let him in. As he walked past, she noticed how he'd shaved and put on what seemed to be his Sunday best for her. That night in the vineyard had led him on, of course it had. What kind of woman does that, then pretends it didn't happen? But what kind of woman talked about sex, especially when it was a mistake?

Sebastian found his way into the small kitchen, and was already at work on making coffee when she met him there.

He took up so much space, Vivien thought. She realized that despite all the men who had come here for her help, none of them had ever been in the kitchen with her. It felt intimate, standing so close, the steam rising from the kettle, the smell of Sebastian's soap in the air. She saw that he'd prepared two cups for coffee, and this gesture struck her as so kind that she touched his arm.

"Vivien," he said, the syllables of her name tumbling from his throat.

And just like that, she was in his arms and he was kissing her again, and to her surprise, Vivien was happy to have it, his mouth on hers and his rough hands already unbuttoning her coat and then her white blouse beneath. The kettle whistled, and Vivien reached over and turned off the stove.

"You have a bedroom here?" Sebastian was whispering.

"I do," she said, taking his hand and leading him toward it.

Later, they lay naked beneath her crisp white sheets. Vivien had never seen a man so hairy, the curly black hair covering his stomach and chest. Although he had arrived freshly shaved, already she saw the blue-black beginnings of hair on his cheeks and chin. The strangeness of him delighted her. She told him this, and he laughed.

"Vivien, Vivien," he said. "How I love your name in my mouth."

"You haven't asked about Denver," she said, watching the slant of the light through the blinds. Afternoon had arrived, she realized.

"I don't need to ask," Sebastian said. "If you had found him, I would not be here naked in your bed."

"I think . . ." Vivien began, but she couldn't finish the sentence.

"Vivien," Sebastian said. "Do you know this little bird that sings? A little yellow bird?"

"Canary?"

"Yes. Ca-na-ry," he said carefully. "Your name in my mouth is a canary. You in my arms makes my heart sing like a canary. You are my little bird."

"A poet, you," Vivien said, turning her head so he did not see the tears that had unexpectedly come to her eyes.

"Birdy," Sebastian whispered, taking her chin in his hand and turning her face toward him. He placed his lips on hers. "Birdy," he whispered again.

For two days, Vivien tended to Lotte and her family. She washed their clothes and swept the floors. She opened the windows to let fresh air in. She made a tamale pie and a chicken pot pie and put them in the refrigerator so that there would be dinner for them during the week. The ways to help the grieving, Vivien thought as she hung the wet laundry on the clothesline outside the kitchen, were similar to helping the sick. Except mourners did not show any immediate signs of recovery.

Lotte stayed in bed most of the time, either sleeping or pretending to sleep, Vivien wasn't sure which. She left her tea and toast on the night table and placed a vase of golden poppies beside it.

"Lotte?" she said late Sunday afternoon.

When Lotte didn't answer, Vivien continued. "I'm going back to town now, darling."

Still no response.

"Lotte, you have to try. If not for Robert, then for the boys."

Vivien waited, but Lotte remained still, her face turned away.

"In time," Vivien said softly as she bent to kiss her friend on the head. "In time."

The ride back to town with Sebastian was quiet, Vivien lost in her thoughts. She looked out the window at the sky darkening, and tried to imagine her future. Would she go back to her routine of weekly trips to the library scouring the newspapers for amnesiacs? Although Sebastian had offered her nothing, she wondered if she might make a life with him. For the first time since the earthquake, she felt a glimmer of possibility. Vivien snuck a glance at Sebastian as he drove, a cheroot between his lips, his face lined and brown from the sun.

"Next week?" he said. "I pick you up again on Saturday?"

Vivien kept her eyes on him. "Why don't you come Friday night?"

"And stay overnight?" he asked, surprised.

"And stay overnight," Vivien said.

On Monday morning Vivien was awakened by the sound of soft knocking on her door. She slipped on her lavender robe and hurried, barefoot, down the stairs. Opening the door, she found the young woman from the other evening stood there.

"You again," Vivien said, frowning.

"I apologize for my sudden departure," the girl said. "My emotions got the best of me."

"I haven't even had my morning coffee yet," Vivien said.

"Should I come back then?" the girl said. She wore a green coat with a red fox collar. The animal's head and amber eyes unnerved Vivien.

"No, no. Come in." She opened the door wider so the girl could enter. "Would you like to join me?"

The girl turned, her eyes narrowing.

"Are you making espresso?" she asked.

"Goodness, no," Vivien said, trying to act nonchalant despite the question. She had not made espresso since David taught her to use that complicated machine of his.

The girl began to slowly remove the bobby pins that held her small green hat in place, her eyes never leaving Vivien as she did. The hat was the type that hugged the top of the head, with a stiff short veil on the front. Sequins sparkled from the veil in the early morning light.

"I don't eat breakfast," Vivien said, heading toward the kitchen. "But I have some biscotti if you'd like."

To her surprise, the girl followed her into the kitchen, boldly taking in everything there: the china in the old cupboard; the three small paintings of cafés in Venice that hung, one on top of the other, by the window; the shadow box that Vivien had made in those first weeks after the earthquake. She had collected broken things from her flat—bits of glass and wood and porcelain—and arranged them in a wooden box. The act of building something out of all of the destruction around her had brought her a strange hypnotic comfort. It was this that the girl fixated on. She stood directly in front of it, examining each item as if it held a clue to something important.

Setting the teakettle on the stove and measuring the coffee into the pot kept Vivien from yanking the girl away from her things.

"When you were here last week," Vivien said, working hard to keep her voice steady, "you had an unusual request."

"Yes," the girl said. "To write my husband's obituary, even though he is still alive." She paused. "He has cancer, you see."

"I'm sorry," Vivien said.

Abruptly, the girl turned away from the shadow box, her finger pointing back toward it. "That red and white porcelain," she said. "Where is it from?"

Vivien didn't look up. She didn't have to. She knew every item in that box by heart.

"A milk pitcher," she said. "That's all that's left of it. It shattered a long time ago."

"I have matching pieces," the girl said. "A small creamer and sugar bowl."

Vivien didn't answer. What could she say? The pattern was a rare one, made in England to commemorate the coronation of Queen Victoria, and never produced again. She knew too that David had given several pieces to his wife as a wedding gift. He had removed the milk pitcher from their home on Nob Hill and used it every morning to froth the milk for coffee.

"I've never met anyone else who owns it," the girl said.

The teakettle whistled. Vivien poured the boiling water over the coffee grounds to wet them, then counted to thirty before she filled the rest of the pot. She tried to make sense of this girl. Perhaps she was related to David's wife. Margaret had died shortly after the earthquake, from cholera like so many others had. In her panic and grief, Vivien had gone to the house, hoping that David was there, alive. But Margaret came to the door, tall and thin and ashen, clutching a pale orange silk kimono closed. She was already ill, too ill to say all the things she wanted to say to Vivien. *I have imagined our meeting for years. And now I am too weak to scream all the things at you that I have screamed in my head.*

Slowly, Vivien pressed the plunger, watching the water turn dark with coffee.

"Where did you get it?" the girl was asking.

"It was a gift," Vivien said.

She poured the rich, strong coffee into cups and placed a few anisette biscotti on a plate. Queasy, she took one and bit into it, letting the licorice flavor fill her mouth. Licorice had healing properties, she knew. It settled stomachs and soothed throats. Some believed it helped insomniacs to sleep.

The girl followed Vivien into the living room, and perched on the loveseat where she had sat during her last visit. They set about the business of fixing their coffees, adding cream and sugar, stirring. Vivien dipped her biscotti into the coffee, and chewed the softened cookie, waiting.

But the girl did not say anything. Again, she took in everything around her, narrowing her green eyes, taking stock. Her hair shone a lovely red as the morning light grew brighter.

Watching her, Vivien became aware of her own dull hair, pulled back into a messy bun, and of how she must look with the deep lines that had developed over time between her eyes and around her mouth. Sorrow lines, that was how she thought of them. She saw these same lines on younger women who had experienced great loss. Not this young woman, though. Her skin was smooth, her cheeks rosy, her eyes lively.

Vivien cleared her throat.

"How sad about your husband," Vivien said. "And so young too."

The girl smiled ruefully. "My husband is quite a bit older than I am, actually."

"Oh?" Vivien managed. She found herself shoving back the idea trying to force its way into her brain. Her hands trembled when she picked up her cup, sloshing coffee onto her lap. She wiped at it halfheartedly.

"He's almost sixty," the girl said. She now turned her scrutiny on Vivien. "Does that surprise you?"

"Older men marry younger women all the time," Vivien said.

The girl simply stared at her.

"I don't even know you," Vivien said. "I certainly am not judging you. Or your husband."

Again, the girl said nothing.

"Tell me about him," Vivien said. She placed her hand at her chest, wanting to slow her racing heart.

"Why?" the girl demanded.

"How can I write an obituary if I know nothing about the deceased?"

"He's not deceased yet," the girl said softly.

"Of course. Forgive me."

"Actually," the girl said, staring down at her lap, "I haven't been completely honest with you."

"Oh?"

"I'm not the one who wants you to write my husband's obituary. He asked me to come. He wants you to write it."

She looked up, her eyes wet with tears.

"Do you think it's bad luck to write the obituary before he dies?" she asked.

"I don't believe in luck," Vivien said. "Bad or good."

"Our maid does," the girl said. "She's always reminding me not to put shoes on the table or death will walk in. She makes me cross my legs if the wind blows from the west. Or is it the east? I can never remember. And if I tell her my dream before I've eaten any breakfast, she covers her ears and hums. I say, 'Fu Jing, how can you remember all these silly rules?' and—"

"Fu Jing?" Vivien asked. Listening to the girl talk, she felt her throat go completely dry.

The girl tilted her head. "Yes," she said. "Fu Jing. I believe it means Fortunate One?"

Lucky Light. Vivien knew Fu Jing meant Lucky Light. She tried to swallow but couldn't. Coughing, she got awkwardly to her feet and hurried into the kitchen for water. Standing at the sink, she let the water run cold, then drank a glass straight down. Still, her throat felt parched. She drank another.

Vivien heard the door slam shut. Without turning off the water, she ran into the living room. Once again, the girl had gone. This time, Vivien ran outside. She stood in the middle of the street in her lavender robe, looking left and then right. But the street was empty. It was as if the girl had vanished. Or had never been here in the first place.

Slowly, Vivien went back inside. There, on the table beside the girl's coffee cup, lay a white business card with black writing. Vivien knew what it would say without having to pick it up and read it. But she did pick it up. She read the familiar words: DAVID GARDNER AND DUNCAN MACGREGOR, ESQ. On the back, the girl had hastily scrawled a note.

*My husband would like to meet you. Please come to our home in San Francisco. Soon.*

Vivien read the address the girl had written below her note. It was her own flat, the one David had bought for her. Trembling, Vivien stood trying to figure out what to do next.

"I have to go," Vivien told Sebastian. "You see that, don't you?"

He had arrived on Friday night with a bottle of Robert's best wine, a small posy of flowers tied with kitchen twine, and a look of such hope it almost broke Vivien's heart.

"You think this girl is . . . what? Married to your *amante?*" Sebastian said. The brightness that had been in his eyes when he'd first walked in was replaced with a flat steeliness.

"I don't know," Vivien admitted.

"And if she is, what will you gain from seeing him?"

"I'll know," she said. "Finally."

Sebastian rubbed his hands together as if he were worrying away a problem.

"What if he's alive?" he said at last. "What if he wants you back?"

These same questions had troubled Vivien since the girl's

departure. Was she married to David? And if so, where had he been all these years? What had happened on that long-ago April morning? Did he want some deathbed confession?

"Would you go back to him?" Sebastian was asking. "After all this time?"

"I . . . I don't know," Vivien said. "I would need to understand what's happened."

"But you might?"

Vivien sighed. "I've waited so long," she said.

At first, she refused to have Sebastian drive her. But he insisted. He insisted she let him take her there right now.

"But we won't arrive until so late," Vivien pointed out.

"Then we arrive late," Sebastian said, putting on his tweed hat and the coat he had taken off so hastily when he'd arrived.

He drove too fast along the dark country roads, and it was with great relief that Vivien saw the city lights ahead. She exhaled, and loosened her grip on the seat. When she directed him through the city streets, it was the first time either of them had spoken.

Once, she had had calling cards printed up with her name and that address on it. She used to write it on letters beneath her name. That address had been home. Saying it now felt familiar on her tongue. At last, after all the time spent getting here, Vivien calmed down.

They pulled up to the house.

"This is it?" Sebastian asked, peering out the window.

Vivien peered out too.

"Yes," she said. "This is it."

The first time Vivien had walked up these steps, she was a twenty-three-year-old young woman in love. The door was open, as if the entire house was waiting for her to arrive. When she'd stepped inside, she paused in the foyer, unsure of where to go or what to do. Dust motes danced in the air in front of the large bay window. Vivien stood and watched them. The air held the strong smell of furniture polish, and she breathed it in, remembering how the first day of school always smelled like this.

Then David had come down the stairs, opened his arms, and said, "Welcome home."

Vivien had run into those arms, and let him swoop her up and spin her around before taking her hand and leading her on a tour of the house. It was a tall skinny thing—"Like you," David had teased her. Those stairs went up three floors, the empty rooms unfolding like secrets and a beautiful stained glass window of a single pink tulip on the landings in between.

"So this is what it feels like," Vivien said, standing in the room that would become their bedroom.

David turned to her, lifting one eyebrow.

"To be happy," she said.

Two weeks later, after furniture had been delivered and the kitchen cupboards filled with dishes and glasses and the bureau drawers lined with pale blue fabric and filled with sachets of lavender and Vivien's clothes hung in the closet on hangers covered with peach silk, she had walked up these stairs again, this time hand in hand with David. At the door, he lifted her and carried her over the threshold. "Soon," he whispered, "you will be my bride."

Even though Lotte, newly married and already pregnant, had warned Vivien that he would never leave his wife for her, Vivien knew he would. The wife lived in the large house on Nob Hill where she'd grown up, an heiress to a shipping fortune. She spent months abroad, traveling with her two sisters to Paris and London to shop and see theater.

"Did you ever love her?" Vivien had asked David one night, months after she'd moved in and made the house her own.

He shook his head. "I thought so," he said finally "But now I know what it feels like to be in love. I can hardly think straight, and when my mind wanders, it always lands on you. I never felt this way with her."

"That's not love," Lotte had reminded her. "That's infatuation. Love is worrying together and enduring each other's moods and smelly socks. It's not all beautiful and romantic, Vivvie. You are living in a make-believe world."

But to Vivien, love was indeed exactly what Lotte called infatuation. It was her heart racing when she heard David's footsteps on the stairs. It was the time spent making herself beautiful for him. It was the feel of his hand on her inner thigh as she drifted off to sleep. It was hope—for the future, for life itself.

"I will wait here," Sebastian said, not looking at her.

Vivien did look at him, though. She knew in that moment that she could never love him, or any man, the way her younger self had loved David. But perhaps she could find another kind of love with him, a safe steady one. She knew too that she would not be able to have that unless she went into the house.

"Sebastian—" she began, but he held up his hand to stop her.

"Tonight it will be finished," he said. "One way or another."

"Yes."

"When you walk out that door, our life together will either begin or it will be finished," he said.

She almost smiled at his melodrama. Vivien had grown fond of the way he saw things in almost operatic terms. But she didn't smile. Instead, she took his hand in hers and brought it to her lips.

"Go," he said, pulling his hand away.

At the steps leading up to the house, Vivien glanced back and saw the ember of his cheroot glowing.

Slowly, she began to climb the stairs. No longer hopeful or young, she was thirty-seven years old, a spinster, an old maid. A woman who had silver strands in her hair and whose days were filled with stories of grief. She could hardly remember what it felt like to be lighthearted. She could only catch a glimmer of that girl who had raced up these stairs and into this house, who had stepped so boldly into an unknown future. Yet here she was, once again at this threshold, unsure of what lay ahead.

Vivien pressed the doorbell. Inside, chimes played a familiar melody. Ah! Vivien thought at the sound. *Ode to Joy.* David had installed this doorbell for her twenty-fourth birthday. She waited, then pressed again, listening to the first notes of *Ode to Joy.* Then silence, followed by footsteps. And then the door creaked open.

A scowling middle-aged Chinese woman stood in the doorway.

Vivien recognized her immediately.

Fu Jing had been a young Chinese girl, the daughter of immigrants who owned a laundry and lived in a crowded apartment in Chinatown when she came to work for Vivien and David in 1905. The woman who stood scowling before Vivien now, although fatter and older, was Fu Jing.

Unsure of what to say, Vivien took a step inside. She could smell garlic and ginger, smells she always associated with Fu Jing, who had often cooked dinner for Vivien and David in a wok, adding fresh gingerroot and garlic to it and stirring them together in oil over high heat. Later, as she served them their dinner, that smell lingered on her.

"Fu Jing," Vivien managed to say.

The woman narrowed her eyes.

"I looked everywhere for you," Vivien said, memories of those horrible days after the earthquake flooding her mind. She'd gone into the chaos of Chinatown, where Fu Jing's family's laundry was in ruins and panicked people fled, unable to understand her questions.

Fu Jing just shook her head. Vivien had never been able to read her expressions, and she could not do so now.

They stood together in the foyer, at the bottom of the stairs. Vivien saw that the banister with its curved railing gleamed with care, and the Oriental carpet that covered the center of each step had been well kept. The deep blues and violets on its pattern of birds and flowers had barely faded.

As Vivien stared up them, the young woman who had come to her house appeared at the top of the stairs. Today, her hair was loose, like Vivien's. But she wore a short skirt that stopped just below her knees, a sleeveless blouse with several long necklaces, no stockings. Vivien had seen such a look in magazines recently, and didn't like it at all. Instead of emphasizing their hips and bust, it made women look flat-chested and hipless, almost like adolescent boys.

"You came," she said as she descended the stairs. "Thank you."

"This was my house," Vivien said, surprised at how small her voice sounded.

"My husband is upstairs, resting. The doctor was here a little while ago. He said the time is near."

She motioned toward the double parlor. "Shall we sit?" she asked.

Without waiting for an answer, she continued into the room. Vivien hesitated, then followed her. The wallpaper was the same, a deep olive green with scenes from ancient Rome depicted on it in line drawings. David had found it when they went to Rome together, delighted that among the Coliseum and Pantheon were lewd pictures of couples in different sexual positions, something guests never noticed, which delighted David even more.

"Forgive me," the woman said. "I'm Ruth. I should have introduced myself that first night at your house."

Ruth turned to the Chinese woman hovering nearby.

"Fu Jing," she said, "bring tea, would you?"

Fu Jing bowed slightly and walked out.

Vivien sat at the edge of a violet velvet loveseat. The one she'd had in this spot was now in Napa in her sitting room.

"I don't know where to begin," Ruth said. "I met my husband five years ago, when I was only nineteen. He was sophisticated. Successful. A lawyer."

At that, Vivien sat up straighter.

"And he had an entire past that I knew nothing about," Ruth continued. "You know how men can be, so secretive. I had to piece everything together myself, with the little bit of information he gave me from time to time. Or from what I found snooping through his belongings. That's how I found that business card I left on your table." Ruth's cheeks flushed with embarrassment. "Maybe you think I'm just a foolish young girl, but I've been jealous of his past, of who he might have loved before me and what he might have done."

"One day we were sitting here, having our afternoon tea, and he was reading the *Examiner*. All of a sudden, his face grew pale and he muttered, 'By God, it's Vivien Lowe. She's alive after all.' And in that instant, I thought that perhaps you were someone he had loved once, before the earthquake."

Vivien got to her feet, certain now that David was here, upstairs.

Ruth stood too. "His life seems to be divided that way. Before and after April 18, 1906."

"Yes," Vivien said.

"When he got the news from the doctor, he asked me to find you. 'She needs to write my obituary,' he told me."

Vivien pushed past Ruth, and almost knocked into Fu Jing in the foyer.

Fu Jing held a silver tray and tea service. Vivien didn't have to look carefully to know that her own initials were engraved on each piece.

"Pardon me," Vivien said as she began to climb the stairs.

"Please! He's resting!" Ruth called to her, but Vivien didn't stop.

The light streaming through the stained glass window spilled across the first landing. How she had loved the effect this made, the way it cast gold and rose here. She threw open one door after another, but each room was empty. Still, the sight of David's study with the heavy mahogany desk littered with papers, the maroon leather cigar box she'd given him for Christmas, the crystal paperweight and gold fountain pen, all of these familiar items, made Vivien pause. She took deep breaths, as if she might catch his scent. But the room smelled of nothing, as if it had not been used in a very long time.

She continued up the stairs to the third floor. There was the sitting room, its door already opened. And across the hall from it, her bedroom. Hers and David's. That door was open too.

Ruth had arrived first, and she stood at the door like a sentry.

"He's very ill," she said softly.

Vivien took a step inside the room. The air smelled like rotting fruit. *Like death,* Vivien thought. Of course everything inside looked different. Vivien had taken the bed and armoire, the lamps and rug, with her when she moved to Napa. Her furniture had been replaced with Oriental pieces: a dark red bed, an ebony trunk with an ivory carving of elephants and tigers on its front. That trunk looked familiar to Vivien, yet she was certain it had not belonged to David.

In the bed lay a man so thin he hardly made a silhouette beneath the saffron duvet. As Vivien neared, she saw wisps of white hair against the embroidered pillow.

"David?" she whispered.

The man's eyes fluttered open.

Vivien looked into them, and instantly she knew.

"Duncan MacGregor," she said, her throat suddenly dry.

Disappointment filled her with such intensity that she sunk to her knees. Not David after all, but his old law partner.

He gave her a wan smile, showing long, yellowed teeth.

"Ah, Vivien," he said, each syllable an effort.

She grabbed his hands in her own.

His hands were so thin she could feel the bones in them pressing against the skin.

Duncan closed his eyes as if to gather strength. When he opened them again, he began to speak in a voice so low and hoarse that Vivien had to lean close and place her ear to his mouth in order to hear him.

"You've come to write my obituary, have you?"

"I don't know," Vivien said. "I suppose so."

"Just in time," he said with a trace of his old humor. "How do we begin?"

"Tell me about yourself," Vivien said, trying desperately to hold back tears.

"I grew up in India," he said softly, "on a tea plantation."

"Yes," Vivien said, nodding.

Duncan continued to haltingly tell Vivien about his education, and how he came to San Francisco and when he met David. She listened, nodding at the familiar stories, until he finally arrived at the day of the earthquake.

"That morning," Duncan continued, "April 18. David and I met in our office at 5 a.m."

"I remember," Vivien said.

He took a few wheezy breaths. "David, my law partner. My friend. In the middle of this dazzling life with you. A lucky bastard, he was. Until the shaking began and everything fell down around us. A support beam gave way and crashed in front of me."

Vivien raised her head to look Duncan in the eye.

"Is David dead?" she managed to ask him, even though she knew the answer in her heart, knew it deep inside her.

"Right in front of my eyes," he said. "An image I see every day. One moment he stood there, so bright and handsome. So full of life. And in an instant he was dead. There was no doubt. It was terrible, Vivien, but mercifully swift."

The weight of all the years of hope made her weak. Vivien clutched the edge of the bed.

"I went to Lotta's Fountain every day," she managed to say, and the words brought back those awful days spent searching the city. At the fountain, survivors—their eyes red and swollen, their faces full of desperation—gathered, all of them hoping to see a loved one, to get information. All of them, like Vivien, hopeful.

"Every day," she said again, her mind now tumbling over the past thirteen years and the lonely hours she'd spent living in grief. Strangers' grief and her own.

"I'm sorry," Duncan said. "I always thought you knew."

"I was told *you* died. Of a head injury," Vivien said.

"Rumors flew during that time, so I'm not surprised. " Duncan said. His face was so gray and gaunt it seemed to disappear into the array of pillows beneath it. "I did get hurt, quite badly. I was in the hospital for almost a year, then I was sent to Arizona to recover more completely."

Duncan closed his eyes. His breaths came out long and shallow.

"He needs to rest," Ruth was saying. "Don't you, darling?"

Duncan lifted one long finger and opened his yellowed eyes. "With his wife dead too, as his business partner I inherited his estate. Please. Take anything you want."

Vivien's gaze left Duncan's face for a moment and took in all of the things that used to be hers.

"I don't want anything," she said.

She had to get out of that room, that house. She had to get fresh air.

"You'll write it?" Duncan whispered.

"Yes," Vivien said. "Of course."

Then she was moving down the stairs, this time not pausing even briefly at the beautiful light coming through the window on the landing, but just moving as quickly as she could, through the foyer and across that threshold and into the street.

There, finally, she could breathe. It had started to drizzle. Vivien tilted her face upward and let the light cool rain fall on her.

David had been dead all of this time. *Terrible, but mercifully swift*, Duncan had said. She thought of the man she had loved for so long. How they had met that long-ago day when she wore her new blue hat. How they had heard Caruso sing. How the very morning he'd left the house and walked off to his death they had told each other that their time together was too short.

It had started to rain, a hard unforgiving rain. Vivien pulled her shawl around her and began to walk down the stairs. She did not look back at the house where she had lived so happily so long ago. In the distance, she heard the rumble of thunder. Vivien paused. She would write Duncan MacGregor's obituary. And then she would sit at the small desk in her room, and she would write the obituary she had hoped she would never have to write.

Ahead of her, Sebastian sat waiting, lit by just the glow of his small cigar.

Vivien inhaled deeply, then slowly, steadily, she moved forward.

# SEVEN

*There is no reason why a woman (or a man) should not
find such consolation, but she should keep the intrud-
ing attraction away from her thoughts until the year of
respect is up, after which she is free to put on colors and
make happier plans.*

—FROM *Etiquette*, BY EMILY POST, 1922

# Farewells

## CLAIRE AND VIVIEN, 1961

"A long time ago," Birdy said, "I was an obituary writer."

"An obituary writer?" Claire said, surprised. "That must have been terribly sad."

But her mother-in-law shook her head. "I comforted people who were grieving," she said with a hint of pride in her voice. "It was a gift, in a way."

Claire nodded. "Yes, I see what you mean."

"I listened to all of their stories," she said. "So many sad stories."

"What I didn't know then," she continued, her voice growing thoughtful, "was that I was comforting myself too. When someone you love dies, after some time, no one listens anymore. I listened."

"Who died, Birdy?" Claire asked.

"Vivien," she said. "Call me Vivien."

Claire sat on the bed beside her mother-in-law and studied the old woman's face. She had been beautiful once, Claire thought. You could see it in her high cheekbones, her straight nose. The lovely hair.

"I'll listen," Claire said.

"Ah, but I promised to listen to you."

"I'm so tired," Claire said with a sigh. "I would like to just sit here and listen for a while."

Vivien looked at this woman, her daughter-in-law. She did not know what had happened between her and Peter, but something had gone wrong. That was clear. And now they'd lost the baby too.

"Do you know the secret to writing a good obituary?" she asked Claire.

Claire shook her head no.

"All the dates and degrees and statistics don't matter," she said. "What matters is the life itself."

"How so?"

"Well, I always began by asking, 'Tell me about your loved one.' Eventually, we always got to the truth."

"Tell me about your loved one," Claire said.

Vivien paused.

"When I was very young," she said at last, "I was walking down Market Street in San Francisco wearing a ridiculous blue hat and pretending to be French. I didn't know it then, but I was hiding behind that hat, behind that persona. My dearest friend was getting married and moving away and I felt untethered. A man stepped into my life that day and grounded me again."

Thinking of Lotte brought it all back and Vivien had to collect herself, to push aside how Lotte's life had turned out. She had never recovered from Pamela's death. One day, Lotte had walked to the river and drowned herself. By then, Vivien had left California. Prohibition and an infestation of crop-destroying insects had closed many of the vineyards, sending Vivien and Sebastian east. She'd heard the news weeks afterwards, and then later, the news that Robert had married Kay Pendleton, the librarian.

She felt Claire's hand on her arm.

"Vivien?"

Vivien opened her eyes and nodded.

"What was his name?" Claire asked. "That man who saved you?"

"David," Vivien said, savoring the name. "David."

"It seems like a million years ago," she added, "and it seems like yesterday. Grief is like that. It never really goes away, it just changes shape. Some days, I don't think about him at all. But I can still have the breath knocked out of me when I taste crab Louis, or hear Caruso sing, or a dozen other things."

"What happened to him?"

"The earthquake of 1906," she answered. "So long ago."

"I'm sorry," Claire said.

"But you see, that isn't the only tragedy." Suddenly Vivien needed to make this clear to Claire. "I wasted thirteen years hoping that he was alive somewhere. Thirteen years holding on to a dream."

"But shouldn't we hold on to our dreams?" Claire asked, feeling almost desperate.

"Not when they keep us from moving forward," Vivien said sadly.

The two women sat quietly, each lost in her own dreams.

Then Vivien's voice broke the silence.

"Tell me about Peter," she said.

Claire looked at her, surprised.

"It's all right, darling," Vivien said. "I can see it in your eyes."

"I've hurt him," Claire said. "I—"

"My son will be all right. And so will you."

Claire rested her head on the old woman's chest, and Vivien stroked her hair.

"Don't waste your one beautiful life," Vivien said softly.


Peter found them like that a few minutes later. He walked into his mother's room with Kathy in his arms.

"Mommy," Kathy said, her voice hushed.

"Kit Kat," Claire said, standing and opening her arms to hold her daughter close.

Beside her, Vivien slept, her breathing shallow.

Claire met Peter's eyes.

"The baby," she said. "She was ours."

She watched the news settle in him.

"I want to go home," Claire said.

"Home?"

"It's time to begin our farewells," she said.

"Oh, Claire," he said.

Claire glanced at Vivien, whose face had grown paler.

"It's time," Claire said.

Claire closed her eyes and breathed deeply all the smells around her. Death hung in the air. But so did the beautiful little girl scent of her daughter, the pungent smell of flowers, her husband's clean soap smell, her own familiar one, all mingled together. Claire breathed them all in.

Then she took the first tentative, terrifying, exhilarating steps into her future.

# ACKNOWLEDGMENTS

As always, I have many people to thank for helping me to tell this story. Gretchen Jaeger helped me with details about vineyards; Nan Young told me about Denver in 1919; Diane and Pablo Rodriguez gave me a lesson in obstetrics in 1961; David Pires and Thom Anderson explained how someone in 1919 would get from San Francisco to Denver by train. The books *The Dead Beat* by Marilyn Johnson, *52 McG.'s* by Robert McG. Thomas, *The Great Influenza* by John M. Barry, and *A Crack in the Edge of the World* by Simon Winchester all inspired my imagination as well as providing necessary information. Kerrie Hoban, Lyndsay Ursillo, Hillary Noble, and Mary Hector who gave me the time in which to write, and Sharon Ingendahl who is a friend and a reader extraordinaire. Thanks too to Gail Hochman and Jill Bialosky, the best agent and editor a writer could have. And to Lorne, Sam, and Annabelle, who always give me the love and support a writer needs.